Tales of the Incorrigible: Flummox or Bust

by

Kevin Bowersox

Dedicated to Jodi.

If I journeyed far through time and space
Across the parsecs wide
I'd have no home, I'd have no place,
Till you were by my side.

Tales of the Incorrigible: Flummox or Bust

Chapter 1

The poster showed a Human male doing a jumping-jack in a clear blue sky. "Two Arms? Two Legs? Too Cool!" the caption read, and from the look on the face of the jumper, two of each did indeed seem to be an invigorating and exciting configuration of limbs.

Next to the poster, a Cranian female (by all measures a Human except for the fact that she was born on Cran 4 rather than Hume 3) leaned against the stainless steel wall. As Flathead and Throom walked past her through the corridor of the Cran port of entry, she stared at Flathead with a look that seemed as if it were about to segue into a disgusted head shake—which it then did.

"Why don't you just go alone?" Flathead whined.

Throom could not help but sympathize with his little friend. This was not at all the planet to make a hot pink squid feel at home. But Throom's sympathy was countered by his not wanting to interview applicants for crew positions alone. "I don't like Cran any more than you do."

"That's not the problem," Flathead countered, "The problem is that they hate me more than they hate you."

Throom could not argue with that. After all, he himself was at least Humanoid. True, his body was large enough that the word "hulking" seemed to have been coined just to describe it, and true, it was made entirely of stone, but the gray granite that comprised him was inarguably Humanoid in shape.

"Arms are for hugging other Humanoids," Flathead read from the next display they passed. It showed a family sharing a group hug. Flathead pulled three of his tentacles away from the task of locomotion and used them to plead with Throom. "Throom, look at me."

They stopped, and Throom looked at Flathead. His friend was about three quarters of a meter tall and very similar to a squid in shape except that his main body (his hub as he called it) was shaped like a shoe box standing on end rather than a pregnant arrowhead. His overall hot pink color was pushed slightly toward purple by a faint blue paisley pattern that covered him everywhere except the undersides of his tentacles.

Flathead had learned to enhance his communications with the faced races by flexing his skin into slight deformations. A crinkle here, a ridge there, a slight tilt of the hub, and he could make his emotions clear to most of the people he encountered. His wrinkles and ridges were now expressing anxiety. They were so effective that Throom almost gave in right there, but instead he hardened his own face and continued down the corridor, forcing Flathead to follow. "Just stay with me and you'll be fine."

They arrived at the shuttle check-in. A balding Cranian male sat behind the counter. "Name and vessel," he droned without looking up from his console.

"Throom of the Incorrigible."

"Business or pleasure?"

"Business."

"And what is your business?"

"*My* business," Throom said.

The little man looked up with his beady eyes narrowed as if he were about to set Throom straight on a few things, but once he saw that he was dealing with a Fraggart, he just swallowed and let him remain askew. He went on to the next question. "How long are you planning to visit?"

"Less than a full rotation."

"Very well. You are all set then," the Cranian informed him. "First gate through those doors. The shuttle will be leaving shortly."

Throom and Flathead started toward the indicated door but the balding Cranian interrupted them before Throom had taken two steps. "Um, excuse me sir." When Throom turned back, the Cranian was glancing over the counter at Flathead. "I didn't realize that this was with you. That complicates things a bit." He sat back down and started tapping at his console.

Flathead flinched as laser beams from a bump on the ceiling shot out and scanned across his surface, no doubt recording his every feature and comparing them to a gigantic database somewhere.

"He's with me," Throom explained, "I'll be responsible for him."

"Yes sir, you will," the little man said, "Which means you are responsible for making sure that it obeys all of the rules laid out here." He placed a word wad on the counter. "Shuttles leave every hour, so you can take all the time you need. If you don't wish to have it confiscated, I suggest you become very familiar with those regulations."

"Have what confiscated?"

"That." The man behind the counter pointed directly at Flathead.

Throom noticed that the man had taken on a tone of greater confidence. In fact he had a definite condescension about him, due most likely to the four guards that had moved in to stand stiffly around Throom and Flathead.

"You can't 'confiscate' him." Throom stepped back to the counter. "He's a Kravitsian citizen and he's our pilot. You have no authority."

"Oh yes we do," the man assured. Then he continued, "It is of utmost importance that it wear this emblem at all times to mark it as non-Humanoid." He slid a small purple adhesive badge of amorphous shape across the counter to Throom. "If it is found within 300 meters of any public works building it will be immediately disposed of. Is that understood?"

"Disposed of?"

"Yes. Disposed of. Is that understood?"

"No," said Throom, "I don't understand that at all."

"Then I suggest you read Grand Ranter Barry's book *The Push for Excellence: Making Cran Great Again*. There is a copy on the word wad I gave you."

"Push," Throom growled, "for excellence?"

"Throom, don't make a scene," Flathead sputtered nervously. "It's their planet."

"Yes it is," the man said proudly. "Now more than ever." Then he recited from memory "Two thumbs up—one on each hand. Hold your single head high and stand for Cran."

Throom narrowed his eyes. He knew the guards' weapons could do little to harm him, but he also knew that going Fraggart on this autocratic speck of overweening flesh would make him miss the interview. Worse yet, he knew the guards' weapons could harm Flathead. A lot.

"It's fine, really, Throom. You don't need to do this. I'm a Caner. I get worse from other Kravitsians. Just let me go back to the ship."

Throom seethed a moment longer.

"Just do the interview," Flathead soothed, "then we can put some deep space between us and Cran."

After counting to ten mentally, Throom grumbled, "All right, I'll see you back at the ship." Throom parted ways with Flathead and walked through the door.

Times like this almost made him regret that he had ever civilized himself.

* * *

It had seemed like a good idea not to accompany Throom, but no sooner had Throom exited through the doors to the shuttle bay, with one last nod back at his old friend, than Flathead felt suddenly very alone, as if he had been dropped behind enemy lines. Now as he flapped down the cold stainless steel corridor even his own reflection on the wall seemed to be mocking him for what he was.

He watched the Cranian female walking toward him. He instinctively pulled toward the wall. When she caught sight of him, she did the same with the other wall, then quickened her pace once she was past. Flathead watched her go, pondering what she might be so afraid of. He was half her size and had no weaponry of any kind. What lies had she been told about him? They must have been pretty awful. Sadly he realized that some part of him was starting to believe them himself, even though he had no idea what they were. He tried to shake it off and move on.

He pulled up to the elevator door and was about to climb up to hit the call button when the doors opened. A group of five or six male Cranians poured out of the box and into the corridor yabbering loudly and incoherently.

Flathead ducked into the elevator, and the doors closed. He climbed the wall to the control panel, but before he could choose his destination, there was a ding. He dropped to the floor as the doors of the elevator opened.

Standing outside, leaning against the call button was the largest of the drunks that had vacated the device as he entered. Three other members of his entourage were gathered around him, the rest apparently having something better to do. They were all looking at Flathead with mischievous grins. "Hey buddy," the largest drunk said, "having a problem?"

"Uh, no. Thanks, though, for asking."

"You sure?" The Cranian's tone suggested he might have troubles he was yet to realize. "Sometimes just being where you don't belong can be a problem."

"Look," sputtered Flathead, "I don't want any trouble."

The big drunk puffed out his incredulity as he stood up straight, tucking his foot in front of one side of the door to prevent it closing. "Who said anything about trouble? We just wanna help." He stepped into the elevator with palms up. "Where you going? Deck one?" He pointed at the deck one button. "Two?" He pointed to two.

"F-four."

"Four," big drunk said and pointed to the deck four button. "Then here, let me help." With that he reached down and, catching Flathead off guard snatched him up by his hub. He then forcefully slammed one side of said hub against the deck four button.

Laughter exploded from the gang as Flathead was tossed into the corner of the elevator. The big one waved as they left and the doors closed. "Have a nice trip."

"And don't come back, freak!" another added.

As the elevator moved toward his destination, Flathead felt relieved. "That could have been much worse." he told himself. But when the doors opened on the next floor down he realized it was worse.

"Still going to four?" a drunk from upstairs asked, a little out of breath and flush with exertion. Without waiting for an answer he repeated the bit of physical humor his friend had initiated, smashing Flathead against the fourth floor button and tossing him to the floor.

Dazed, Flathead saw what he was in for when the button for the next floor down lit up, followed by the one below that.

Chapter 2

Throom sat at a dingy yellow table in a Spammy's restaurant holding up the laminated menu in front of him in a way that suggested he might be reading it. He had no intention of ordering—eating for him was as impossible as it was unnecessary—but if they thought he intended to order it might buy him some more time before they threw him out as a vagrant.

He looked around the otherwise unoccupied dining area. Most of the booth's chairs had rips in the well-worn sparkly green plastic upholstery. Stained stuffing fibers stuck through like scabs.

On the walls were several nondescript landscapes, a poster of a person Throom assumed to be High Ranter Barry, and one pancake that had somehow become attached near the ceiling.

On the floor, besides a spattered condiment package and a napkin, sat a crude wooden box filled with rusty scrap metal, shards of glass, and tubes of industrial adhesives. A handwritten sign on the front read: Creative Fun Zone – Create at own risk.

He would have to speak again to the Cap'n about choosing better rendezvous points. These places were always so awful, not to mention awkward for a non-eating stone golem like himself. He knew, for instance, that the booth he was sitting in was never going to be the same, probably requiring comprehensive repairs, yet he was not going to order so much as a pecker nugget.

He had considered tipping the waitress as he often did, or ordering food and just not eating it. But after he saw the staff kick a man out because he was missing a finger he decided he didn't care about such things this time around.

He realized he had been sitting there staring into space when a voice interrupted his thoughts by asking "Are you Lou Greasly?" The deep, firm voice belonged to a Humanoid with a washboard forehead and impressive physique.

The new arrival had long brown hair and a neatly trimmed mustache and beard as dark as deep space. He was in some sort of quilted jumper that was tiled with pockets, or possibly flaps, most of which were held shut with toggles made from large fangs. The fabrics used varied in color from a dark earthy green to a rusty brown, but all had the same texture of tightly packed irregular striations. Piping as thick as Throom's thumb enhanced the manly tapering of the recruit's torso as well as the broadness of his shoulders. He carried in his hands a sealed cylindrical container filled nearly to the top with murky water.

"Actually, I'm his first mate, Throom." As Throom extended his hand to the new arrival, he noticed that in the jar floated some sort of sea creature that was shaped roughly like a leaf of romaine lettuce. It was reddish purple in the middle, growing to light pink at the scalloped edges. To his astonishment, the floppy red lettuce in the jar sprang to life and plastered itself to the side of the container. Its color changed to a dark maroon, and words appeared in a lighter shade across its surface.

"I am Kurplupt," the words said. Obviously the thing was intelligent.

Throom considered a moment. Was the jar occupant introducing itself or complaining of fatigue?

Throom looked to the holder of the jar for some help in comprehending what was supposed to be happening. The holder of the jar would not meet his gaze. Throom looked back at the lettuce. Words were now scrolling across it.

"... of the school of Shuuupt of the sphere of Tullusht of the pod of Shluuurptptpt of the..." The words continued far beyond Throom's interest in them.

After waiting long enough that he felt the requirements of basic decorum had been satisfied and exceeded, Throom decided to speak. "I'm happy to meet you, Kurplupt," he interrupted, certain now that Kurplupt was a name.

The letters were replaced by a series of dots, and then, "I was not finished," appeared in the center of the lettuce.

"That's all right. We can get the rest when we're filling out W-4s."

"As you wish. I am honored to share your sphere," the words spelled out. The ridge-headed person set the jar on the table, and because Throom's body took up so much room on his side of the booth that the table was pressed firmly into the back of the opposite bench, the one outside the jar simply stood at attention by the table, hands behind his back.

"So you must be the other recruit I was supposed to expect?" Throom asked the jar carrier. The jar carrier did not meet his gaze.

The lettuce displayed a number of words in all upper case. "DO NOT ADDRESS MY BEARER!" they said.

"I'm sorry, I was just..."

"Klorf is my bearer—a form of transportation—nothing more."

Throom looked at Klorf to try and gauge the bearer's feelings about this, but Klorf continued to stare at the mysterious pancake. Throom looked back to Kurplupt and read the scrolling words.

"Flapulates often use the services of cling-ons when traveling on liquid deficient worlds. That does not mean that the cling-on has suddenly become worthy of representing our race."

Throom seemed lost for a moment. These two beings were of the same race? He decided not to risk enraging the jar being with further questions, however, and instead took refuge in the business at hand. "Well let me explain this first, since it is sometimes a deal-breaker," he said. "There is no regular pay for this position. We of course supply full life support during your incumbency. But beyond that you are only entitled to a cut of any prize we find. Do you find that acceptable?"

"A cut?" the jar-thing asked.

"A portion, a share."

"Of what proportion?"

"All crew members, including the Cap'n, get an equal portion of whatever is left after expenses."

No words appeared on the being. Throom assumed it was mulling it over.

"Are those parts of the deal acceptable to you?"

"Yes," appeared on the flapulate.

"Before you ask, I can't tell you what the purpose of this mission is. The Cap'n will tell you all about it if you sign on."

"Understood."

Throom opened his mouth to ask Klorf a question but caught himself and asked Kurplupt instead. "If we took you on, would Klorf be expecting a share?"

"What Klorf expects is immaterial."

"I see." Throom fidgeted causing great moans of strain from the bench. "What position are you wanting to fill? It was unclear from your correspondence." It had not been unclear at all, but now that he had met Kurplupt, he was certain there had been some mistake.

"I wish to be chief of security."

Or maybe not. Throom looked at the salad bar escapee floating in a jar. "Security of the ship?"

"Yes, why not?"

"Well, it's a very active job. I mean, a very physically demanding job." He paused to let the rest of the problem blossom in the mind of the flapulate. The seed found no purchase. "The Incorrigible is an air-based environment. Roughly four to one nitrogen/oxygen."

"Go on."

"Well... you wouldn't be in charge of a team. You would actually be all of security." Still no sprouting. "You might have to physically subdue various beings." The flapulate was still not getting it. "As in chasing, shooting at, fighting with."

"I am aware of these things."

Throom had to lay it out for him. "So how would you do that?"

"My bearer would assist me."

"So Klorf would be doing your fighting for you?"

"Of course he would," the flapulate informed him, "I'm in a jar."

"I see that. Well, just to play the bad guy for a minute, if Klorf is doing all the dangerous work, why wouldn't we just hire Klorf?"

In response to this, Klorf started, and Kurplupt seemed to flatten himself even closer to the glass, giving Throom quite an eye full. "Are you insane?! Klorf is a cling-on. When the great croosian traders swim through the profound pressures and darkness at the core of the water moon Vadnu, the cling-ons are the parasites that even that most hostile environment will not dislodge. They are unrefined. They are coarse. They are barbaric. Only the repulsive fact that they can take near vacuum-pressure gases into themselves and derive oxygen from them makes them of any use to us. What you suggest would be as if I offered to hire, instead of you, the chair you sat on."

Throom processed this information. He could not fathom what it must be like to live in Vadnu. There was no other place in the galaxy like it—a moon made entirely of water from surface to core and on through to the surface again— a planet-sized drop of pond water teaming with life and hurtling around a lifeless gas giant and twin suns in an intricate dance that gave it just the right amount of energy to sustain life.

"I see." Throom nodded. "If we took you on, what sort of life support would you require?"

"My environment vessel is self contained. All I need is to absorb full spectrum light for a short time each day. Klorf can operate all of the necessary equipment."

Throom nodded. He wasn't sure what this thing considered "full spectrum" in regards to light, but he knew they had the ability to provide anything considered visible by any known species and at a minimal power cost. In general, photovores were the best deal available when trading energy for person hours. Even if Kurplupt himself were useless in his job at least it would not cost much to have the thing on board, and Klorf looked as if he might be very useful.

"By the way," Throom segued, "I notice that your jar does not have one of those stickers on it."

"Of course not!" Came the immediate response.

"Do they not realize that you are sentient?" It would make sense that any Cranian would assume that anything in the jar would be at best a pet of Klorf.

"They do not."

"And how long have you lived here?"

"We do not live here." The response was abrupt. "We were… laid over here after a term of employment ended several months ago."

"They left you here, on Cran?"

"The term of employment ended with unexpected abruptness."

Even with Throom's short exposure to Kurplupt, this too made sense. So was he really going to bring this strange thing on board? Technically that was entirely up to the cap'n, but Throom knew that realistically it was entirely up to him. He had been the one to hire Penny, the latest recruit to their crew made at their last stop and every other hire since he joined the crew so long ago. This was his decision.

Could it be called a decision, he wondered, if you lacked the courage to say no?

"All right then," Throom began, but before he could finish the sentence he was interrupted.

"Throom! You overgrown pigeon perch. You haven't changed a bit," a cheerful voice exclaimed.

Throom turned to look at the source of the voice, and his stone jaw dropped. "Hardegar?"

Hardegar nodded his rotting head vigorously. Bits of decaying skin on his forehead and cheek flapped as if in greeting. "The one and only!"

Hardegar was of average build and height for a Human— or at least average build and height for a Human found preserved for decades at the bottom of a peat bog. He wore baggy trousers and his shriveled arms protruded from the short sleeves of an overly spacious shirt that was decorated with large flower shapes in bright colors.

"I thought you were dead," Throom uttered blankly.

Shrugging and nodding his hairless head, Hardegar admitted, "I am—been dead since Endrosia. Poisoned you know." Then brighter, "Don't drink the water, eh?"

Throom was unsure what to say. "So, uh, how've you been?"

"How have I been? I've been dead!"

"Okay, but... uh..."

"It's the damned implants," he explained sheepishly. "The control unit malfunctioned and won't shut down. I keep going through tissue regeneration, but its not working so well any more." He flicked at one of the flaps of dead skin.

"That's terrible."

"Yeah, the thing I miss most is my brain. Well, second most." He winked his right eye but found he had to open it again by hand. "Most of me is still in my Brain Bubble 3000, but I'm pretty sure I had some really nice memories in wetware. Oh well, I'm sure it's in a better place. Absent from the body, at home with the Lord."

There was an awkward silence.

"So," Throom ventured at last. "Cran is a long way from Endrosia. What brings you here?"

"Nothing in particular—just kicking around waiting for the old batteries to go down."

Throom nodded in recognition. While he was not exactly battery powered, he was powered by the slow decay of an irreplaceable clump of heavy elements deep in his chest. So it was the same in every way that mattered. While most living things could, in theory, keep living as long as they took in food they could derive power from, his energy source was strictly limited.

Another moment of silence. Throom searched for something to add. "Well, I guess you're lucky, right? I mean if you have to be dead, you should at least stay active."

"Lucky? Look at me, Throom."

"Uh, yeah." Throom said uncomfortably, noticing that he could see completely through portions of one of Hardegar's arms.

"So how about you? How's the old stalactite hanging?"

"I can't complain. Still on the Incorrigible."

"And why wouldn't you be? Beautiful ship."

Throom nodded agreement. "In fact I'm here recruiting right now, so... It was nice seeing you again, Hardegar, but I need to get back to work."

"Sure thing," agreed Hardegar as he pulled up a chair and sat down. "Let's get started."

Like a stink bomb in an airlock, realization filled Throom's mind. He had been told to meet a recruit from Vadnu and one other. Throom felt some of the minerals in his torso gain density as he realized that the tattered bag of bones in front of him was that other. "Huh?" was all he could manage to say.

"I'm throwing in with you again," Hardegar said brightly, "if you'll have me."

Throom tried and failed to look excited at the prospect.

* * *

As they entered the elevator on the starport and started their ride down Throom could not help thinking that he was far too soft-hearted for someone made entirely of stone. He had at least a dozen reasons to reject the recruits he was coming back with, yet here he was, coming back with them.

Klorf stood next to him with a scaly duffle bag of some sort over his shoulder and a jar full of ego in his hands. Next to Klorf was a marionette of science with what remained of the mind of an old co-worker. These were the people he would be trusting with his life if push came to shove. Well at least he knew he could rely on the cap'n and Flathead. The thought of Flathead gave him enough of a jolt of realization to pique Hardegar's curiosity.

"What is it, Throom?"

"Nothing," Throom responded. "I'm just realizing I'm not sure if our pilot got back to the ship all right. I'm hoping he did."

"He didn't." Came a muffled voice behind him.

Throom turned but saw no one else in the elevator. But then a hot pink bulge of flesh emerged from a slot in the wall intended to hold waste items. Throom tried not to show his revulsion as the rest of his old friend squeezed out like psychedelic toothpaste onto the floor.

Klorf was instantly on guard with the jar tucked under one arm and his other held out between the new rider and Throom.

"It's ok," Throom assured, "this is Flathead, our pilot."
Then to Flathead, "Who did this to you?" It was clear from
his tone that he intended to do the same to them.

"A bunch of drunks were harassing me. I hid in there."
Throom relaxed a little. Harassing his friend was
still bad, but not as bad as stuffing him into a tiny trash
receptacle. He watched as Flathead regained his shape and
composure.

Then Flathead caught sight of Hardegar and was back in
the bin.

Chapter 3

"As beautiful as I remember," exclaimed Hardegar as the group approached the Incorrigible.

"Mm-Hmm," agreed Throom vaguely.

"Very retro."

"She's a classic all right," Throom agreed. "One of the last ships in the 'Defiant' line. After the Incorrigible, there was only the Stubborn, the Headstrong, and the Pig-headed Jerk. Then they quit making them because they were officially out of names."

There was, of course, no way for any of them to know that the ship was shaped very much like a huge 1957 Buick Roadmaster. The designer of the Defiant line, Snell Smarkly, had made a career out of no one knowing that. He had dug into the ancient archives and chosen a random land-car design from Hume three and used it as the basis of his entire line.

He even found that the ad campaign that had been used to sell the original carbon fuel burner was so usefully vague that it adapted perfectly to each new ship in his line. When the Incorrigible was up for sale it was billed as "The Newest Defiant Line Ship Ever," as had every other ship in the line, including the first. It was the "Ever" that seemed to impress people.

The glossy ship sported sleek lines and swept-back tail fins. A thin chrome stripe ran a bit above the spherical black lift pods that took the place of tires, then dipped down sharply just in front of the rear pod like an elegant check-mark. The Incorrigible's body was two tone—mostly yellow but red from the undercarriage to the chrome stripe. Near the front, four elliptical portholes accented the space above the stripe and gave a faint impression that the pod was rolling forward at speed. The "grill" was resplendent with chrome and glass—being the forward observation deck.

On the side, where windows would have been if it really were a Buick, was a logo made of bold stylized lines suggesting a planet and something like a comet swooping around it and heading away. Intermeshed with the logo were the words Galactic Guard Lite. The motto "To Swerve and Deflect" curved beneath it. Next to the logo like a footnote was the abbreviation "Ret." Beneath the entire emblem, in much larger letters, was the name of the ship—Incorrigible.

They all grabbed luggage off the trolley and headed up the gangway extending down from an opening just aft of the forward lift pod.

Cap'n Lou Tok Greasly was there to greet them when they came aboard. Or rather he happened to be shuffling through the corridor in his underwear as they came aboard. One hand scratched absently beneath the waistband of his baggy boxer shorts and the other rubbed down his face and off his cleft chin. His blue eyes were bleary. His greying sandy brown hair, normally wavy but disheveled, was now disheveled but wavy.

"Hey," he mumbled as he passed.

"Who's that?" Klorf asked, apparently at the behest of Kurplupt.

"The cap'n," Throom admitted. "He'll be better after he has a cleaning and a coffee."

A female yelp from down the corridor drew their attention to where the other new recruit, Penny, had come around the corner to nearly collide with her under-dressed boss. The petite, black haired woman now had her back to the wall as the cap'n shuffled past, tipping an imaginary hat to her. As soon as she could, she quick stepped over to Throom and the others. "Is that normal?"

"Normal in general or normal for Cap'n Greasly?"

"On this ship," she snapped, somewhat annoyed.

Throom held up a hand palm down and moved it like a teeter-totter.

Penny looked like she was assessing whether it was too soon to jump ship.

"It might take him a little while to adjust to having a woman on board," Throom offered.

"Hey," Flathead chimed in, "he was wearing shorts, wasn't he?"

Hardegar spoke up. "Remember when he talked to that Lumarian diplomat for three minutes before he realized that they were on a video feed? And he'd been sitting in the cap'n's chair the whole time, naked, clipping his toenails?"

Throom and Flathead chuckled.

"That caused a war, didn't it?"

"A minor skirmish," Throom corrected. He looked to Penny, who was taking in Hardegar's appearance. "Oh, forgive me. Penny, this is Hardegar. He was a crew member back in the day, and he's returned. Also, he's dead."

Hardegar held out his hand, but Penny reserved hers and turned to Klorf.

"The flapulate in the jar is Kurplupt." Kurplupt pressed against the jar and began listing his full title and lineage. "That's his family..." He paused politely to let her read but then decided they could not wait for the entire list. "His bearer, who we should not address directly, is named Klorf."

Although he had not known Penny for very long, he could tell that this last statement had rankled her. Her eyes narrowed, and her head ticked to the side, making the pull tab of her forehead zipper tinkle.

Throom suppressed a feeling of revulsion once again at Penny's strangest feature—in fact her single odd feature. The beautiful, bright eyed, Human female had an old fashioned zipper across her forehead. Interviewing her had been difficult once he had seen it, and while he was becoming a bit more used to it, it still made him uneasy. Just the fact that most of the races in the galaxy were bags of water with organs floating around in them was bad enough. But to see one that seemed to have easy access to those spongy, wet innards right on her face added a new level of ick.

He was sure that in time he would adjust to it. After all he had just seen his old friend Flathead ooze through a slot he would not be able to fit his own hand into and had managed to not let on how disgusting it was. Surely he could get used to this. In fact, some part of him was strangely compelled by it. He had never actually seen a zipper before, they had become obsolete centuries ago, and he wanted very much to see how it worked. But before he could ask that, he would have to feel comfortable acknowledging in words that it existed. Both of them would have to be much more comfortable with each other. Personal observations of that sort required time and tact.

"Is that a zipper?" Hardegar blurted out.

Penny's mouth dropped open, and her expression went from shock to hurt to anger. She seemed to have a number of candidates come just to the point of speech only to be rejected as undiplomatic. Finally she simply turned and walked briskly away.

"Well, was it?" Hardegar asked Throom. "What's it for?"

Throom could only shrug and lead them on to their cabin assignments.

Chapter 4

"Thanks again for doing the interview, Throom," Greasly said as he and Throom stood outside the briefing room. Though the cap'n's hair was still unruly, noticeable improvement had been made. Improvements had also been made in his clothing in that he was actually wearing some.

He wore his old uniform which consisted of black boots and baggy black riding breeches with a spazzer holstered on his right thigh, a plain white tee shirt under suspenders formed from colored rectangles (the color sequence of which indicated his rank and several of his achievements), and over all, a jacket that could be best described as a thigh length cutaway duster of worn brown material with shiny copper buttons—all unbuttoned. The jacket bore on each arm a patch of the same "near miss" emblem of the Galactic Guard Lite that was born by the ship, but minus all of the wording.

"Not a problem, Cap'n."

"I would have done it myself but, you know—hangnail."

"Mm-Hmm"

"They can be very painful. You're lucky you'll never know."

The cap'n's excuses had become progressively more inane over time, and Throom felt that it was now little more than a running joke. He was sure he detected a subdued smirk on the Human's face.

"Well," Greasly said, "shall we get this party started?" He turned and walked into the briefing room door. A second later, while he was rubbing his nose, the door opened.

"Throom, you've got to work on the timing of these doors," he grumbled.

"I tried, but the minimum is hard-coded."

"Well, chisel it out," he snapped as he entered the briefing room. All the new recruits plus Flathead were there, seated at the long table that took up most of the room.

"You can sit down," Greasly enjoined, but no one was standing. "I'm Cap'n Greasly. Welcome to the Incorrigible. She's a fine ship, and now she's got a fine crew." He paused for a moment lost in a troubling thought. "Again," he added, then snapped out of it.

"I run a lax ship," he stated as he paced with his hands clasped behind his back, "but I expect everyone to do their share. Everybody. Got that?"

Hardegar and Penny nodded. Klorf looked at the floor. Kurplupt signaled "Yes" in red letters.

"What the hell is that?" Greasly asked, pointing at Kurplupt. Then to Klorf, "Can you talk? You're not a mime, are you?"

Throom interrupted, "Cap'n, Kurplupt is the one in the jar. Klorf is only his transportation. They are sort of a symbiotic pair."

"Really?" Greasly completely ignored the text scrolling across the flapulate. "Well, I've had security officers that were pickled half the time, but this is ridiculous!" He looked at the others ready to accept praise for his witty remark. He got none. "Because of pickles... in jars."

They all looked around nervously, unsure what pickles and jars had to do with each other. Who would bother pulling individually wrapped pickles out of their box and putting them in a jar? What purpose would it serve? Greasly's love of history had bitten him in the ass again.

"Tough crew," Greasly remarked. "Anyway, we'll sort all that out later." He waved his hand in the general direction of Kurplupt.

"The mission," he continued, "The mission is locating and retrieving the final cargo of—drama pause— Bartholomew Methane."

At the mention of the name Bartholomew Methane, all of the recruits gasped, except for Kurplupt, who just stopped ranting.

"*The* Bartholomew Methane?" asked Hardegar in awe. "You don't suppose there are two sons-of-bitches unlucky enough to have that name do you?"

"The most notorious pirate that ever lived," Penny stated as a question.

"That's the guy," Greasly confirmed. "Rumor has it that his ship went down when he was finding a hiding place for some of his most valuable spoils. That's what we're after."

"So what have you got?" Hardegar queried.

"The Incorrigible, thirty thousand moolas, and you." The cap'n said. "Sound's like a song, doesn't it?"

"No leads?"

"I know right where it is."

"You know right where the wreck of Bartholomew Methane's ship is?" Hardegar asked with cautious optimism.

"I know right where the lead is. I happen to know because I won it playing poker. It's an old electronic log made by Bart, himself."

"You have one of his logs?"

Greasly sat down. "Had. I lost it on the next hand. But I know who has it now, and—more importantly—I know where he keeps it." Greasly grinned slyly, then noticed that text had been scrolling across the flapulate. "What's that, Kurplupt?"

Greasly spoke the words as he read, "How do you know the owner of the clue hasn't already retrieved the..." Greasly rubbed his eyes then pointed at Klorf. "You."

"Klorf," Throom supplied.

"Klorf, can you speak?"

"Yes, I can."

"Talk to me through Klorf," Greasly instructed Kurplupt.

The words "NOT ADDRESS MY BEARER" faded from the flapulate. After a moment the security officer reluctantly pulled itself away from the side of the jar facing Greasly and went to the side facing Klorf.

"Very well, captain," recited Klorf.

"Not captain. cap'n," corrected Greasly. "I was in the Galactic Guard Lite, not the Galactic Guard."

"Cap'n," Klorf amended.

"And I know, because I know the man who has it. His name is Ratner Groat." Greasly pulled out a crumpled piece of paper bearing a photo of a slick looking Human with a pencil thin mustache, and spread it out on the table for all to see. "His stupidity is only surpassed by his vanity. There's no way he could figure out the encoding scheme, and it will still be months before he will admit that fact and have someone else figure it out for him."

"He looks dishonest," pronounced Penny. "His eyes are so close together." Greasly smoothed out the paper some more. "Oh, that's better," she said.

He pulled another crumpled piece of paper out of his pocket and spread it on the table. "That's his ship, The Other Woman." He looked at the paper somewhat wistfully.

The Other Woman was another Smarkly "original", this time based on an ancient trailer, that in turn seemed to have been based on an ancient toaster. It was pretty much a silver box with rounded corners, four spherical lift pods, and a triangular brace protruding out the lower front.

"She was my first ship. That bastard tracked her down just so he could have her, and I couldn't." Greasly sighed. "I had a lot of good times on The Other Woman."

"Excuse me," interrupted Kurplupt by way of Klorf, "are you talking about stealing the log from him?"

"Yes," stated Greasly.

Klorf looked at Kurplupt then at Greasly. "Okay."

"He's on his way to Oon," Greasly continued, searching through his pockets. "His course requires him to stop briefly near Slavin seven. Damn it! Where is that map? Throom, Do you have a copy of his course?"

Throom entered something into a console, and the course of The Other Woman appeared on the wall behind Greasly. Greasly looked over his shoulder, then quickly turned around in his chair to face the projected image.

"What the hell?" Greasly yelped. Then beaming at Throom, "I didn't know it could do that. You are a genius, man!"

Greasly hopped up and pointed out the Slavin system. "This area here is controlled by the original Slavinites. It's theirs by treaty—their laws, their courts. Intergalactic law does not apply in this zone."

"And theft's legal there?" asked Hardegar, looking particularly gruesome in the half-light.

"Of course not, but neither is gambling. So anything you lose in a game of chance is legally still your property. And," he added significantly, "it is also perfectly legal to break and enter to retrieve stolen goods—frontier justice sort of thing. So as long as we get the log back while The Other Woman is in this zone, we don't break a single law. Any questions?"

"But didn't you get the log through gambling?" asked Penny.

"Yes."

"So do you really own the log according to Slavin law?"

"Are you a lawyer?"

"No."

"Any other questions? Good. Let's Flitz!"

"My master has a question," entreated Klorf.

Greasly stopped on his way to the door and looked at the ceiling with his shoulders slumped. "What is it, Kurplupt?"

"How can you be sure the log is genuine?"

"That's a good question. The answer is: I just can."

"But how?"

"Look, I just know it. We have to leave it at that. Okay?" The recruits mulled that over.

"Look, I just feel it. My gut tells me the log is genuine. You are all going to have to trust me on that point." He turned and left.

The recruits looked at Throom and at Flathead. Flathead was the first to speak. "I know this probably won't help, but that's good enough for me."

Throom jumped in to bolster Flathead's recommendation. "Flathead is our pilot, and he is very factually oriented. It means a lot for him to say that he trusts the cap'n." He looked around the room. "But then again, you have no reason to trust me either." He shrugged. "It's a risk. There is no way around that fact. Either you take a chance, or you don't."

The new recruits each considered their options.

"I'm in," Penny threw in at last.

"Me too," shrugged Hardegar.

"As am I," added Klorf for Kurplupt.

"Good," said Throom. He tapped a console, and a blue line was added to the image. "This is our course."

"That's longer than Ratner's course," Penny pointed out. "Shouldn't we try to be there before him?"

"We will be," stated Flathead confidently.

"That red dot," explained Throom, pointing out a red dot located on the blue line, "is a translation into normal space of our current position in Flitzville."

"We're already in Flitzville?" Penny sounded amazed. "I didn't even feel the Flitz drive kick in."

"She's a good ship," Throom boasted.

"She must be if we are already that close to Jordanis!" exclaimed Penny.

"That's thanks to our fine pilot." Throom motioned toward Flathead. "He could find a straight path through a plate of spaghetti."

Flathead blushed purple.

"But why are we going to the Jordanis system at all?" Hardegar queried.

"We have to recruit the sixth crew member."

"Anyone I know?"

"Ever hear of Willy Smith from Elvis three?"

"Willy the Wisp?"

"Yes."

"Willy the Wisp, that stole the jeweled hose clamp of Thran?"

"Yes."

"I heard he ended up in a Jordanian prison waiting to be executed."

"Exactly."

Chapter 5

As the sleek-lined Incorrigible floated gracefully—guided by Flathead's skillful tapping on the console—toward the surface of Alankhus (fourth planet in the Jordanis system), the cap'n sat in the command chair of the bridge staring intently at the front display, his face alight with the glow of victory.

The victory that glowed on him was not his own, however, but rather that of the protagonist in the historical drama he was watching: "Sherlock of Hume Three." The series reenacted the achievements of an ancient Human that solved mysteries using a technique called reasoning. The stories of his exploits had been told for ages, even though the technique never really caught on.

Greasly smiled as Sherlock slapped the titanium cuffs on Moriarty and pushed him into the hansom cab to be taken to the Scotland Yard reprogramming center. As the hansom cab started its carbon fuel engine and drove down the cobblestone street, Sherlock's busty sidekick, Watson, opined in her thick English accent, "Well, Holmes, England is a safer place once again because of you, eh, wot?" Music swelled, and there was a flash of white on the screen as the entire list of credits scrolled past in less than a second.

Greasly pondered those simpler times. There were still discoveries to be made back then that didn't require massive quark twisters or spin deducers the size of small moons. A man could work miracles with something as primitive as a microscope or an MRI. All one needed to do was nab a criminal with a little DNA evidence, and people thought you were a god.

People took too much for granted these days. Some didn't even realize that it used to take lifetimes to travel between the stars. Well, the Amish did. They still used solid fuel boosters for space travel—plodding through endless space in their black spaceships with large orange triangles on the back. How tedious their lives must be—waiting minutes for a burrito cooked with microwaves.

"Throwbacks," he mumbled. Then, as if suddenly realizing what he should have been doing, he blurted, "Flathead, what's our ETA?"

"Ten minutes," Flathead responded.

"Ten minutes," Greasly repeated, the gears of his mind clearly working. "And port processing, another what?"

"Five minutes, tops. It's all automated."

"Fifteen minutes. Damn it!" He rose and started to the door. "Not enough time for another episode," he grumbled. The door slid shut behind him.

* * *

After landing, the crew assembled in the forward port airlock. Greasly looked over the three members of the away party.

A wig of brown hair had been affixed to Throom's head and his entire body had been painted to resemble a light-skinned human. Even his eyes were a reasonable facsimile of Human eyes. Naturally the pupils never dilated or contracted, but, to the casual observer, Throom could pass as a Human—though a fairly creepy and lumpy one.

Hardegar, after spending some time in a tissue regeneration bath, had increased his dermal integrity. All of the visible gaps in his flesh were healed over, at least, but he still looked like he had crawled out of a zombie bargain bin. In fact, Throom looked to be the more Human of the two.

Penny had tried to hide the zipper on her forehead with some makeup but only managed to change it from a zipper to a ghastly looking scar with a pull tab.

"Well," Greasly began, "all I can say is you are damned lucky Alankhus has the dress code it does. Hoods up."

The three were wearing the bulky hooded robes that the people of Alankhus considered morally requisite in order to either hide the shamefulness of, or protect the sanctity of, the Human body—depending on who you asked and what mood they were in at the time. The three pulled up their hoods, and suddenly each looked like any Alankhus native.

"Keep alert out there." Greasly nodded to Flathead, who opened the exterior airlock doors. "Heads down, hoods up."

The world outside was standing on end—perpendicular to what should have been level. Along the right edge of the door, a tan city, seemingly carved out of the desert sands, looked to be balancing on its side. Along the left side, fluffy clouds moved slowly upward.

Flathead attached an extendable ladder to the right edge of the exterior hatch and let it unroll. It fell toward the city. Throom, Hardegar, and Penny had a hard time maneuvering themselves onto the ladder, what with the shift in gravitational pull and the bulky robes, but they managed it.

After the three were on the ground, they spent a few moments reorganizing the world in their heads. Once they got rid of the feeling that they were standing on a wall and got used to the idea of seeing the Incorrigible standing on its nose, they started off toward the city.

"Do they always make ships land like that here?" asked Penny as she looked at the other ships around them—all of which were parked nose-down.

"Well, the law says all ships have to land facing the Shrine of the Descension, where the prophet Alan Moon Hammy landed for the first time," Throom explained, "which happens to be on the other side of the planet."

They got through the gates of the city easily by keeping their heads down and their hands together in front of them back to back—the Mooner attitude of prayer. Once inside they moved through the crowds, scouting out positions and working out the final details of their plan.

* * *

It had been a long time since Throom had seen a place filled entirely with featherless bipeds. Jordanis was even more exclusive in that way than Cran. At least Cran would allow non-Humanoids to enter the cities and spend money, though on a short leash (often literally). Jordanians considered anything even touched by non-Humans or Humans with mutations to be tainted and impure.

Throom looked around the sun-baked market square, wondering what would be the best way to do this. His goal was to commit the most heinous of all Jordanian crimes and then escape without the true nature of his body being discovered.

As Throom pondered, a nearby merchant jumped up from his seat inside one of the crudely constructed wooden booths. He pressed the backs of his hands together in greeting. "Brother, in Alan's name I greet you."

Throom quickly mimicked the greeting and went back to surveying the crowd.

"You look like a man in need of a good slave," the merchant suggested, presenting with a wave of his hand three slaves seated at the back of his booth. He clapped his hands, and the slaves rose to their feet.

"No slaves today," Throom said curtly.

"Would you like to browse my online catalog?" The merchant turned an ancient terminal toward Throom so he could use it. Throom looked in disbelief. The thing actually had what the ancients called a key rack and a moose. He thought sarcastically that he was surprised they were not connected to the display by wires. He had no idea how they would be used. He had to snicker to himself at the quaintness of it.

"No, thank you."

"These are the most excellent servants on all of Alankhus. They were taken from the Northlands where winters are harsh. That breeds strength!"

"No, thank you."

"They are docile and obedient to a fault—no backtalk here my friend." He looked around cautiously then added in a conspiratorial tone, "and none of my slaves have the wasting disease." He winked and pointed subtly to the vendor across the way.

"I heard that!" the other vendor complained.

"He heard nothing," the merchant assured Throom.

"I have no need for slaves."

"Perhaps not now but take one home with you. You may find a use later."

"No, thank you." Throom was growing angrier.

"Maybe a frozen slave or two to save for the harvest?" It was all Throom could do at this point to keep from crushing the merchant's head like a grape. "My merchandise is the finest. They keep well and are very well educated. This one can do simple calculus and basic astro-navigation. This one is very skilled at computer use."

Throom was momentarily intrigued. He had never thought of slaves as having skills of that caliber. "What about her?" he asked with a nod to the remaining slave—a lean and shapely Human female with seductive, dark eyes.

The merchant half laughed, half leered, "You're joking right?"

"No, what skills does she have?"

The merchant laughed again and waited for Throom to laugh, too, but Throom did not. He looked around to see if any of the black robed Ears of Alan were in the area, then motioned Throom closer and whispered a few of her more juicy skills into his ear.

"Why would she do that?" Throom asked in shock.

"She will do that and anything else you desire."

"I would want her to do that?" Throom was quite out of his element now. His people had nothing that even slightly resembled mating.

The merchant shrugged. "To each his own. Most men would pay dearly for it. But you, sir, don't have to. She is very reasonably priced."

Throom looked at the merchant askance then at the dusky slave. Then he realized that he had just been given the perfect opening. "What about Alan?" he asked. "Would he like that?"

The merchant stiffened somewhat and looked around. Throom was starting to think he had succeeded already, but then the merchant leaned forward. "We are told that he was a man," he put forth suggestively.

More was needed, apparently. "And he did have the required appendage," Throom continued.

They were clearly getting into an area that made the merchant uneasy, but he did have to agree.

"Penis," Throom clarified. "That is the appendage I mean."

The merchant cleared his throat. "Yes," he said, "his body was perfect in every way—lacking no attribute."

"In fact," Throom pressed further, "he had two."

The merchants jaw dropped.

"Penises, that is."

The merchant was frozen for a moment in shock then shook his head and smiled again. "I'm sorry, I misunderstood you for a moment. Yes, we are told that the ship of the high prophet did have two pinnaces."

"Not pinnaces—penises," Throom corrected, "as in schlongs, weiners, cronznasters. The Most High Prophet, Alan Moon Hammy, had two penises—one on each hip."

The merchant's flesh went white. Even the slaves stared at Throom, aghast. "I'm afraid you are mistaken," the merchant offered.

"No, no, no," Throom turned to address the crowd in general and asked in a loud, clear voice, "Isn't it true that the Most High Prophet, Alan Moon Hammy, had two penises—one for each hand?"

A profound and venomous silence fell over the crowd. Throom heard the merchant behind him hurriedly closing up shop and running for cover.

"And in the middle, the parts of a woman?" Throom added for good measure.

Somewhere, something made of glass shattered as it slipped from the grasp of a stunned Mooner. A low murmur spread through the crowd. Expressions of shock or anger or both spread out before Throom like endless sand dunes.

To Throom's amazement, a nearby Mooner with a gold tooth turned to face him. "Go, wise one!" he urged. "The Ears of Alan approach! Go now!"

Throom blinked at his benefactor in surprise. The Mooner grabbed Throom's robe to pull him away. Naturally the Human could not budge him. He stared at Throom in awe.

The Ears were coming closer. Throom tore himself away from his unexpected aide and ran. More Ears, alerted by the divine spirit—as received via divine spirit transceivers—poured in from the side streets and ran after him like the swiftly pursuing vengeance of Alan that they represented. As he rounded a corner, one of them tried to intercept him, and Throom deftly flung him into a pile of animal dung.

The people were starting to clear a path for him, and he could see the city guards forming ranks at the gate to bar his exit. The guards leveled their primitive lead-flingers at him and were about to open fire when an ice cream van rolled down the hill, crashing completely through Alve's Slave Salve booth. It came to rest against the side of a stall selling lashes for self flagellation, effectively cutting Throom off from the gate guard's line of fire and letting him get another 40 meters closer to them without being shot.

At the top of the hill down which the van had rolled, Penny casually disappeared into the confused crowd.

The next step for Throom was to get through the gate, but first he had to get past the wreck of the van. There were too many people in the street to go around it, and smashing through the thing would tip his hand as to his strength.

Instead, Throom altered his course and, head lowered, rammed directly through the flimsy stand next to the van like a vengeful bull. As luck would have it, the large hand painted sign reading "Kustah's" fell from its place and blocked the path Throom had made, forcing his pursuers to take the long way around the van.

Now, only a few meters of space and the heavily armed guards were between him and the gate. The guards leveled their automatic rifles and were about to open fire, when Hardegar ran between them and their target, flailing his arms and scolding Throom. The guards immediately began yelling at Hardegar to get down. Throom picked up Hardegar and threw him at the guards. This gave Throom just enough time to slip through the gates before they were able to fire again.

Throom felt some of the lead pellets spattering his back as he ran toward the Incorrigible, but he was far enough away from the guards that they wouldn't be certain they had hit him. The guards were a ways back, but still in pursuit, when he climbed into the ship.

The cap'n was there waiting for him. "Get 'em good and mad?" he asked.

Throom looked out the door and to the right. The guards were about twenty five meters below, screaming and shaking their fists. "I think so," he said. "Uh oh, they're climbing over... er... up."

"Flathead," the cap'n requested. Flathead rubbed two tentacles together in gleeful anticipation then flapped a few times on a control panel. Outside, the artificial gravity around the climbers altered so that they fell away from the ship. As they approached the limits of the AG generators, real G began to kick in. The net result was a graceful arc of plummet from the side of the Incorrigible through the roof of a nearby building.

"I love doing that," Flathead chortled from the outer door where he had run to watch the fun. He reeled in the ladder.

The cap'n patted Throom's back. "So now we wait."

Chapter 6

In a little under two hours after Throom's escape, the Alanic Guard had joined the City Guard and the Ears of Alan in surrounding the Incorrigible. Overhead, the black and heavily armed "Earplanes" circled.

The Divine Overseer of the city contacted Cap'n Greasly over vidyacker. "Blasphemy is the oldest crime on Alankhus, and there has never been a blasphemer that has escaped the prescribed punishment."

"I understand that, but it was an honest mistake," the cap'n lied.

"It does not matter," the Overseer explained, as if it were completely logical. "The words have sullied his spirit; he is a blot on the pure face of Alankhus."

"So let us go, and we'll take the pimple with us."

"But this is blasphemy! By not punishing him, we would take ten-fold the sin on ourselves. The sacred hymn of punishment is very clear. Everybody must get stoned."

"When would the stoning occur?"

"Well, we have quite a backlog right now, so it is hard to say. We have a notorious thief scheduled for today. He has been waiting for three sacred orbits—about four galactic standard years. But we bumped him up because of his notoriety. We thought it would be a good draw for this year's stoning festival to have Willy the Wisp and Torm the Fog on the same bill."

"So it sounds like it would be several years before you actually got around to stoning Throom anyway. Why don't I just promise to have him back here before then?"

"Outrageous! The very thought is absurd."

"But I need him on my crew. We are already under-staffed as it is!"

"Then you should have kept him from blaspheming the Most High—blessed be his rockets. That is the most serious offense on Alankhus!"

"Really?" Greasly had to keep himself from smiling. "More serious than theft?" he asked with faked surprise.

"Much! Every blessed soul on the planet is crying out for his blood."

"Then trade me Willy for Throom."

The Overseer pondered this. "Why would you want him? He's a thief."

"Let's just say he would be a reasonable substitute for Throom."

"Hmmm. A blasphemer is always a more popular stoning than a thief, and this blasphemer..."

"Sounds like a win-win solution to me."

"But Willy does have a tail..." the Mooner pondered.

"Blasphemy," Greasly coaxed. "Did they tell you what he said about Alan?"

"Let me offer it up to Alan in prayer." The Overseer pushed a button and the vidyacker went dark.

Greasly turned to Throom, who was sitting off to the side. "Are you sure you can take a stoning?"

"From Humans?" Throom snorted and rolled his eyes, revealing the granite he had not painted at the edges of his eyeballs.

Chapter 7

The exchange was made in front of the ship. Throom was bound with the archaic metal hand restraints that had been taken off of Willy, then led by the Mooners back to the city gates while the cap'n shook Willy's hand.

"I'm actually quite honored to meet you. Your reputation is very impressive."

The dark robes of Alankus suited Willy. He was roughly Humanoid, though about half the size of a full grown man. His neck, rather than coming out the top of his shoulders, came out the front of them giving him a perpetually stooped posture, as if cringing. His hair was dark, and in spite of its sabaceousness, stood out in unruly tufts here and there. His eyes were small, dark, and shifty. As he pulled his hand back from greeting the cap'n, his arms went into their natural rest position—bent with his hands near his chest like a squirrel or kangaroo.

He squinted at Greasly. "Hose clamp," he suggested in a hoarse, whispery voice.

"Well, yes, the hose clamp. But even before that."

A lengthy prehensile tail snaked around from under Willy's robe and scratched behind his ear. "Well. Thank you," he rasped.

"Not at all."

"Why have you done this thing?" His voice was like a lonesome wind through a graveyard.

"Because I need your services," confessed Greasly.

Willy nodded. "Of course."

"Believe me, for you this will be nothing." Greasly turned and started up the ladder. "Especially considering what you get in return." When Greasly reached the top he entered the airlock and looked back down the ladder. His heart plummeted. The ladder was empty. "Fark!"

"What is the nature of this service?" The wispy voice came from behind Greasly. He screamed and turned quickly to see Willy standing there with his shifty eyes scanning the airlock.

"Jebus! Don't do that!"

"Do what?"

"Sneak up on me like that," Greasly spluttered. Then, "How did you...?"

Willy's head cocked to the side, and his tiny eyes blinked at Greasly.

"Anyway," Greasly continued, regaining his composure, "I want you to sneak onto a ship and steal something for me."

"And...the catch?"

"That is the catch." Greasly was leading Willy through the interior of the Incorrigible as they spoke. "Of being set free. It's that easy."

"You waste my talents," came a whisper from Greasly's left. Greasly turned, but there was no one there. "I am as omnipresent as shadow, as inevitable as death, as silent as the grave."

Greasly turned all around trying to find Willy. The voice kept moving, but he saw no one. "Maybe so, but that's still what I need done."

Greasly heard Willy whisper in his right ear, "I will do what you ask."

He turned quickly but saw only the storage room they had been walking through. "Good," Greasly said.

Suddenly there was a clattering, a girlish scream, and a thud. Greasly turned to see that Willy the Wisp had fallen over a storage box. He was ignobly struggling with his face pressed into the floor, his stubby legs and snake-like tail flailing. Greasly moved to help him, but Willy jerked to the side, pulled himself to his feet, and brushed himself off.

Willy laughed self-consciously. "I'm a little out of practice." His voice was different now—more nasal. "Look at that!" He pointed behind Greasly. Greasly saw nothing, but when he looked back, Willy was gone.

The faintest shadow of a whisper of a doubt crossed Greasly's mind.

Chapter 8

"Stop!" the black-robed Ear commanded. He stretched with his hands on his lower back trying to catch his breath. In stoning arena number two seventeen, the circle of stone throwers stopped throwing. As the cloud of dust began to settle, the crowd watching the stoning held their breath.

Throom had indeed been a large draw. Even on such short notice, the seats were filled, and a crowd had even formed around the stoners on the stoning grounds itself. No one had complained about the substitution once they heard what Throom was guilty of. In fact they had a record number of stoners sign up and pay the premium to enact the justice of Alan on Throom the Blasphemer—an act that was proving more difficult than they had imagined.

The stoners were very weary at this point. Some were bent over with hands on their knees, others grasped their sides in pain, and still others were spread out on the ground in exhaustion.

The Ear walked to the pile of stones in the center of the circle. He caught his breath, then called out, "Remove." He gestured feebly at the rocks, unable at the moment to think of the word for them.

Several guards came forward and started digging into the stones, handing them back to the crowd. Eventually they uncovered the top half of Throom, who was buried up to his chest in the dirt with his hands at his side in the traditional Jordanian being-stoned position. His head was slumped forward. There was no sign of movement.

An argument broke out between two stoners that both claimed to be the owner of a custom made Justice Bringer

420, but they were too tired to put much effort into the squabble.

Throom's slumped form was dirty and battered. When Throom painted himself, he had used the same paint used on the outside of mining ships—the rubberized kind that was designed to resist impact after impact—but even a mighty mountain can be ground down by grains of sand over time. After three stonings, the paint was beginning to chip in several places. To the casual observer, however, the chips appeared to be only spots of dirt.

"Tell me he's dead this time."

The guard bent down to pull back Throom's head by the glued-on wig.

Throom suddenly opened his eyes and smiled, full of energy. "Sorry about that! I dozed off. Where were we?"

The Ear threw up his hands and spoke heavenward, "Your will be done, Alan." Then, with a dejected wave to the guards, "Release him."

"What? So soon?" Throom complained, wanting to rub it in. "Rest up a while and give it another shot," he urged, but they were already digging him out.

Later, as Throom walked through the exhausted and dumbfounded crowd, one of the first faces he passed was the gold-toothed benefactor that had been there when he committed the crime. His new admirer dropped to one knee with his hands in Mooner prayer.

"Stand up and stop that," Throom snapped. He immediately obeyed.

Throom spoke to one of the stoners, "You know, you've got a good arm, but you need to follow through. Get your back into it."

The Alanic guards were wearily urging Throom to leave. He moved on, shouting one last piece of advice over his shoulder as he did, "Be the rock!"

Chapter 9

After Penny and Hardegar had gotten back on board at the arranged rendezvous point in a tiny village south of the city, the Incorrigible entered Flitzville and headed toward Slavin. Actually, when discussing Flitzville, it would be more accurate to say that it headed in a long series of seemingly random directions that would eventually cause it to be located in the normal space coordinates occupied by the Slavin system.

As they sat in the briefing room discussing the last mission, Greasly was all but staring at Hardegar and how his skin was darker and more taught.

"What happened to you?" Greasly asked at last.

"I got tanned," Hardegar beamed. It seemed to be harder for him to form words, as if his skin had hardened.

"I didn't know that dead skin would tan."

"Not that kind of tanning," Penny put in, "like they do to animal hides."

One end of Cap'n Greasly's lip curled up in disgust. "Really?"

Penny nodded. "There was a tanner in the village. God, it smelled awful."

"How does it feel?" the cap'n asked Hardegar.

"It's a little stiff, but I'm sure I'll get it broken in," reported Hardegar. He tried to blink but could not manage it.

"Well, anyway. . ."—the cap'n slapped his knees and addressed the room— "everyone did a great job back there. Especially you, Throom."

Throom grinned. The paint had been removed, and he was back to his old stony self. "It was nothing."

"True enough, but thank you anyway. So here's the current situation. I have verified Groat's destination as Slavin. We have the universe's best pilot and navigator on board, and Flathead tells me we will arrive at least one hour before Ratner. The only tricky part now will be to locate The Other Woman before they Flitz again. That's where you come in, Penny.

The Other Woman uses an old multi-fractal-modulation Flitzdrive. They put off a similar sub-ether resonance to the reverse-lateral-luminance drives that replaced them. So if there happen to be some of the old RLL drives in the area, you will only have about five minutes to weed out the RLLs and spot The Other Woman's MFM drive among them. Any longer than that, and there's a good chance we won't have time to pull this off before they Flitz again."

"No problem," she said, "all I have to do is—"

"Don't explain," the cap'n interrupted, "just do it. Any questions?"

Penny blinked, a little taken aback, but his tone had not seemed malicious. She was discovering that Greasly had a curious way of being able to do things like that without upsetting her. Or at least not too much. Or maybe it was just that after the first thing he had ever said to her, everything else seemed like an improvement. "Is that for decoration or what?" he had said in reference to her forehead, even before "Welcome aboard", or "Glad to meet you."

"No, is that?" she had responded curtly in reference to the Galactic Guard emblem on his shoulder.

At the time, she had not cared if it cost her her position, but he had just smiled, said "mostly", and went on as if the exchange had never occurred.

"I have a question," Klorf said for Kurplupt. "Why is the thief not at this briefing?"

"Who said he isn't?" asked Greasly.

"He's right behind you," Willy attempted to whisper menacingly in Klorf's ear, but before he could finish the word "behind", Klorf's hand shot around and lifted him from the floor by his face. His nasal, muffled voice seemed to whine something about "lemming dough" as his small arms and legs worked uselessly like the limbs of an up-turned beetle.

"This," asked Klorf incredulously, "is Willy the Wisp?"

"Yes," admitted the cap'n. "Put him down, Klorf." Then he caught himself. "I mean Kurplupt."

The flapulate was already on Greasly's side of the jar. The words "YOU WILL NOT ADDRESS" were scrolling across it. Greasly just ignored them.

Klorf dropped Willy, who fell gracelessly onto his butt. Willy sat there rubbing his nose and glaring at the burly cling-on.

"You were very fast, my friend." He squinted meaningfully. "This time." Then he stood and pointed at the far corner of the room. "Look!"

Klorf's gaze did not move from the little man. Willy grew nervous—his eyes darting around the room.

"Kurplupt is talking to you!" he blurted out at last, pointing to the jar.

Klorf's eyes narrowed suspiciously. He tried to glance as quickly as he could at Kurplupt who was, as it happened, still trying to communicate his outrage to the cap'n. The instant he was out of Klorf's view, Penny saw Willy dart behind the chair next to Klorf but did not see him exit the other side.

When Klorf looked back, Willy was apparently not visible to him either. He growled and scanned the room with his dark eyes.

"Willy has been incarcerated for a long time," the cap'n rationalized. "He's a little rusty at what he does, but still, The Other Woman should prove no problem."

"But how do we get him on board?" It was Hardegar asking.

"It's taken care of," the cap'n assured them.

Chapter 10

The thing tumbling through the heatless vacuum of space appeared to be a shipping crate.

"Shall I blast it?" asked the young Nootian eagerly. Nootians were built the same as Humans, but their average height was about 1.6 meters, and their skin was a shiny cherry red. This particular Nootian had very short blonde hair and an impish look in his eyes. His crimson hand hovered eagerly over a button—an actual old fashioned button—marked "Blast It, Baby." All around him on the walls of the bridge were psychedelic light patterns.

"Hold on, Cookie," Groat could see, as the crate tumbled slowly end for end, that it had writing on it. "Zoom in, Jones."

An amorphous jelly covering one of the consoles twitched, and the magnification of the view screen increased. Groat waited for it to tumble around again. This time he could read it clearly. It said: "Danger! Thranian Pecker Beasts. Do not thaw before cooking."

"Wow!" Groat exclaimed. "Hey, Toby, can we get a yoink beam on that?"

"I believe so," responded his Xemite first mate. Toby was a tall Humanoid with pale green skin and roughly the face of a Human, as long as the Human in question had only one large eye. This facial deficiency was more than compensated for by the fact that each of the dozen or so stalks coming out of the top of his head sported a functional eye at the end.

"Then reel it in."

The Xemite nodded his head and began flipping and pressing the ultra-retro buttons and switches of The Other Woman. A glittering lime green beam shot out from the ball of the trailer hitch and passed through the tiny cube. The trajectory of the rolling cube altered, curved, and bent into the glittering beam.

* * *

Meanwhile, on the bridge of the Incorrigible, Cap'n Greasly grinned with satisfaction. He turned to Throom and raised his eyebrows a couple of times. "He took the bait, Throom."

"Yes, he did," acknowledged Throom.

"He took the bait," he repeated—this time to Hardegar. Hardegar tried to nod, but his neck skin was still too stiff.

"Penny," Greasly prefaced.

"He took the bait," she finished.

"Yes, he did." He was beaming. "He certainly did."

"Kurplupt wishes to understand the technology they are using," said Klorf.

"The yoink beam?" Greasly seemed surprised that Kurplupt had never seen one before.

Penny jumped in with the answer. "There are a few different models. We have a Simpson model, but from the green sparkle, I can tell they have an old Cartesian model. That kind works by directing a stream of molecular screws all rotating in the same direction. As the screws pass through the target, each imparts a small force in the direction opposite the screw's line of travel. The net force is sufficient to pull most objects toward the source of the beam but still harmless to most living matter."

"It does tingle, though," Hardegar threw in.

"I'm afraid that is a common misconception. The screws are actually far too small to be felt."

"Misconception, my ass," countered Hardegar.

"I beg your pardon!" Penny flushed at the affront. "And what exactly makes you an expert on the effect of yoink beams on *living* matter anyway?"

"First of all, I used to be living, and second of all, I have actually been yoinked." He paused to let that sink in. "Have you?"

She only glared in response.

"It tingles," Hardegar concluded triumphantly.

"Hey, do you guys mind?" complained Greasly. "You're interrupting a perfectly good gloat here."

* * *

Back on The Other Woman, they were busy taking the bait.

"We have a solid lock on it, Sir," reported Toby—his three-fingered hands busy with the buttons, switches, and knobs on the striped-fur-covered console. "Where should we put it?"

Groat stood up from the red velour captain's chair and straightened his green satin shirt. He brushed off his checkered golf pants and decided, "How about the starboard cargo bay?"

Toby nodded several of his eye stalks and got to work maneuvering The Other Woman into position.

"Come on, Cookie, and grab a gun."

Groat ducked under the tassels along the top of the doorway and left the bridge. Cookie followed eagerly behind, his canary yellow teeth showing out of the grin on his scarlet face as he grabbed a weapon.

Minutes later, a panel on the outside of The Other Woman opened—breaking up a painted message that read: "If the ship's a rockin' don't try to raise us on the hailing frequency." Through a window in the inner door, Groat watched the cube tumble into the cargo bay and land gently—guided by artificial gravity. The outer door closed. Groat turned to face Cookie. "Let's go."

He pressed the button to open the door. It slid open with a sexy female sigh. They entered the cargo bay and readied their weapons.

"I'm ready when you are," said Cookie, standing near the crate.

"Okay now, if there happens to be a thawed pecker beast in there, don't hesitate. Just shoot."

"Got it."

"And Cookie."

"Yeah?"

"Aim for the pecker," he said solemnly. "They're helpless without it."

Cookie nodded.

"I'll be right over here." Groat ducked behind a piece of loading machinery.

"Hey, why do I have to open the thing?" Cookie complained.

"Because I'm a Human, and you are a Nootian."

"So?"

"Well, let's just say there is more than one reason they call them pecker beasts."

Cookie rolled his eyes and shook his head. "That thing is the weakness of your race, Groat—always has been." Then, as he turned and readied himself to open the crate, "You should have it removed like we do."

"Just open the crate."

Cookie operated the mechanism and stood back, gun readied, as the side of the crate fell open. The crate was empty except for a few empty packing boxes. Cookie entered the crate and kicked the boxes around but found nothing else.

Cookie and Groat relaxed.

"Fark," Groat sighed after examining the crate inside and out. He shrugged. "Oh well, it was worth checking out."

He walked out of the cargo bay with the Nootian at his side. "You have any idea what an order of pecker nuggets goes for on Oon?"

* * *

"He's in," Penny reported from her console on the bridge of the Incorrigible.

"Great! Flathead, bring us into their sensor range," Greasly commanded. "Make it close, she was built for comfort, not..."—he realized too late that he had started down the wrong cliche—"...sensoring," he finished apologetically.

"Aye Cap'n." Flathead flapped in the course.

"Oh, and not too fast. Give Willy time to find the thing."

Chapter 11

Jones bubbled and hissed.

"Put it on screen," Groat commanded. The view screen, which had silver silhouettes of nude women at each of the lower corners, suddenly filled with an image of the Incorrigible.

"Lou Tok Greasly," Groat muttered mostly to himself. "What the hell do you want?"

Jones shivered and let out a long, slobbery stream of air.

"Okay then, patch him through."

The image of the Incorrigible was replaced by Cap'n Greasly. "Hey, Ratner."

"Hey, Greasly. Come back to lose more money?" He smiled with perfect teeth from under a jet-black pencil thin mustache. There was a twinkle in his brown eyes.

"No, I came to win the pink slip to that floating brothel of yours."

"You hold on to your dreams, Greasly."

"Actually, I just happened to be in the area and wanted to talk to you about that log you won off me."

"Talk."

"I was just wondering if you wanted to cut your losses. I have a contact from the Galactic Society for the Preservation of Hoaxes who would be willing to buy it."

"Nice try, Greasly."

"No, really. I'm willing to make you a handsome offer."

Groat pushed a button, and a shaken martini rose up out of the armrest of his captain's chair. He sipped at it, licked his lips, then spoke. "Go ahead."

"Well, I thought maybe I could come aboard and talk about it." Greasly riffled the deck of cards he was holding.

Groat broke into a laugh. "You are so predictable, Lou, but there is no way you're coming over here. I'll come over there."

Greasly looked concerned. "But we just painted here. It's full of paint fumes, and The Other Woman is much more comfortable than the Incorrigible."

"You got that right! But you're not coming over here while I have the log on board. I'm not stupid."

Greasly looked angry. "You're saying you don't trust me."

"That sums it up."

"Fine. You can come over here, but if you asphyxiate it's your own damn fault."

"Be over in a few," Ratner concluded in a self-satisfied tone. "Jones." The blob twitched, and the view screen went dark.

Ratner looked at Toby. Toby's large eye and several of his small eyes blinked back at him. "What?"

"Why even talk to him? He seems to have nothing to offer, and he clearly wants the log," Toby reasoned. "It makes no sense."

"He's an old friend." Ratner shrugged. "Sort of," he modified. "It won't hurt to humor him. What could he do? He might cheat me. He would certainly lie to me, but he would never kidnap me or resort to extortion. I'll just humor the old has-been."

"Humor," Toby asked, "or taunt?"

Ratner Groat lost his fight against smiling. "You know me too well, Toby. It makes me think you've been on this ship too long. Jones, put Stuart on the screen."

The view screen was suddenly filled with a sea of billowing flesh covered with a tightly stretched and brightly flowered muumuu. A floppy-jowled, greasy head was poking out the top. "Stuart," Groat said. The head turned toward him with an air of annoyance.

"What?" Stuart snapped.

"You still working on decoding the log?"

"Of course I am. What else would I be doing?" A fat finger poked out from one of the folds of the muumuu and jabbed at a console. A screen changed its image before Ratner could be sure what the old image had been, but whatever it was it had had a lot of flesh tones. "I'm running several decryption programs against it now."

"All right." Groat was about to have Jones disconnect him when he was struck by a realization. "Stuart?"

"What?"

"Have you lost weight?"

"Probably. It's impossible to get a proper meal on this tub."

"Well, it looks good on you." He motioned to Jones. Stuart sneered as his image disappeared. "Ready the shuttle, Cookie."

"Ready the shuttle, Cookie," Cookie grumbled under his breath as he headed for the shuttle bay.

On the way to the shuttle bay, Groat got nervous and detoured to his cabin. After checking to make sure he was alone, he opened a storage chest. He picked up the log of Bartholomew Methane and satisfied himself that it was real and still in his possession. He tossed it back in and closed the chest.

As he was leaving his cabin, he had a strange feeling that he was being followed. He entered the cabin again and looked around. After convincing himself that he was only being paranoid, he shrugged and went to the shuttle bay.

Chapter 12

Ratner Groat and Lou Tok Greasly sat opposite each other at a card table in the rec room of the Incorrigible.

"Double low reach-around fisbin Chicago with aces wild," announced Groat, dealing the cards from behind his stacks of poker chips.

Greasly's stacks were not nearly as impressive as Groat's pile or even as impressive as his own had been when the first hand had been dealt. Greasly picked up his hole cards and arranged them carefully.

"You know I've been here quite a while and haven't smelled paint yet," goaded Groat.

"Really?" Greasly sniffed the air. "You can't smell that?"

"No."

"Hmm." Greasly shrugged. "Twenty." A mechanical arm emerged from the table and quickly transferred twenty moola's worth of chips to the middle of the table.

"Call." Groat dealt the next round of cards as the arm added the proper number of chips to the pot. He turned over the next card as the fisbin. It was a four of clubs. "Puppy paws," he announced.

The two of them got up and walked around the table several times. When they sat back down, they had swapped seats. The mechanical arm slumped briefly, then—setting gintResolve to INTMAX—swapped their chip piles at high speed. The cards stayed where they were. Each player picked up his new cards.

"So have you had a chance to look at that log you took from me?" Greasly probed.

"You mean the one you won off that prospector two minutes before I won it off you fair and square? Forty."

"I think that's the one. See your forty and raise ten."

"Call," said Groat.

There was another round of dealing and another fisbin— Queen of hearts this time. "Lady love," Groat heralded with a smirk, "Jacks wild."

"Did you happen to bring it with you? I'd like to look at it."

"I bet you would." Groat shook his head at Greasly's ham-handed tactics.

"What would it be worth to you?" Greasly pressed.

"To let you see it?"

"Yes."

"For how long? Long enough to make a copy?" Groat asked sarcastically. "Your bet."

"Roughly, yes. Sixty." The arm quickly transferred some chips then stopped, turning it's hand partly sideways like a curious puppy's head. It gently tapped Greasly's left hand, which was resting on the pile of chips it needed to get to. He moved it, and the chips were quickly transferred.

"More than you've got. Raise twenty-five."

"How do you know what I've got? Call."

Groat provided another round of dealing—this one face up—and another fisbin. "The gravediggers spade. Damn," he complained as the mechanical arm used his chips to double the size of the pot. "Whatever you've got, it's not enough."

"Don't tell me you think it's genuine." Greasly tried to muster incredulity, but acting was not his strong suit.

"Don't try to tell me you think it's not. One hundred. I'm not totally stupid, Lou."

"One hundred!?" Greasly repeated in shock.

"That's right."

"Fark!" Greasly reluctantly said, "call." Another round of dealing. Another fisbin—a black seven.

"Eclipse. No betting." The mechanical arm folded back for a well-deserved rest. Groat dealt the last round. He flipped over the last fisbin—the slop fisbin. It was a ten of diamonds. "Damn. Taxes."

Smiling smugly, Greasly turned over the next three cards and added their values. "Seventeen."

Back in action, the arm added seventeen of Groat's moolas to the pot. "Last round of betting. You have an ace showing."

"I'll bet everything I have left," offered Greasly, "and you don't even have to match it, but if I win, you sell me the log for ten thousand moolas."

"No, Lou. Just bet."

"Everything here plus five thousand," Greasly blurted.

"No. No. No. Just bet." Groat was pretending to be annoyed, but a glint in his eye showed he was having fun as well.

Greasly shrugged and bet five.

"Raise one hundred," Groat said smugly as he pushed a stack in manually. The arm flitted back and forth, momentarily confused.

Unseen by Groat, Hardegar poked his head into the room and nodded at Greasly as best he could.

"Fold," stated Greasly. The mechanical arm was a blur of motion as it transferred the pot into orderly stacks on Groat's side of the table.

"Fold? You can't be serious. You stand to more than double your bet." Groat eyed him suspiciously.

"Will you throw in the right to buy the log?"

"No."

"Fold."

"Come on, Lou, don't be that way."

"There's no 'way' about it. Take the pot." He gathered the cards and removed their moola pods from the slots in the table. "It's been nice seeing you again."

Groat was very suspicious now. "It's not like you to take no for an answer."

"Isn't it?"

"No."

"I don't accept that 'no'. " He was up and herding Groat to the door, slapping Groat's updated moola pod into his hand as they moved.

"What is it? What just happened?" Groat looked around the room for clues.

Greasly sighed. "Okay, look. I just wanted to make one shot at getting the log from you. I did. Didn't get it. Now I've got things to do, okay?"

They were at the door of the cargo hold. Greasly helped Groat through.

"What would you put up against the log?" Groat asked.

"Nothing. Thanks anyway."

"Now I KNOW something's wrong."

"Really?" asked the cap'n blandly as he tapped a console. The door slid between them. He spoke to Groat via the interyacker, "The outer door is going to open in 30 seconds."

Glowering now, Groat patted his belongings over to make sure they were all there. He grabbed the key to his shuttle and pressed the button.

By the time he got back to The Other Woman, the Incorrigible was gone. He ran through the wood paneled hallways to his cabin and threw open his storage chest.

The log was gone.

He stood and pressed a button to page Cookie.

"Cookie here."

"Cookie, that bastard stole the log. I don't know how he did it, but track him!"

Just then he looked again at his storage chest, and there—as clear as day—sat the log.

"Hold on." Groat picked up the log then looked so violently around the room that one or two of his hairs broke loose from their gel. He weighed the log in his hand. It was real enough.

He shook his head. "Never mind," he said to Cookie, "my mistake. But I want you and Toby to check the shuttle over for bugs or tracers."

He broke communications then, scratching his head, walked over to fix himself a drink.

Chapter 13

The first action Greasly took once he had possession of the log was to take a two day Flitz into deep space, so that he could focus on decoding the log with little worry of Ratner showing up. Then with parting words of "Take care of the ship. Take care of yourselves. I'll see you when I see you," he disappeared into his cabin with the log. From that point on, even if you saw him outside the cabin he was so absorbed in his thoughts that he might as well have still been in there.

At first the crew seemed to be enjoying the extra time to themselves. The first few days, Throom would find Penny lounging in the observation deck reading something trashy while snacking and drinking a beer. By day four, however, he instead found her pacing in irritation, and by day five she was disassembling sensors to try to improve their sensitivity. Between that endeavor and Flathead running himself through advanced piloting simulations, the bridge was busier than Throom had ever seen it.

Because he never slept, Throom had even more time to fill than the rest of the crew. He read a lot, watched info-vids, listened to info-squawks, and inched his way through the vast steaming pile of logic that was called the ship's non-vital control layer, looking for a way around the troublesome door delay other than rewiring all the mechanisms. All this was in addition to keeping up regular maintenance on the ship.

Throom found the care and upkeep of the Incorrigible to be a very calming and rewarding thing even though it was—no actually, *because* it was—so diametrically opposed to his internal makeup. In addition to the feelings of accomplishment, he also got the exhilaration that comes from self-discipline. It also occasionally gave him some bonding time with other members of the crew, since some of his tasks required more delicacy than his stone fingers could deliver. Usually, Flathead was his go-to person for such things, but today Flathead was busy, so Throom asked Hardegar to help him change the secondary inthripulator on deck 2.

Throom popped the floor panel up out of its securing snaps and set it to the side of the corridor. The sub-floor area that was revealed was a roiling snarl of cables entangling strange devices of diverse shapes and sizes.

"Is this it?" Hardegar asked, rapping his knuckle sharply on a hefty looking cylindrical device.

"No," Throom said, moving Hardegar's hand away from the device, "that's a gravitic generator. Very expensive."

"Okay, so what am I looking for?"

Throom pointed out a prolate spheroid (what an ancient North American would call a "football" shape) about 10 centimeters long that was formed out of a fleshy pink material. Across the top, two puffy "lips" ran the length of it. "It's inside this veneral pod. It opens where those two ridges butt up against each other along the top."

Hardegar looked at the pod then pulled back to give Throom an odd sideways glance, "Are you serious?" he asked.

Throom was not sure what to make of the question. "Of course," he said.

With a shrug, Hardegar reached for the pod.

"Be careful, though, Hardegar," Throom warned. "You need to warm it up a little so it opens. Just move your finger back and forth along the seam for a while."

"You want me to be gentle," Hardegar confirmed then shook his head for some reason, smirking. "Okay."

"It's just that it's new and hasn't been opened before."

Throom wondered at Hardegar's laughter. Maybe his Brain Bubble was beginning to break down.

"This is really taking me back," Hardegar mused as he stroked the seam. His expression had changed to one Throom found cryptic. He was biting his leathery lip and his eye lids seemed to be getting heavier.

"I can do this part if you want," Throom offered.

"No," Hardegar snapped. Then a bit later, "There. It's starting to open."

"Okay, now at one end you'll find a little button. Move it gently in a circle."

Hardegar sat up looking around. "Okay, what's going on here?"

"What do you mean?"

"You're recording this, right? The other guys are laughing their asses off right now, aren't they."

Throom held up his hands in a shrug. "I don't know what they're doing."

"But this is a prank, right?"

"No." Throom stared at him in puzzlement.

Hardegar looked Throom over and apparently decided he trusted him, because he knelt back down and went back to work on the veneral pod. His expression gradually changed again. "I'll tell you what, Throom. Prank or no, this is really activating my erectron."

Throom had no clue how to respond to that. He mentally tried several responses but rejected them all, ultimately just nodding and smiling. Luckily the pod opened completely at that point and changed the subject. In keeping with the retro theme of the Incorrigible, when the pod split open it did so with a hydraulic hiss and its interior was filled with bubbling, backlit fog. In the midst of the fog was what looked like a small, translucent, yellow sea cucumber with long, fibrous spikes.

"That's the inthripulator, I bet," Hardegar offered.

"Correct. You can just pull that old one out."

The inthripulator made a slurping tearing sound followed by a snap as Hardegar plucked the rubbery thing from its resting place. The spikes along the underside had all been inside deep holes in the veneral pod.

"Good. Now this is the delicate part," Throom said as he took the inthripulator from Hardegar and gave him the replacement. He then gave him a thin, plastic tool. "You need to put the new one in the recess but guide all the spiky things into those little holes."

"Got it. Does it matter what side is up?"

"No. Just start at one end and lay it down into position as you go."

Hardegar got to work.

"Thanks again, Hardegar. I know this is tedious. I'm sorry I interrupted you."

"No sweat, Throom. I was just sitting around reading the Bible anyway."

"You really have changed," Throom mused. "I can't imagine the old you doing that."

"Reading the Bible?"

"Reading," Throom specified.

"Probably not. Back then I was too busy to read." As Hardegar worked, a nostalgic grin grew on his face along with some of that odd expression Throom had seen earlier.

"I remember," Throom assured him. "I mean, I'm no judge of things like that, but some of your stories made the cap'n blush."

"Those were some wild times," Hardegar admitted with pride, "but I'm a Christian now. I'm settling down. Walking the straight and narrow path."

Throom had read the Bible, so he understood the allusion. "That must be hard for you."

"Being dead makes it easier, but yeah," Hardegar paused his work to point at Throom. "Worth it, though. I don't want to be on the wrong side when the apocalypse starts. You shouldn't either. You should convert." He thrust his finger forward again as if to refresh his point then went back to work.

"To Christianity?"

"Of course. We're the oldest apocalyptic religion in the universe, Throom. I think we know something about it, don't you?"

"I guess that's one way to look at it."

"I mean, even if you and I don't live to see the end times—which are coming very soon, mind you—you should still be worrying about staying out of Hell."

"By becoming Christian."

"Of course." Hardegar finished the installation and sat up. "You give your heart to Jesus, and you stay out of Hell. I mean, that's cheap at twice the price."

Throom was less than sold on the idea. "Well, I'll think about it," he said noncommittally, then with a motion to the pod, "Just push the two halves up until they join."

Hardegar closed the pod, kissed his fingers and touched the lips of the thing. "Night-night baby," he said.

Throom assumed this must be some odd human superstition. He replaced the floor panel as Hardegar sat back and continued his soul pitch.

"Not only that, Throom, but it gives your life meaning. Gives you a purpose."

"I already have one of those," Throom said, trying but failing to hide his dislike of the fact.

"I mean a higher purpose, though."

"Higher in what way?"

"I don't know, like ultimate, I guess." Hardegar shrugged. "The reason you were created."

"I know the reason I was created," Throom assured him. "I know my ultimate purpose, and it is not something I'm proud of."

"How can you say that?" Hardegar was shocked. "What do you think your purpose is?"

Throom looked him straight in the eye. "My purpose is destruction."

"No, man, no. Why would you think that?"

"I can't not think it, Hardegar. It's built into me," he explained. "My designers didn't want there to be any doubt over such a basic concept, so every Fraggart has that knowledge from the day they are created, and there is no way to change it or forget it. In fact if you beat any of us in a game we go into a mode where we state our purpose along with a list of all of the engineers of the slag pits on Frag. No one knows why."

"Whoa whoa whoa," Hardegar snapped as he leaped to his feet. "Designers? Engineers?"

Throom stood from his squatting position. "Yes," he said with an implied "so what?"

"You mean you're a manufactured intelligent life form?"

"Are you serious? We worked together all those years and you never realized I was a MILF?"

"No!"

"Well I am," Throom bent to gather the tools.

"Wow. Well never mind then."

"Never mind what?"

"I'm sorry I tried to convert you."

"Why?"

"Well you don't have to worry about any of that. Manufactured beings don't have a soul, and you can't go to Hell if you don't have a soul."

Throom was stunned. Both at the nerve of an animated corpse telling him he had no soul and at himself for being offended. A few minutes ago, he probably would have argued against the existence of the soul himself, (at least a detachable one) but now that someone was telling him that he didn't have one, it all seemed different. Suddenly it felt like he was being demoted—sent to the back of the shuttle. "Look," he said deliberately, "If anyone has a soul, I do."

"Don't get mad, buddy," Hardegar spluttered. "It's just a fact of nature."

"Doesn't the book of Oprah say that all sentient life has a soul?"

"Yes, and spirit, and mind."

"So your own Bible says I have a soul."

"Well," Hardegar seemed uncomfortable. "It does specify sentient."

Throom blinked at him. "Are you serious?"

All Hardegar could do was shrug apologetically.

"I'm not even sentient!?"

"Well you just said it yourself," Hardegar pointed out. "To be sentient you have to have a soul, spirit, and mind." Hardegar held up a finger for each attribute, then pulled one back. "You're one short."

Throom stood agape at how Hardegar had taken his logic and turned it inside out and stomped on it. He finally had to shake his head and start over. "You just told me you thought I was a naturally occurring organic being all these years." Throom held up a finger. "You're standing here having a conversation with me." A second finger. "Yet you're telling me I'm not sentient?"

"It's complicated, Throom."

"Not really," Throom insisted. "If you tell someone they're not sentient, and that pisses them off, then odds are they're sentient!"

"Who's sentient?" Flathead asked as he flapped up the corridor behind Throom.

"Oh, hi Flathead," Throom said. "We're all done. Thanks for checking."

"All over but the shouting, it sounds like."

"I was just a little upset because I found out that Hardegar here doesn't consider me to be sentient."

"What?" Then to Hardegar, "Are you serious?"

"Well first off, did you realize that Throom was a MILF? I just found out."

Flathead was so floored by this question that he had to fall back on reruns for his response. "Are you serious?"

"Yes, he's manufactured," Hardegar assured him. "Aren't you, Throom?"

"I meant are you serious that you didn't know." Flathead clarified.

"Oh."

"And," Throom interjected, "Hardegar informs me that MILFs do not have souls and are not sentient."

"That's ridiculous," Flathead opined. "Of course Throom is sentient. What ship would have a non-sentient first mate?"

"Good point," Throom commended, holding up three fingers.

"He might not have a soul, but he is definitely sentient."

"Exactly," Throom concurred, then caught himself. "Wait. What? You don't think I have a soul either?"

"Of course not; only Kravitsians have souls."

"And Humans," Hardegar added, glad for the support.

"No," Flathead rejected. "Just Kravitsians."

It was Hardegar's turn to be taken aback. "Are you actually trying to tell me that Humans don't have souls?" Hardegar blustered. "We invented souls, you little..." he searched his hardware for some analogue for Flathead that was more insulting than squid.

"Actually, the Hub invented souls," Flathead corrected gently, "and he gave them exclusively to those who were not tempted by the errant limb."

"Huh?"

"It's very simple," Flathead went on. "In the beginning, all was shapeless and without definite form—in short, floppy—and the great Hub saw it was good. And he created eight Kravitsians to live in this perfect world. But one of them was tempted by the rebellious limb to take hard parts into itself."

"The rebellious what?" Hardegar asked.

"Limb," Flathead waved one of his tentacles in the air as an example. "The one that rebelled from the all-loving Hub and detached itself to roam the world creating mischief—the progenitor of firmity."

Hardegar was struck by a thought. "That's practically a serpent."

"I never thought of that before," said Flathead, intrigued. "Interesting parallel."

"But why would any of this mean that I don't have a soul?" Hardegar snapped back on subject.

"Because the soul was a special gift to the seven that did not rebel. For those seven, the great hub first removed one limb so that we might remember the transgressor then gave to us alone the gift of a soul."

"Only you," Hardegar said incredulously.

"Spoke 3, section 42, stanza 10," Flathead cited. "To you who stood firm against firmness, I grant you alone for your pureness, self knowledge and reason that lives on when even your body's consumed in the furnace."

Hardegar was about to object, but then stopped, blinking. "Was that a limerick?" he asked blankly.

"No," gasped Flathead, "it is written in the holy form of the Floppy."

"Which also happens to be a limerick," Throom put in.

"Yes," Hardegar concurred, "believe me, it's the one form of poetry I know, and that was a limerick."

"Really?" Flathead tried it out. "There once was a man from Nantucket." Then in comparison, "To you who stood firm against firmness" he continued the comparison all the way through to "And carry it home in a bucket."

"See?"

"Just because it has the meter and rhyme scheme of a limerick doesn't mean it's a limerick!" snapped Flathead petulantly.

"Actually, I think it does," Throom soothed, patting Flathead's flat head.

"Well, that's just the way it translates, anyway," Flathead grumbled. "In Kravitsian it sounds nothing like that." He began to recite the same verse in Kravitsian—a language made up entirely of slaps and slides of the tentacles.

As Throom listened, he definitely heard the rhythm of a limerick, but he didn't want to belabor the point. "Anyway," he said, "So now we know I don't have a soul and neither do Humans."

Hardegar objected, "Human's do have souls," he insisted, "no matter what your poem says. It says so right there in the Bible."

"Poem?!" a shocked Flathead ejaculated.

Throom decided this was his stop. He knew that at this point neither side would be able to support their position with reasonable arguments, and it would devolve into a shouting match. "Look, guys," he said, "I'm going to have to leave this debate in your capable hands and tentacles. I might not have a soul, but I do have work to do." He turned and headed off down the corridor.

"Don't go away mad, Throom," Flathead called after him.

"Yeah," Hardegar agreed. "I really wish you did have a soul."

Throom kept walking.

"It's nothing personal," Flathead and Hardegar called after him in unison.

Chapter 14

18th day in deep space

Throom entered the cap'n's cabin and stopped, momentarily certain he had entered a trash chute by mistake. The floor was covered with crumpled paper, food wrappers, and food. The debris seemed to climb the walls, since they were covered with scribbled notes stuck around in no discernible pattern. Across from the door the cap'n was hunched at a console, his back to Throom and haloed by the light of the display as he tapped in information.

"Cap'n?" Throom prodded. "Do you need anything?"

Greasly turned abruptly to face Throom. "What?!"

"I asked if you needed anything."

Greasly looked lost, like it was the strangest thing he had ever been asked in his life. Then, in an instant, he stood with his finger in the air and lunged at the wall of notes. Scanning them with ferocity, he found the one he wanted and plucked it from the wall. Then he was back at the console again. "You'll have to get it yourself, Throom. I'm busy here."

Throom considered trying to correct him but envisioned it taking the better part of an hour to get the concept straight. Greasly was a grown man and the cap'n of the ship. If he needed anything he could get it himself.

Throom exited into the corridor and went next door to his real destination, Penny's cabin. He activated the panel to announce himself, and soon the door slid open.

"Hey, Throom." Penny greeted. "Something wrong?"

"Not really. Well somewhat. I'd like to talk to you for a minute."

"Uh-oh," she said as she motioned him in.

Like most of the cabins on the Incorrigible, the cabin was three by three meters with the space taken up by a fold down bunk on one wall, a pull-down desk on another, and dozens of cubbies, each with a door that operated similar to an ancient roll-top desk. Since both the bunk and desk were down, there was little room for a massive Fraggart and a woman to stand.

"Do you want to sit?" Penny offered, motioning to the bunk.

"You have your cabin set to 1G. I'd crush it."

"I can lower the gravity."

"No. Please don't bother. I can stand indefinitely."

"I sure can't," she said and boosted herself up to her bunk. "I think I know what this is about."

"Klorf?"

"I knew I shouldn't do it." she admitted.

"Kurplupt is very unhappy. I don't think I've ever seen so many capital letters in my life."

"I'm so sorry, Throom. It was unfair to you."

"I get it, Penny. You know I do. You know I want better for Klorf." He searched for words.

"I know, Throom." She smiled at him with a softness he would have thought impossible a couple of months ago. "I'll stop trying to talk to him."

"Thank you," he said and turned to leave. Then stopped and turned back. "You know, I think that we are having an influence even when we play by Kurplupt's rules.

"How's that?"

"Just by how we all treat each other. Sometimes the most life-changing thing that can happen to a person is just to see that there are options. That there are other ways of doing things."

Penny smiled. "I hope you're right, Throom."

"Me too."

"Say, while we're on the subject of Kurplupt and his rules, would you mind telling him that no one is getting on or off the ship while we're floating in deep space and he can stop demanding ID from us all."

Throom groaned. "Okay."

"And speaking of that. Are we supposed to have IDs?"

"No," Throom confirmed. "Never have."

"Kurplupt might need to hear that, too."

Chapter 15

19th day in deep space

"In accordance with my position as head of security," Klorf recited, "I demand that official IDs be issued to all duly vetted members of the Incorrigible crew." He and Throom sat at one of the mess tables with Kurplut between them, pressed against the top of his cylinder. A beam of light from above shown down onto the cylinder.

"I don't understand why we would need them," Throom complained.

"To ensure security," was the response.

"But Kurplupt, we have a crew of only five," Throom reasoned, being careful not to count Klorf.

"Yes."

"You can't tell us apart?"

There was a pause.

"Kurplupt? Do you have trouble telling us apart?"

"I must admit that the similarity of your forms has proved a challenge," Klorf read at last.

"Really."

"That is, however, not the reason I insist on IDs being issued."

"So what is it?"

There was another pause followed by, "A few weeks ago I caught a glimpse of what I believe to be an unauthorized life form on board."

"An unauthorized Humanoid?"

"Not Humanoid."

"Are you sure it wasn't just a rat?" Throom suggested. "What did it look like?"

"I believe the closest analogue would be a Stragite."

"Stragite?!" Throom was familiar with the spider-like Stragite race. But the odds of something that size going unnoticed for months at a time were extremely slim. "You saw a Stragite on the Incorrigible?"

"Perhaps, but a very small one."

"How small?"

"The size of my bearer's hand." Klorf held up his hand.

Throom relaxed a little. "So not a Stragite. Possibly a very large spider."

"Spider?"

"Look it up in the archives," Throom said. "Generally not dangerous. Though one that size could be unsettling to some Humans." He remembered being ordered to dispatch one only the size of his thumb by Greasly. He had instead kept it in a box and put it out of the ship at their next stop.

"If it actually is a spider."

"Hold on," Throom said, "now that I know what has you worried, how would having IDs help?"

"In case the life form has the ability to disguise itself."

Inside, Throom was shaking his head. "Kurplupt," he said, "shape shifting of that level is unknown in the galaxy. It only happens in fiction."

"Are you certain?"

"Very. It defies a number of natural laws. If you see this thing again, try not to frighten it off and contact me to come take a look."

"Very well."

"Not the cap'n," Throom specified. "Me." That should assure the thing is dealt with in the most humane way.

"I will."

"In the meantime, work on telling the rest of the crew apart, would you? If you look carefully you should find small differences between us."

Throom left and went directly to Penny. He asked her to run a scan of the entire ship looking for any unauthorized life form. She reported that she had found nothing.

At worst a spider, Throom thought. *If not just a trick of the... whatever Kurplupt uses for eyes.*

Chapter 16

25th day in deep space

Ever since Kurplupt told him he had seen an intruder, Throom scanned the floors more than usual when walking through corridors, so he didn't notice when Hardegar walked past him with an ornate new look.

"Hey, Throom," Hardegar said as they passed.

"Hey," Throom responded and walked on.

"Dude!" Hardegar called after him.

Throom stopped and looked back. He stepped closer to try to process what he was seeing.

"Notice anything?" Hardegar hinted, rubbing a hand across his scalp, which was now a frenzy of intricate design.

The patterns began just above the point between Hardegar's eyes and spread up and out, in the shape of a widow's peak, to cover the back of his head. They were made up of strings of tiny five-petaled flowers, mandalas, and fleur-de-lis. The overall effect was one of stately ferocity, Throom thought.

"What happened?" Throom asked.

"Penny did it. I was complaining about how shiny my head was since Jordanis. She mentioned she had done a lot of leather work on her homeworld. I helped her put together some tools and viola!" He presented his inwrought noggin.

Throom took in the waves of intricacy. "Impressive," he said honestly, leaving *If a little disgusting* to his inner thoughts.

"I know, right?" Hardegar said, obviously beyond pleased with it himself. "Hey, she could do you too! I mean she might need harder tools, but I bet she could."

"Not necessary," Throom assured him. "If I really wanted a design I could make my own."

"You a stone carver?"

"Fraggarts can make small adjustments if we concentrate long enough. It was meant to let us regrow limbs by reassigning some of our mass. But if we work at it we could add patterns. I've seen other barbarians do it."

"Well there you go!" Hardegar seemed to be expecting him to sit down right now and redecorate himself.

"I'm not going to, though."

"Why not?"

Throom was befuddled. "Wa... Huh?"

"Why not do it?"

"I don't want to."

"Why don't you want to?"

"I don't know."

"Then how are you sure you don't want to? What is it? You have something against body designs?"

"No."

"Then why not do it?"

"Ok," Throom admitted, "Maybe I'm not in favor of body designs on my body."

"How could you be against beautifying yourself?"

"I..."

"If I want my body to be a work of art, what right do you have to condemn me for it?"

Throom had the feeling that this conversation had taken off and left him behind. He crossed his arms and decided just to listen. Curious where it would go without him.

"This isn't just a fad, Throom. This was a commitment. It took Penny hours and hours of work to do this and she hasn't even started dying it yet."

"Mmm Hmm."

"I can't undo this, you know. It's not like a tattoo that I can switch on and off or change any time I want. Feel it." Hardegar held his head forward. A bit reluctantly Throom touched it briefly.

"I see," Throom said. "It's carved in."

"It's part of me."

"Okay."

"So I'm a little pissed off that you hate it. People like you always have to shit on self expression. You probably support uniforms in schools!"

Wow, Throom thought, *This conversation has rockets!* Maybe it was time to reign it in before Hardegar took a matter declumpinizationizer to him.

"I like it, Hardegar."

"You do?"

"Yes. It has a... savage propriety."

"Really?"

"Yes. Really."

"So are you going to do it?"

Throom threw up his hands. "I don't have time for this, Hardegar."

"How long does it take?"

"Not reconfiguring myself. This conversation. I don't have time for this conversation."

Hardegar clearly doubted that. "What else do you have to do?"

"Anything. Anything, Hardegar. I would rather be doing anything than having this conversation. Okay?"

"Sheesh," Hardegar exclaimed. "Fine! You like it though."

"Yes."

Hardegar smiled, turned, and headed off to show someone else his new "do".

Throom wished again that the cap'n would finish the decoding. Any more boredom could be the end of them all.

Chapter 17

28th day in deep space

Throom was in the mess, poring over the programming code and the schematics for the door control system. He always made a mess when he was doing programming, so the mess seemed the appropriate place for it.

When working on this sort of problem, Throom always had to have the information printed out rather than on a console like most people. Somehow being able to touch the information put him in the proper state of mind to deal with it all. He had just gathered up a section of the internal sensor control code and tossed the thick pile of papers aside when he was very surprised to hear it squeak. He turned in time to see something scurrying out from under a blanket of printouts and off the edge of the table.

Throom was standing and in pursuit quicker than one would ever expect a Humanoid boulder to move. The spider thing sped up the wall and into an air vent. Without the ship in emergency mode, that vent would be open to a similar vent in the corridor. He had actually just seen the design specs a few minutes ago.

Throom dashed through the door—or rather into it. He growled as he stood for a second, waiting for the door to open. It slid to the side only as far as the dent shaped like his face would allow, but that was enough for him to get through sideways.

The entire ship reverberated as Throom ran through the hallway. As he turned the corner, he saw the thing moving swiftly down the next corridor. He was after it in a flash. It

turned a corner with Throom right behind. He rounded the corner and ran full face into Klorf.

The glass cylinder Klorf was carrying shattered; water and terror stricken flapulate flew everywhere. Klorf slid several meters down the corridor on his back. Throom lost his footing and fell face first. He tried to scramble to his feet but his right foot slid out from underneath him, smearing something slick across the floor. He caught himself and was up and moving again even before Klorf realized what had happened.

A minute or two later, Throom had to admit to himself that he had lost the spider thing. He was heading back to check on Klorf, when he heard the scream. It was a deep male voice filled with rage and sorrow, and it seemed to go on forever as it trailed slowly into deep sobs. Throom's first thought was that Klorf had fallen victim to the spider in some way, but the emotion in the cry was not right. His eyes widened even further as he realized what it must mean.

When he rounded the corner, he knew at once that his worst fear was true. There was Klorf bent over a long dark streak on the floor that had once been his master.

As Throom approached, he saw that there was faint lettering across the streak, stretched out and hard to read. He could just make out the letters as they slowly faded away. They spelled out two words: AVENGE ME.

Chapter 18

The fatal collision had occurred just outside Penny's cabin.
After making sure Klorf was unharmed, she had stepped
next door to summon the cap'n. Hardegar appeared at the
scene before Greasly opened his door.

"What happened?" Hardegar asked Throom.

He tried to answer, but the words would not come.
Instead he turned to Klorf. He was on his knees.

"It was an accident, Klorf." Throom pleaded, "I'm so
sorry."

Klorf said nothing. It was strange to see someone that
had been so strong and so forceful look so utterly lost
and devoid of connection to anyone or any place. Throom
wondered what exactly it was that made a person look like
they belonged. One moment you look normal and the next
you look like you were superimposed into the scene, a cheap
effect in a holovid, something a child would instinctively
circle in a picture entitled "What's wrong with this picture?"

Throom could offer nothing else to the cling-on. Maybe
the cap'n would know the right things to say.

"Yeegh!" Greasly said with a cringe.

Hardegar nodded as if he guessed that summed it up.

"So is this all of him?" The cap'n asked.

Throom surreptitiously glanced at the bottom of his foot.
"I think so."

Greasly sighed. "Well, let's scrape him up. I'll tell
Flathead to set a course for the nearest planet."

"Are we going to bury him there?" Throom asked.

"Kurplupt was a Clammy. I doubt he would want to be buried," Penny interjected.

Klorf glared at Throom. "To be in contact with soil would defile his essence."

"We're just landing to ship him home by Feral Express," said Greasly. "Let the Vadnus flush him, or whatever they do." He addressed Klorf directly. "You can get passage back, too, if you want, or we would be honored to keep you on as security officer. It's up to you."

Klorf seemed unsure how to answer, rattled by all the rapid changes.

"Don't say anything now," suggested the cap'n, seeing Klorf's distress. "Think it over and tell me when we land."

Klorf nodded.

"Shouldn't we say a few words?" asked Penny, nodding at the smear that used to be Kurplupt.

"You mean other than 'get a mop'?" the cap'n responded.

"Well, yes." Penny hugged herself and shifted her weight nervously.

"We'll have a service when we send him home," assured Greasly, putting his hand on Penny's shoulder. "Everybody should be thinking about what they want to say. Okay?"

"Okay," she nodded.

"I want you all to know that if there is one thing you can rely on during your stint on the Incorrigible, it's a decent funeral." Greasly smiled a brief comforting smile and turned to go back to his work.

Chapter 19

The crew of the Incorrigible stood in a grassy clearing on Seria of the Slavin system. Crisp, melodic avian calls filled the air. A gentle breeze caressed the grass, evoking sensuous waves and stirring up the sweet green smell of pastoral life. All around them a deep, tall forest watched on.

Above the tops of the trees, glinting in the warm sun, peeked the upper rim of the great cylinder of Amphora, the fabled city-in-a-can that was the planet's only claim to fame. The crew stood in a circle, feeling a little buoyant in the 0.9G gravity of the planet.

Greasly looked into the forest and blew a silent whistle that bore the Feral Express logo on the side. Then he turned toward the group and intoned the traditional opening for star-faring funerals, "Bow 'em if you got 'em."

The Humanoids bowed their heads.

"We are here today to say good bye to Kurplupt of the spawn of Chump of the roe of Flippy-flop yada-yada-yada. He was a good friend and an able security officer. He will be missed. Would anyone like to say something?"

There was silence for a moment, then Flathead spoke up. "I would."

Throom noticed with alarm that one of Flathead's tentacles looked as if it were fading. It had changed from the usual hot pink to a pale sepia. As he spoke, that tentacle rubbed absently against his other tentacles. His voice was softer—more feminine.

"I barely knew Kurplupt but liked him," cooed Flathead. "He was the most floppy member of the crew. I loved to see him undulate through the water. He was so graceful, so flowing, and so filled with the promise of blissful union."

"Uh, Flathead," cautioned Greasly, now also aware of what was happening.

Penny, Klorf, and Hardegar were staring at the Kravitsian with shock and puzzlement.

"To flow, to bend," Flathead continued, lost in reverie, "in subtle suppleness and sublime flow of motion."

"Flathead," Greasly tried again to interrupt.

"To move in harmonious undulation to that blissful release of egg and—"

"Flathead!" Greasly barked. Flathead stiffened. "Cut it out!" Greasly looked around, embarrassed for his pilot. "Jebus! You're getting me hot over here." He straightened his collar. "Maybe you better go ready the shuttle."

Flathead blushed purple. "I'm sorry," he said with remorse. "I sort of... I'm sorry." He flapped up the gangway into the shuttle.

The cap'n whistled softly. "Looks like we gotta get her back to Kravits Rock."

"Her?!" Penny asked in surprise.

"For now at least. They only take on a sex at mating time, and it's fairly random which one they take on," Greasly explained. "Anyway, back to Kurplupt. Does anyone have something else to say?"

"I do," offered Hardegar.

"Okay," Greasly allowed then added, "keep it clean."

"I know that Kurplupt was a Clammy, but I'd like to share a part of the real Scripture that seems appropriate." Hardegar cleared his throat and referred to the electronic book he carried. "For The Lord, who said, 'Let light shine out of darkness,' made his light shine in our hearts to give us the light of the knowledge of the greatness of The Lord. But we have this treasure in jars of clay to assure us that this power is from The Lord and not from us. We are hard pressed on every side, but not crushed; perplexed, but not in despair."

He lowered his book. "Just like Kurplupt faced danger in his fragile vessel, so do we. I just hope he knew that even though we seemed so different from him, we were really the same inside. And I hope we can all remember that a person is a person, even if they are smelly and live in a jar."

Most of the meaning was lost on Throom, but the brittle jars analogy struck home, even though he was far from brittle himself. He had known many fragile jars over the years that had broken, losing the life inside them like water poured out in a desert. He puzzled over the intentions of the passage but noticed that the others seemed to be comforted by the words. It was as if they had all forgotten that Kurplupt had been hard pressed and very much not "not crushed." How hard it must be for the fragile to come to terms with the precarious walk of their lives.

Finally the cap'n spoke. "Thank you Hardegar." He was clearly impressed. "That was damn close to being profound."

Hardegar shrugged shyly.

"Penny?" Greasly asked.

She thought it over then nodded. "I didn't know Kurplupt very well at all. The most contact I had with him was when he was asking for our IDs every twenty minutes." There were smiles and light laughter of recognition. "But I do think that I know him enough to say that the big tragedy of his life seems to be that he never appreciated what he had." She breathed in as if preparing to jump off a precipice then continued. "I find it very sad that he never really appreciated having such a fine, loyal, and trustworthy servant as Klorf."

Klorf looked up suddenly to meet her gaze. Throom could see that he was shaking and was unsure how to interpret his expression. Surprise certainly was there, but there was something else. Was it outrage? Anger? And if so, directed at whom?

"He was lucky to have you, Klorf," she finished, unabashed.

Klorf looked at the package Greasly held—the package that held Kurplupt's remains—then at the ground. "Do not speak of things you do not understand," he growled.

"Klorf, I do understand. It was nobody's fault—least of all yours."

"She's right, Klorf," the cap'n piped in. "If you had been lax in your duties, I wouldn't be asking you to stay on as security officer."

He looked at Hardegar. "Any ancient words of wisdom for this situation, Hardegar?"

"Yes," he said nodding. "From the book of slogans: 'Shit Happens.'"

Penny and Greasly grunted in agreement.

"If it was anyone's fault..." Throom began to suggest, but he was finding it hard to finish the sentence. "It's mine," he said at last—head hung in shame.

"Yes, that's right," exclaimed Penny brightly.

"True," agreed the cap'n.

"Fark, yeah," concurred Hardegar, "Throom squished him."

Throom looked at all of them in shock.

Penny was the first to recant. "But it isn't," she ejaculated, "anyone's fault."

"Of course not," concurred Hardegar.

There was a rustling in the trees, and a hunched over Humanoid with wild hair and a snarling mouth popped out into the open. He was "dressed" with animal hides strapped seemingly to random locations on his body.

"Ah," announced Greasly, "Feral Express." He walked toward the wild man and tossed the package onto the ground.

The wild man ran up on all fours and hopped around the package, poking and prodding at it skittishly. Greasly explained exactly where the package needed to go. The wild man seemed to take no notice. He bounced up and down a couple of times then lifted his leg and showered the package with a stream of urine.

"Okay then, thanks!" Greasly said cheerily.

As Greasly returned to the group, the wild man circled the package, kicking his legs back to throw dirt and uprooted grass over it until it was shallowly buried. He then howled a long mournful howl and loped into the woods.

"Well, that's taken care of," the cap'n said as he returned to the group. "Shall we go?"

Everyone except for Klorf started up the gangway. They stopped halfway and turned to look back at him. He was looking back at the shallow mound of dirt and grass.

"Are you coming with us?" Greasly asked.

"We would like you to come with us," Penny rephrased the cap'n's words.

Klorf looked at the group then back at the buried package. A large wolf had emerged from the woods and was sniffing the air.

"Come on, Klorf," urged Hardegar. "They'll get him back."

Klorf glared briefly at Throom then hung his head for a moment. He started up the gangway as the wolf dug up the package and ran into the woods with it hanging from his snarling maw.

"So how is breaking the encryption coming?" Hardegar asked Greasly as they boarded.

"Oh, didn't I mention that?" the cap'n responded. "I broke it the other day. I'm almost finished reading it."

"You're kidding!" Penny exclaimed.

"Nope. Looks so far like it must be somewhere near Frag."

"Great," said Throom with a disappointed sigh.

The exterior door began to close.

"And the best part is that the rumors are true," Greasly continued. "He was definitely carrying some high value items when he went down."

They all smiled at that except for Klorf.

The shuttle lifted gently off Seria and headed toward the Incorrigible. As they exited the atmosphere, Klorf stopped conversation dead when he turned to Throom and spoke.

"I want you to know that I do not hold you responsible for the death of Kurplupt. I have tried to, but I cannot."

Throom was surprised and pleased by this. "Thank you, Klorf. I'm very glad to hear that."

"But I am still duty-bound to kill you."

"Oh," said Throom. "Now?"

"Whenever it is convenient for you."

"I see. Well, can we put that off for a while? Give ourselves some time to think it over?"

"That will be acceptable," conceded Klorf.

Throom tried to read Klorf's face. "Are you joking with me, Klorf?"

"No," replied Klorf, obviously thinking the question odd.

"Oh." Throom was becoming uncomfortable and confused.

"I do not wish to," Klorf clarified.

"Then don't do it," suggested the cap'n.

"I have told you, I am duty-bound."

"Can it wait until the mission is over?"

"Perhaps," said Klorf, "but if I see an opportunity to take his life, it is cowardice not to take it."

The cap'n nodded. He looked at Throom. "That sounds manageable doesn't it?"

Throom had to admit that it did. He knew that any weapon powerful enough to hurt him would be unusable on board the Incorrigible. He should have plenty of time to try to talk Klorf out of his obligation.

"Okay then," Throom said to Klorf, "thanks for the warning."

"I'm afraid it must be the only warning I give you."

Throom shrugged. "Fair enough."

Chapter 20

"Personally I don't understand it," Penny said later on the ship. They had set a course for Kravits Rock immediately on arriving and were now in Flitzville. She and Klorf were in the mess, eating a meal together. "You should really be grateful to Throom." She nibbled a Notable Raul brand Flavo-Fibe. "I know you don't feel comfortable with the idea, but he did liberate you."

"I did not ask for that," Klorf admonished, then took another bite of his Krill Puffs.

"No, and he didn't mean to do it. But aren't you glad it happened?"

"Of course not," he snapped at her. "What you suggest is treason." But Penny felt his anger was not quite genuine; at least he wasn't angry enough to stop talking to her.

"I'm sorry, Klorf," she said softly. "I'm being pretty insensitive about this I know. It's just that slavery is something that I—"

"I was not a slave," Klorf interrupted. "I was a servant."

"Were you free to quit?"

"Servants do not quit."

"But could you if you had wanted to?"

"It is not done."

She sat back and shook her head. "I think we both know the answer, Klorf. You weren't free to quit."

"You may phrase it that way if you wish," he grumbled.

"My phrase for it," she said with a little sarcastic laugh, "is slavery."

Klorf stood and wiped the crumbs off of his hands. "I will not sit here and listen to you denigrate ten thousand years of Vadnu history and culture." He walked forcefully to the door, which was jammed open because of the face-shaped dent that Throom had put into it. He stopped without looking back. "Thank you for speaking with me," he proffered then left without further comment.

She sighed, stood, and started cleaning up.

Suddenly the lights went out. She was in complete darkness. She grabbed the edge of the table to keep some sense of place. The emergency lighting kicked in all around the bottom edge of the walls. Were they under attack? There should have been a call to arms in that case. But what if there was no one left to raise the alarm?

She got up and ran into the hall, heading for the bridge. Music started to play over the communications system, then stopped, then started again, then changed style. The hatch in front of her slid shut and locked along with all the other hatches in the area.

"Oh crap," was all she could think to say.

The lights were back on. Then off again. She heard the hatches open, but everything was pitch black.

She waited for the emergency lights, but none came on. She seemed to feel the infinite vacuum of space as if it were pressing in on the ship, ready to tear through the fragile hull in the wake of a laser beam or solid projectile and suck the life out of her—freezing her bones and the lives inside her.

Desperate, she unzipped her forehead. Now she could see the heat patterns of the hallway. She ran through the hallways again as the music changed erratically.

She entered the bridge and saw Throom just ahead of her, stepping very carefully and feeling his way in the dark. From the way he was reaching as if to find a hatchway, she thought he must not realize yet that he was already on the bridge.

She turned and saw a fiery snake caressing the control panel. She realized at once that it was Flathead's amorous tentacle, giving off a lot of heat. She sighed in relief and started to laugh. "Flathead, snap out of it!" she shouted.

Flathead came back to herself and realized where she was. "I'm sorry...I didn't...oh no," she blubbered in her now fully feminine voice. She started to flap at the controls with a more practical purpose this time.

Penny turned to Throom. He had turned to the sound of her voice and was feeling outward trying to find her. "Penny?" he called.

"Yes, stand still a minute, Throom. Flathead's turning on the lights." It was in that instant that the lights came on figuratively as she realized the implications of her statement. Unfortunately, it was also in that instant that the lights came on literally. Her hand flew to her mouth in terror, but it wasn't her mouth that she should have covered.

When the lights came on, Throom's first instinct was to swipe the spider from her head, but he could only stare in stunned silence when it quickly retreated inside Penny's skull by way of her open zipper.

Chapter 21

Cap'n Greasly sat in the briefing room, tapping the table
with a stylus and staring at the spider-like thing before him.
"Look," he said at last to Penny. "It doesn't really matter.
I mean you're still a member of the crew. None of that has
changed." He poked the stylus under the spider-thing and
lifted it off the table. This seemed to anger it. It scurried up
Penny's arm to her shoulder.

"It doesn't like that," Penny said a bit apologetically.

"You can talk with it even when it's not..." he motioned
at his head, "home?"

"I just know it doesn't like that. Would you?"

"I don't know." Greasly mulled it over. "Maybe."

He leaned back in his chair and looked at Throom,
tapping his stylus again. "Well, Throom, you do get our
money's worth. Next we'll find out Hardegar has a colony
of intelligent maggots living in his chest."

Throom leaned forward and spoke to Penny. "But why
didn't you just tell me?"

"It's a personal thing, It wasn't any of your business."

"Yeah, Throom, people don't have to give up all privacy
do they?"

"Generally no," Throom granted, "but having a spider in
your head seems like a special case."

"First of all, it's not a spider; it's a Goober," Penny
corrected.

Throom was shocked. "What?"

"But the people of Goob are Humanoid," Greasly
pointed out.

"Like me?" she asked leadingly.

"But without the..." He motioned across his forehead.

"No, they don't have..."—she motioned across her forehead, mocking Greasly—"but they do have..." she motioned the same motion but at the back of her head. "I'm a mutant," she divulged with a small amount of embarrassment.

"No kidding?" exclaimed Greasly. "All Goobers have zippers and spiders?"

"Zippers and riders."

"Riders, eh?"

"That's a rough translation of the name. The Goobish word is Cootie."

Throom was confused. "So which of you is the Goober?"

"We both are. It's a symbiotic relationship." She smiled at the rider on her shoulder. "At least ours is." She turned back to the others. "When we reach a certain age, we go through a rite of passage where the zipper is added to the opening and one of the offspring of the parents' riders is zipped inside."

"So what do they do, scoop out your brain?" asked Greasly.

"We don't have brains, not in the same way Humans do. Our consciousness is spread throughout our body rather than a single spot." She said this with neither pride nor shame.

"Why a zipper?" Throom inquired.

"Tradition," Penny said. "It's been that way as long as anyone can remember. They say that the ancients used a zipper so that the ridden could change riders."

"But you don't change riders anymore?" asked Greasly.

"You can," Penny shrugged. "Most don't though. In fact in some places on Goob, the parents actually sew the zipper shut."

Throom was smiling and shaking his head. "Sewing," he said. "Sewing a zipper."

"I hope you don't mind us asking all of these questions," Greasly tendered.

Penny smiled. "It's okay." She was happy to see that the cap'n was at least capable of retroactive tact.

"You said your relationship is symbiotic. What is it you get from each other?"

"Well, the riders get Humanoid bodies. The ridden get a copilot, or in some cases, a pilot. It depends on how much control you give it."

"So, what's its name?" Greasly smiled.

"Riders don't have names."

"How about Crawly?"

"Why give it a name?" Penny complained, "Just treat it like part of me. That's what it is. Do you name your body parts?"

Greasly shot a warning glance at Throom, who wisely opted to refrain from speaking.

"Let's just say that, if the part is important enough, it has been known to happen. If I had a body part that could crawl out of my head I would definitely name it."

"Well, I would not," she said flatly.

"I'd name mine..." he pondered it. His face lit up. "Athena!" he burst out. He raised his eyebrows a couple of times. "Now that's cool right? Get it?"

They only stared at him blankly.

"Cretans," he mumbled, "Though I bet that's lost on you too." He gave it up. "Well, I don't have any more questions. Do you, Throom?"

Throom thought it over. "Actually I do. You said the only reason that you didn't tell us about your rider was that it was personal, but I asked you to run a scan on the ship, and you lied and said you found nothing."

"I did not lie," she parried. "I said I found no unauthorized life forms. I gave you exactly the information you asked for, and it was entirely accurate. My rider is part of me, and I'm authorized."

"That's stretching the truth a bit, isn't it?"

"If you had asked Klorf to run it, and he didn't report Kurplupt would you say he stretched the truth?"

Throom leaned back. "You're not going to be that way about every assignment I give you, are you?"

Penny laughed and shook her head. "No, Throom, I won't."

"Well, we should be hitting Kravits Rock before long." The cap'n stood to signal that the meeting had ended. "You ever been to a Kravitsian orgy?"

"No," she said with one measure of repulsion and two of curiosity.

"Well, you're about to have your chance. They only happen every seven or so years, you know. It's quite a sight—planet-wide flap and wriggle!"

"The colors are amazing," Throom conceded.

"I'll consider it." Her rider crawled home. She zipped up.

"Maybe something epic," suggested the cap'n out of nowhere as they walked down the hall, "like Omnitarsi the Mighty—Bringer of Feet!"

Chapter 22

"Fascinating," remarked Throom as he reclined in the reinforced portable chair.

The cap'n was sitting beside him sipping on a drink—dark glasses on. "You got that right."

Penny was less at ease. She looked at the two, then at the motley mountain of squirming, slimy Kravitsians. A few minutes ago, the instant the outer doors had opened, Flathead had flittered across the hundred or so meters to the mound and taken a high, arcing leap to land in the squirming mass with an audible "ploint".

Now she was lost somewhere in the pile, no doubt lost in passionate ecstasy as well, while Penny, Throom, and the cap'n (the cap'n had specifically not told Hardegar they had landed, and Klorf had refused to join them) sat sipping cool drinks and watching the whole thing. Penny pulled her collar together and held it shut with one hand.

"The colors!" praised Throom.

"The smell!" raved Greasly, breathing in the lilac-like aroma. "Smell that," he urged Penny. Then, when he saw how uneasy she was, he cajoled, "Oh, lighten up."

"It doesn't seem right," she murmured.

"They don't care at all, believe me," he assured her. "It makes no difference to them if we're here or not."

She looked again at the huge mound of roiling flesh, easily twice again the size of the Incorrigible. At mating time the male Kravitsians also changed color but not to any one set color. So hundreds of different colors and patterns were mixing, twisting, disappearing from the surface, all glistening with the sweet-smelling fluid. In the silence she could hear a thousand soft, metallic sighs punctuating the silence like the rhythm of rain.

"The funny thing is that between orgies, the Kravitsians have a strict caste system. Half of those buggers wouldn't be caught dead in the same room with the other half. Now look at them—Shemps, Jeffies, Caners, Porkies, Mooks..." The cap'n laughed. "Sex makes strange bedfellows!"

Penny did find that amusing but wasn't about to let on.

Greasly breathed in deeply. "Smell that!"

She grimaced.

"It's no different than smelling flowers. Flowers are a plant's sexual organs, you know. The smell of spring is a flower sex party in your nose."

She looked again at the slimy mound and shook her head. "It's different," she insisted.

"Not much." He shrugged, laid back, and sipped his drink.

After a minute or two, her curiosity did what Greasly could not. She somewhat timidly sniffed the air and gasped in astonishment. When she breathed it in deeply it was like a cross between lilac scent and a cool drink of water on a hot day. It entered through her nose, and she could actually feel it flowing down into her lungs and outward to her very fingertips. It filled her entire body with cool, relaxing... peace. There was just no other word for it. She would have thought that it was some sort of hormone if she had been in the mood to analyze anything critically. She suddenly wasn't.

She caught Greasly grinning at her. "See?" he chuckled.

She nodded, smiling freely. She leaned back and let it roll over her.

After a few minutes of reverie, she reached up and unzipped her head. Mini-Penny, as Greasly had eventually insisted on calling it, crawled out and rested itself on her forehead.

"Wow," she sighed. Greasly laughed.

Throom couldn't help feeling a little left out. He had no sense of smell, and the hormones had no effect on him, so he was suddenly feeling as if he were intruding. He spoke. "So when do we all get to hear what you've learned about Bartholomew Methane?"

"Anytime," the cap'n answered. "I'll tell you now if you want. He's an interesting character."

"Sure," agreed Throom, happy for something to make the moment a little more cerebral.

Greasly cleared his throat and began. "Well, the weirdest thing is that you probably see him every day."

"What?"

"That's because the infamous pirate is none other than a certain famous spokesperson for a common brand of snack products."

Penny turned her head to look at him lazily. Mini-Penny crawled to high ground on her left ear as she turned. "Really? Who?"

"I'll give you a hint," he said. Then in the patented inflection said, "My Nuts!"

Penny's eyes widened at mention of the ubiquitous tag line from the hilarious line of holovid commercials. "Notable Raul?"

"None other."

"You're kidding," accused Throom.

Greasly shook his head.

"I love his Flavo-Fibes!" Penny said dreamily.

"Of course, Notable Raul isn't really his name, but it is his face—or was. I mean...Jebus, where do I start with this?"

Greasly closed his eyes for a minute. Throom was about to nudge Greasly's elbow when he started talking again.

"Okay, like I said, Bartholomew Methane's real name is Raul Grimshaw. That was his name when he was in advertising. He was a real hot toddy in advertising. He was voted King Liar by Intergalactic Sales magazine four years in a row, but his crowning achievement—and the one that wrecked his life—was Notable Raul.

"The odd thing is that he just sort of lucked into the whole thing. The guy that was working it had gotten killed by a zero-tolerance stoplight, and all his work was incinerated with him. Grimshaw had to whip up the whole campaign from scratch overnight.

"That's why he had to use his own visage to program the holovids. He didn't have time to buy one. He had intended it to be a stop-gap sort of thing, but everyone loved the ads— so much so, in fact, that they insisted on using him in them! He was very careful what contracts he signed, though. He would never sell them his visage outright. He made sure he had a real sweet ride!"

"But, wait a minute," interrupted Throom. "Bartholomew Methane died 50 years ago. Notable Raul has been around a lot longer than that."

"Yeah, when was this all happening?" Penny asked with her eyes closed.

"Roughly two hundred years ago."

"Two hundred is a nice number," Penny sighed dreamily. "I'm thinking of two hundred pieces of chocolate!"

"So anyway," the cap'n continued.

"But. . ." Throom was even more confused. Greasly held his finger to his lips and shushed him.

"Patience, my mafic friend." He closed his eyes again. "So anyway, Raul let them use his visage as long as he was on the account. The ads were farking hotcakes!"

"Hotcakes," Penny repeated hungrily.

"Everything was going great until Grimshaw got tired of it all and tried to retire and take his visage with him. The Notable Raul Corporation—they had split off from the main company; I don't remember that name—but anyway, Notable Raul Corp really wanted the rights to Notable Raul. So what they did was. . ."

Greasly froze as he heard the sound of clothes fasteners being undone. He looked at Penny. She was removing her top, leaving only a flimsy camisole.

"Go on," she moaned lazily and flowed back into her chair. "I'm hot," she drew out the "h" in "hot" sexily.

He blinked a few times then laid back and tried to continue, but he was having trouble looking away from the sensuous curves under Penny's camisole. "Um... what was I talking about?"

"What did they do?" Throom assisted.

"Who?"

"The Notable Raul Corporation."

"Oh, those bastards." He laid back and looked into the pinkish cyan sky, a full measure of disgust entering his voice. "Remind me to tell you sometime what they did to Raul Grimshaw."

"Okay," prompted Throom, "why don't you tell me?"

"I will." He weakly pounded his fist on the arm of his chair in determination. "See, they could sue him if he used the Notable Raul character for anything else. He hadn't, but then one night when he was at a dinner party, one of the waiters poured hot soup in his lap. 'My Nuts!' he yells, and bam! They nail him for stealing their intellectual property."

"That's terrible," Penny pouted.

"It's worse than that," the cap'n continued, "because the courts only gave him probation. So the bastards set him up again. This time they made sure he was served underdone pecker beast. They kept doing that sort of thing until he was broke and therefore defenseless. Then the courts threw the book at him. The Notable Raul Corporation was awarded exclusive rights to Raul Grimshaw's visage. They even forced him to change his name."

"Change his name? But there are lots of people named Raul!" Penny argued with kittenish indignance. "I know three of them myself. There's Raul, and Raul, and oh, what was his name?"

"Raul?" Throom and Greasly suggested in unison.

"Oh, yeah." She smiled and rubbed her cheek against her soft shoulder. "I'd forgotten about *Raul*." She said the name with gusto.

"Uh, anyway," the cap'n whimpered, pulling himself away from the sight.

"But why would they care about the name Raul Grimshaw?" Throom asked. "They never use it in the ads."

"Spite. Those Notable Raul bastards were pretty bitter that it took them that long to get him where they wanted him, so they pulled some strings and got the court to assign him a new name. Bartholomew Methane was born. If he hadn't thrown himself on the mercy of the court, they would have named him Peter Boyle."

Penny tsked at that. In her current state, it was perhaps the sexiest sound Greasly had ever heard. His ears and face were hot, and he was breathing more heavily.

"Ahem. Cap'n," Throom put in. It snapped Greasly out of it.

"What's that?" He turned to Throom.

"A cap'n should keep a healthy distance from his crew," Throom reminded him in a tone that made it clear that he was repeating the cap'n's own words back at him.

"Oh," the cap'n laughed a little, "yeah."

"Is that when Methane became a pirate?" Throom led.

"Actually, he just went into hiding to avoid the mandated plastic surgery, but some company thugs tracked him down and gave him a scar and ruined one of his eyes. That was when he decided that he would turn pirate. They had taken everything from him—his money, his house, his name, his fertility. All he had left was a scar and an eye patch. They had made him into a man with nothing to lose—and there is nothing more dangerous." The cap'n heard Penny's pants being slipped off. "Almost nothing."

"Don't look," Throom warned.

With difficulty, the cap'n complied. "He started by pirating music, then worked himself up to holovids. Things really took off when he downloaded a ship, then used it to steal a better ship: the Flummox. He put together a crew and started boarding freighters and stealing their goods. His log doesn't say how he got so good at catching the freighters just as they exited Flitzville, but he was the master."

"Oh, that would be easy," Penny purred. "Hyper pre-retro tachyon micro flux. It always happens when real space is penetrated. It's like the universe saying 'oh!' " The "Oh" was a quiet but surprised little yelp. She giggled.

"Maybe we should go in," the cap'n proposed weakly.

"Definitely." Throom was already up.

"Oh, but I'm really enjoying myself," Penny whispered loud enough for Greasly to hear.

"Maybe you and I better go in," Throom suggested to the cap'n.

"If we leave her here, she's likely to jump in the pile and suffocate," the cap'n countered.

"So, you go in," Throom retorted.

"Let's all go," Greasly sighed. He got up. She was lying there in panties and her camisole. He would never have guessed that she wore such dainty undergarments. They looked like Oonian silk—tantalizingly translucent.

"If you want me to go, you'll have to help me up." She held out her hand—a sly grin on her face.

The cap'n looked at Throom. Throom shook his head. But the cap'n thought he was too close to refuse without offending her. He hopped over his chair, knocked a small portable table out of his way, then hurried over to her and held out his hand. When she put her hand in his, a wave of passion flowed over him. It seemed to be the softest hand he had ever touched. She pulled herself up and stood directly in front of him—so close he could feel her breath on his lips. He breathed it in, and it seemed sweeter than the smell of the Kravitsians.

"Come on, guys," Throom asserted, trying to herd them toward the ship, "let's go." He moved behind them and pushed them toward the ship.

Penny grabbed her clothes. They walked—she and the cap'n each more aware of the other's movements than their own.

Throom moved past them up the gangway to open the door, and when he turned around, they were naked on the ground, with Mini-Penny skittering around them in alarm.

Throom knew enough about Humans to know that unless he was willing to turn a hose on them, there was nothing he could do at this point. He averted his gaze and went sheepishly into the Incorrigible.

*   *   *

"Why didn't anyone tell me we landed?" Hardegar complained about an hour later.

"You'll have to talk to the cap'n about that," Throom grumbled.

"Where is he?"

"Uh," Throom wasn't sure if he should tell him but couldn't come up with a lie in time, "outside," then, as if he had broken the dam on his reservoir of truth, "with Penny. They're humping like insane monkeys," he ejaculated.

Hardegar's jaw dropped. His face ran through a long sequence of expressions as he adjusted to the news. Throom wasn't sure what all of them were, but he knew shock, anger, and disgust were in there. He settled on a smile of admiration. "That lucky son of a bitch!"

Throom frowned at being denied a partner in disgust.

"Can you show me how to work the external monitors?" Hardegar asked conspiratorially.

Throom only hung his head and shook it from side to side. "Humans."

"What?" Hardegar asked defensively.

"Just go out the forward starboard gangway, and you'll have a front row seat," Throom suggested derisively.

"I really shouldn't," Hardegar said as he headed for the forward starboard gangway.

When Hardegar got to the exit and opened the door, Penny and Greasly were there, ready to come in. They were both dressed, but had a rumpled, well-used look to them. Both of their faces were flushed, and they seemed a little short of breath.

Greasly noticed the way Hardegar was looking at him."Whew," he exclaimed unconvincingly, "it's quite a walk up here."

Flathead pushed her way between Greasly and Penny and into the ship. She made her way down the corridor with a strange hobbling gate as if her tentacles were sore.

"So, what'd I miss?" Hardegar asked pointedly. He self-righteously tapped his finger on his chin while waiting for the answer.

Penny said nothing but went quickly to her cabin.

Greasly pushed past Hardegar with a mumbled, "excuse me," and went to his.

Hardegar looked out the door at the mountain of Kravitsians as it dissolved into thousands of sheepish individuals. He grumbled and narrowed his eyes as he closed the door.

Chapter 23

After its crew had rested for a day or two, the Incorrigible lifted off of Kravits Rock and slid gracefully into the pinkish cyan sky. But rather than heading straight into space, it followed the gentle curve of the planet until it came to a huge blanket of green that reminded Greasly of a Sargasso Sea floating in the atmosphere.

As the Incorrigible lost altitude, Greasly could see that the patch of green was actually made up of thousands of balloons, and that underneath the balloons hung thousands of porous shapes, mostly spheres, connected to each other with hole-filled tubes. Even from this distance the cap'n could see the movement of colored specks across the surface— Kravitsians going about their daily lives.

Perhaps it was just the result of his recent paroxysms of emotion, but Greasly felt as if he could cry looking at it; there were so many people, so many lives, yet so lonely and so fragile—clinging to the monotony of their daily lives while dangling precariously above certain death.

"Thank you, Cap'n," said Flathead in a quiet female voice.

"We can stop if you want."

"No. It looks better from here," she said, somewhat sadly. "Besides, I'm not really welcome anymore."

The view shifted and the sea of balloons fell away as the Incorrigible headed into space.

"Do you want to talk about it?" Greasly asked without looking back.

"It's nothing you don't know. I chose a career far outside my caste."

Greasly shook his head. "That's so wrong—to have your life locked in for you by an accident of birth."

"But in my culture there are no accidents." She sounded almost as if she believed it. "Everything happens for a reason."

Greasly turned to look at her. "Well, in reality there are accidents." He turned away again and added, "Stupid, pain-in-the-ass accidents."

"On Kravits Rock they say that people believe in accidents because they don't like what they would have to admit if there were none."

Greasly untangled the meaning of the statement. "You know what?"

"What?"

"I liked you better as a male."

Flathead did not respond, but Greasly thought he detected a new violence to her flapping of the controls. The Incorrigible climbed out of the atmosphere.

The door opened, and Throom entered the bridge. "Hey Flathead," he greeted the Kravitsian genially. His greeting to the cap'n was made palpably cold by its lack of existence. He moved to a panel in the wall, removed it, and began poking around at the circuitry inside.

Greasly got up and walked over to peer in over Throom's shoulder. "What are you doing?" he asked innocently.

Throom's eyes narrowed. "I'm working on fixing the doors," he asserted with barely disguised annoyance.

"Ah, finally."

"Some people on the ship don't have the self control it takes to wait for a door to open," Throom sniped.

Stung, Greasly returned fire. "That must be how someone's face got imprinted in the mess door."

Throom was obviously holding back a nasty response.

"Well, keep up the good work," the cap'n directed. "I'll be in my cabin."

He went to the door, but it did not open. He waited a minute—not wanting to give Throom the satisfaction of his having to ask permission to leave his own bridge.

Finally, Greasly gave in. "Throom?"

"Yes, Cap'n?"

"Can you let me out?"

Without a verbal reply, Throom allowed the door to open. Greasly turned to go but found himself face to face with Penny, who was on her way in. He struggled for the appropriate words.

"Uh, hi." That seemed appropriate, if not impressive.

"Hi," she returned, trying not to look at him.

He stepped aside and awkwardly motioned her in. She stepped in without touching him and went to her control console. Greasly turned to go, but the door slid shut centimeters in front of his nose, which crumpled as the door stopped his forward motion.

Throom smiled at his own perfect timing.

"Throom!" Greasly growled.

Throom messed around in the wiring then turned to Greasly and shrugged. He went back to work. "I should have it open in a few minutes," he called over his shoulder.

Annoyed, Greasly went back to his cap'ning chair. After waiting a few uncomfortable minutes, he turned on the holovid.

Writhing bodies in contorted sexual positions appeared before him, panting and moaning in passion. He quickly turned it off. He tried surreptitiously to look back to see if either Flathead or Penny had seen it. They had. He laughed nervously.

"I wonder who was using this last?" He forced another laugh. "Whew!"

He looked at Throom who was also looking at him. Throom shook his head and went back to work.

"Hardegar!" Greasly proclaimed too loudly. "Hardegar— that's who it says was using this holovid last. See? Right there. Hardegar." He shook his head. "That guy!"

Greasly gave up the holovid idea. He got up and paced. His mind was racing. What should he say? He wanted to do the right thing—to save her any embarrassment, but what would do that? Should he talk to her openly about it? That was his policy on everything else, but somehow this felt different. Maybe that was because this had been his fault?

His fault? He had not intended it to happen. He had never seen anyone react so strongly to a Kravitsian orgy. His intentions were no more insidious than giving her a bouquet of flowers, but he had gotten far more than a thank you and it seemed as though he had cheated her somehow.

What was she thinking now? Was she thinking he had cheated her? Would it only cause her more pain if he brought it up? Or would she be more upset if he didn't say anything about it? He watched her as she worked and could not decipher her expression.

The door opened, and Hardegar entered. He looked around. "What's this? Old home week?"

Greasly walked quickly past him to the door, but the door did not open. He looked back at Throom, who was still fiddling with the circuits. He glared at the Fraggart's stone back.

"Okay if I watch a holovid?" Hardegar asked.

"No!" the rest chorused unanimously.

Abashed, Hardegar shrugged. "Okay."

Hardegar walked toward the door. Greasly stood close by—ready to duck through with him. For that very reason, Greasly was certain, the door did not open.

"Throom's working on the door," Greasly explained to Hardegar with a hint of sarcasm.

"Oh."

Hardegar walked aimlessly around the bridge for a while. Greasly pulled up a chair next to the door.

Hardegar pulled a handball out of his pocket and began bouncing it off the wall. He did this until he became aware of the annoyed glares from Penny and Greasly. Grumbling to himself, he put the ball away and went back to pacing.

The door opened but shut again before Greasly could get out of his chair and through it. Greasly repositioned the chair directly in front of the door and sat hunched over, ready at any second to leap through.

"So, how was Kravits Rock?" asked Hardegar. "I hear it was rockin'." He glanced at Greasly with his mechanical eyes.

Penny's jaw clenched noticeably as she worked.

Greasly shook his head slightly—not taking his eyes off the door. "I'm sorry I didn't tell you we landed, okay?"

"I didn't say anything about that," Hardegar snapped.

"You were thinking it though, weren't you?" Greasly accused. He knew Hardegar would have difficulty admitting how much he wanted to watch the orgy, but something inside Greasly felt very much like twisting a knife.

"No," Hardegar replied, trying for nonchalance but achieving nothing. "I might have, though, if I had known there was a floor show."

Penny stopped her routine scans and slowly looked up at Hardegar. He froze like a thieving raccoon in a flashlight beam.

She spoke slowly and clearly. "It was nothing you could relate to anyway." She went back to her work.

"Rrrow!" Flathead commented unexpectedly.

Penny started. "I thought you were on my side," she said to the cubic squid.

"I'm not on any side." Flathead shrugged, not even stopping with her calculations. "It was perfectly natural for me to be there. I have no issues with anyone."

"Oh no? No issues?" criminated Penny incredulously. "Yet in the same breath. . ." she seemed to realize that breath did not really apply here, ". . . er in the same paragraph you intimate that our being there was unnatural."

"I didn't mean that."

"Then why say it at all?"

Flathead shrugged again; a double shrug this time—two limbs on each side.

"Well, you must have meant something."

Greasly rolled his eyes. "Jebus! Now we've got the women fighting."

"Oh, bite me!" Flathead and Penny yelled in unison.

Greasly sat up in indignation. "Hey! I am the cap'n of this ship!"

"Bite me, Sir!" Penny amended sarcastically.

As she went back to work she casually slid her palm against the tentacle offered by Flathead in congratulations.

Greasly narrowed his eyes at the pair of them, but then the door opened again. He leaped, but it was shut by the time he made contact with it. He sat back and seethed as he rubbed his nose. "Throom, I really don't know why you are so pissed at me."

The words took Throom by surprise. As he thought about it, he had to admit to himself that he didn't know either. He had just been very angry at the cap'n ever since the incident at Kravits Rock. Was his true Fraggart nature, in spite of all of his efforts, coming through? Or could it be jealousy? Had he been around Humans so long that their mental ailments were rubbing off on him? The very possibility of that only made him angrier.

"Throom could never be mad at you, Cap'n," Hardegar assured, switching targets. "He's a total butt-kisser. He'll even sell out a friend for you."

Now Throom's anger turned to confusion. He pulled his head out of the electronics to look at Hardegar. "What are you talking about?"

"Greasly says, 'don't tell the zombie we've landed,' and you just do it." He held his hands in the air to demonstrate the lightness with which Throom had "just done it".

"I thought you didn't care about that," pointed out the cap'n.

Hardegar winced. "I don't, but he didn't know that."

There was a pounding on the door. "Klorf." Greasly said. He readied himself to rush through when the door opened. Throom didn't open it. The pounding came again.

Hardegar nodded exaggeratedly. "Okay, fine. So now I'm a zombie."

"What?!" asked Throom.

"We never said that, you did!" complained Greasly. There was more pounding.

Hardegar narrowed his leather eyes and pointed around the room. "But not one of you denied it."

He was pelted with disgusted statements, all indicating that he should take a more realistic point of view and give them all a collective break.

"Fine! Gang up on the dead guy!"

"You stupid ass!" the cap'n added, just as everyone else stopped complaining so his comment rang clear in the new silence. Even the pounding had stopped.

"Who the hell do you think you are to call him that—oh ass of asses?" Penny challenged scornfully.

"Whoa," warned Flathead, "calm down."

"Don't tell her to calm down!" Hardegar snapped.

"I will if I want, dead boy!" Flathead retorted with two of her tentacles balling up in attack position.

Klorf pounded some more. He may have been yelling, too, but only the sound of the pounding made it through.

"Both of you calm down!" Throom intoned.

"You stay out of this!" Hardegar enjoined.

"Yeah. Clam up, pebbles!" Flathead agreed. She put another pair of tentacles in attack position, this time between herself and Throom.

"You slimy little hermaphrodite!" Throom exclaimed in shock.

In an instant the insults were flying so fast and thick that they formed into an unintelligible wall of sound, punctuated by Klorf's pounding.

Greasly stepped back from the situation as he always did when entering crisis mode. He was losing control. He looked at his crew. They were actually about to physically attack each other. Flathead was up on top of the console taunting one and all to come closer and get what's coming to them. Penny was shoving Hardegar in the chest, and Throom was obviously about to lose his decorum and go Fraggart on their asses.

"Wait! Wait! Don't you see what's happening?" he cried, thinking fast. "This isn't like us!"

The name calling died down to a trickle of expletives as each of them gave Greasly half an ear.

"I've seen this before," he lied. "There must be something else on board—a presence of some sort."

The insults petered out. They were all listening to him now. Klorf's pounding was the only other sound.

"Think about it!" Greasly pleaded, exactly as if he knew what he was talking about—a skill he learned in officer school. "Are any of you acting normal? Throom yelling insults and about to pound Flathead? Penny being mean and callous? Hardegar openly defiant? Flathead ready to knock the vitals out of any and all?" They were silent. He walked to the center of the room. "This is exactly what it wants," he intoned meaningfully.

"What what wants?" Hardegar asked.

"A gritch," Greasly invented the name on the spot. "It's on this ship, and it's controlling us. The more we fight, the more we feed it." They looked at the door, interpreting the pounding in a new light. "That's Klorf." Greasly assured, trying to avert disaster.

Hardegar grabbed some spazzers out of a supply cabinet and distributed them.

"Can you open the door, Throom?" Flathead requested while aiming two spazzers at the doorway.

"Right." He quickly went to the wiring he had been working on. "Ready?"

They all nodded, except for Greasly, who was coming up with the rest of his plan.

The door slid open, and Klorf's voice entered the room first. "What is your situation?" he was yelling. They all breathed a sigh of relief and lowered their spazzers. Klorf entered and looked around. "What has happened?"

"There's a gritch on board," Hardegar informed him. "An intruder."

"I knew it!" Klorf exclaimed, barely able to contain his glee. "Since we landed on Kravits Rock I have been unable to lose the feeling that something unauthorized was on board."

"It feeds off anger," Flathead added.

"It made the cap'n and Penny have sex just to piss us off!" Hardegar piped in.

Klorf's eyes narrowed, and his fists clenched.

"Don't get mad, Klorf. It only makes it stronger," Throom urged.

"I'm not angry," Klorf insisted, but Greasly didn't like the way his eyes kept darting back and forth between he and Penny.

"I'll run a scan," offered Penny, setting down her spazzer and rushing to her console.

"Uh," Greasly hadn't thought of that, "yeah. But you might not find anything. They say these things are pure energy of a kind that—"

"Got it!" Penny reported triumphantly.

"What?"

"It's on this level. In one of the storage rooms."

Hardegar, Klorf, Throom, and Flathead gathered around the display. Greasly stood where he was, trying to get a grip on reality again. How had his imaginary nemesis just managed to show up on Penny's scan?

"We should come from two directions so the shuttle hole is its only escape," reasoned Klorf, pointing out the routes on the display.

"Sounds good," Penny agreed. "Everyone get yackers, and I'll track it from here."

"Right!"

They broke up, and in a few seconds they were armed and heading down the corridors of the Incorrigible.

The cap'n looked over Penny's shoulder. Sure enough, there was a seventh presence on the ship. It must have come aboard on Kravits Rock while they were distracted. Then it occurred to Greasly. "Wait, that's Mini Penny!"

She tapped her forehead. "Uh uh," she said, "it's moving."

Greasly thought at first she was talking about Mini Penny, but then she pointed at the extraneous blip. It had left the storage room and was headed aft—toward the shuttle hole.

Greasly was pondering what the blip might be with growing unease. Had he stumbled upon the truth in making up a lie? What if it were a stowaway? Would they stop when they saw it? What if it was a race they didn't recognize? They would assume his lies had been true. He grabbed a yacker.

"Just spaz it. Does everyone hear that? Spaz only."

"We hear you." The voice was Hardegar's.

"Starboard group speed up," Penny instructed. "We don't want it to run up to the second level."

"Spaz only," Greasly repeated. A knot was forming in his throat.

"We heard you!" Hardegar exclaimed.

"Starboard team, you're too late, it's headed up the ramp to second—wait—it's turned around. It's going into the airlock," Penny relayed excitedly.

"I see the door closing," the voice was Klorf's. It was followed by his rapid footsteps. There was a pause, then, "I don't see it."

"Me either." It was Throom.

"It's there. It's in the aft starboard airlock," Penny promised adamantly.

"Let's open it." It was Hardegar's voice.

"Okay, ready?" Throom asked. The other two responded affirmatively. "Damn," Throom exclaimed. "It's blocked the door with something."

"I think it's messing with our heads again because I'm getting really pissed," Hardegar growled.

Flathead said, "Let me at that."

"I know what I'm doing," Klorf growled.

"I'm on my way down," said Greasly to Penny as he turned to go. He wasn't even to the door before Klorf's voice came across the yacker.

"Oops."

"What happened?" No response. Greasly tapped his yacker. "Klorf, what was oops?" Still no response. "Explain oops, Klorf."

"The ship is secure," Klorf reported.

"Klorf," the cap'n asked cautiously, "what happened?"

"I jettisoned it, sir."

"I told you to let me," Flathead nagged.

"Unintentionally," Klorf continued.

The cap'n went white. "Penny?"

"Yes, Cap'n?"

"Did he just say. . . " he could not make himself say the words.

"He jettisoned it," she repeated, puzzled by the cap'n's response.

"I had intended to capture it alive," Klorf said.

"Space law gives us full right to eliminate any unauthorized presences," Penny offered. "A gritch is surely on the galactic noxious beings list anyway, right?"

"Quick, run a scan and see what it was. It might still be close enough."

"We're in Flitzville."

"What?" His hopes of at least understanding what he had done vanished.

"We entered Flitzville a few minutes ago. Whatever it was, it could be anywhere by now—most likely deep space."

Greasly nodded. "I'm gonna go lie down for a while." He took off the yacker and tossed it on a console.

"Cap'n?" Penny called after him as he was leaving.

He stopped and looked at her. "Yeah?"

"Are you okay?"

"Yeah, sure." He turned to leave again.

"Really?" she asked, somewhat softer. He turned to look at her. "Klorf was only doing his duty. I'm sure he didn't mean to..."

Greasly shook his head as if to say "Don't worry about it."

"Lou?" She interrupted his exit again. He looked up at her. She seemed to be fighting for words that weren't there. She settled for smiling at him.

He smiled back—a weary, somewhat sad, smile. "We'll talk later, okay?"

She nodded.

On the way back to his cabin, he thought about Penny. She really seemed to be concerned about him. She was certainly a woman of extremes. She could be as fierce as an oblejag and as soft as the fur behind a kitten's ear, efficient to a fault but still wild enough to please him in ways he hadn't even thought of until she did them. He shook his head—dangerous thoughts.

Every cap'n knew about the Kirkian dilemma. They taught it in officer's training. For a cap'n to fall in love with a member of his crew dramatically increases the odds of that crew member dying, often within an hour's time. No one could explain why it happened, but numerous historical studies had shown that it was a very real effect.

And even if she survived the dilemma, there was the soap opera syndrome. Whenever any two members of a starship crew are in a relationship that is healthy and happy, at least one of them, and often both, will inevitably become marginalized and uninteresting to the point that they have to have an affair to avoid fading into the background. Scientists studying these effects had proven statistically in numerous studies that there is a fundamental universal force that wishes fervently for people to be happy but won't tolerate them for long after they are.

He flopped down onto his bunk. What or whom had he just killed?

He sighed. Even if he ignored the altruistic motives for avoiding Penny, he was left with an even stronger reason. She was far more than he deserved.

Chapter 24

The "trunk" of the Incorrigible popped open, and the tire-shaped shuttle craft hovered out into space—the chrome and plastiglass of the hubcap glittering in the light of the Solian sun—and gracefully glided toward the planet below.

"Spazzer," listed Throom.

"Check," Klorf, Penny, Hardegar, and the cap'n responded in unison.

"Discombobulater."

"Check."

"Heat flinger."

"Check."

"Remote yacker."

"Check."

"Last will and testament."

"Check."

"Klorf, do we have the matter declumpinizationizer?"

"Yes, we do," Klorf confirmed.

"Good, you carry that. Is that everything?" Throom pondered.

"Literally," complained Hardegar.

"By the time this is over, you'll be glad for it," the cap'n intoned seriously.

"Sporks!" blurted Throom.

"Check."

"I can't believe I almost forgot sporks," Throom murmured, shaking his head in disgust.

"It's been a while since you went on a mission like this," Greasly comforted.

"I still have the feeling I'm forgetting something—something important."

"Is all of this really necessary?" Penny bellyached. "Entire governments have been overthrown with less equipment than this."

"But we're not overthrowing a government," the cap'n pointed out without looking at her, "we're going to Sol."

"I've been to Sol. It was the most boring month of my life—nothing but office workers and bureaucrats."

"Ah," Greasly put a finger in the air. "That's Sol Prime. That's the Sol they let the entire galaxy see. We are going to Sol Deux—Sol Prime's dark secret." He turned to face them all and spoke in excited tones. "The civilization of Sol did not start where it is now. It started here. Everything you say about Sol was once true of this planet, but then it fell into darkness, chaos, and barbarity. Only a few million escaped to the new Sol and rebuilt their civilization. The rest..." He looked around the control room at the attentive faces. "...remained."

The rest of the crew looked at each other to see if anyone was getting his drift.

"What do you mean fell?" Hardegar pressed.

"Well, you know how anal the Solians are, right? I mean, in the annals of anality they take the anal cake, but they were even worse before. There were over thirty thousand different agencies all keeping a very careful eye on something or other. It was regulated up to a Xemite's eyeballs—the little ones, not the big one. Nothing happened in old Sol without three different permits and six different licenses. Hell, sometimes you had to have a permit just to get a license! And it was like this because it was exactly the way the Solians liked it. Solians felt that they had created the perfect society. It was a masterwork of process and information all intermeshed and supporting each other in a beautiful cathedral to bureaucracy—Solian perfection—and it was all brought down in the space of a year by one lone Solian."

Penny knew he would not continue until somebody asked it. "Who?"

"Nobody knows his real name. It's lost to history. But he's called Solian 7 by anyone that knows about him. He was the one Solian that was born into this perfect society that didn't like it. In fact he hated it. He hated all of the rules and regulations and checks and double checks and... well, you've been to Sol," he said to Penny. She nodded in understanding. "But he couldn't leave. He was a Solian that hated Solian society—something that had not happened in thousands of years. He was the evolutionary twitch that brought down the whole house of cards because it drove him mad, and he thought he should return the favor."

"What did he do?" asked Klorf.

"He got a patent."

"A what?" asked Throom, sure he had misheard.

"A patent."

"On what?"

"On the concept of seven," Greasly announced importantly. "That's why he's Solian 7."

"You can't patent a number," Hardegar scoffed.

"On Sol you could. They liked everything imaginable to be somehow regulated—even concepts like a number. Of course, all of those sorts of patents were held by a central conceptual property ministry that was divided up into numerous administrative bodies which elected steering committees which... you get the picture. They owned and operated all of the basic concepts."

"But they missed one?" Penny queried.

"No, they owned one, they missed seven," Greasly corrected.

"No, I didn't mean the number one—I meant one as a number, er, as a quantity."

"I'm trying to tell a story here, do you mind?" Greasly complained.

She narrowed her eyes at him.

"Anyway they missed one, and Solian 7 found it. Of course, having such a basic concept in the hands of a single, insane Solian mixed things up a bit, and by mixed things up a bit, I mean destroyed them utterly. Effectively, nothing could happen legally without his permission, and he didn't give it.

"Oh, a few replacements for seven popped up, like the movement to replace it with 4+3 or the open-source seven substitute gnuChimpZilla, but the legality of those would take decades to determine. In the meantime, everything stopped.

"Most of the Solians went as mad as Solian 7 had. There were only a few handfuls in cities all over the planet with just enough rebelliousness in their blood to break a rule in an emergency. They stole ships and took off to colonize another planet while this one burned, and out of the ashes of this great crystal city of logic and order, monsters have grown." He was grinning in anticipation of the exciting time they were going to have. "Screaming pink bone-crushers. Yellow puss maggots the size of a man. Rat-faced scab melons. Cool stuff, guys!" he said, trying to get through to them. "We finally get to blast some stuff!"

His crew looked at each other nervously, except for Throom—who looked apologetic.

"Is that why we're here?" Penny demanded.

"Sort of," admitted Greasly sheepishly, "but mostly to get some information on the Flummox."

"What the hell is a flummox?" Hardegar inquired.

"It was Bartholomew Methane's ship," Penny answered in an annoyed tone.

"What? I was supposed to know that?"

"He told us all that on Kravits Rock."

"No," he corrected pointedly, "he didn't tell all of us. Klorf and I weren't invited to your little screw-apalooza, remember."

"Oh, Christ!" she snapped. "Will you shut the far—" She caught herself. "—fuck up about that?"

In spite of themselves the group giggled.

"What?" she queried.

"Penny, we're all adults here," Greasly assured her. "It's okay to say fark."

She smiled sheepishly despite her efforts not to. "Okay, shut the fark up about that," she amended, but not with feeling.

"Anyway," Greasly began, in an attempt to take back control of his conversation, "we need to find the registration record of the Flummox to find out as many technical details as we can about it. Anything that will help us spot it on Frag."

"Why is that information here?" Klorf asked.

"Wouldn't it be on Sol prime?" Penny continued his thought. "The central ship registry is on Sol prime."

"But two hundred years ago this was Sol prime." He tapped the side of his head to indicate how brainy he was.

"So?" Hardegar asked.

"So... the Flummox was registered over two hundred years ago," Greasly reminded.

"How is that possible?" It was Klorf asking. "What ship has a career of a hundred and fifty years?"

Greasly sighed in exasperation and went back to his seat. "You two catch these guys up on the story, all right?"

Throom snapped out of his deep thoughts. He had been only half listening. He had been trying to remember something— something important. There was something important that he should be remembering, but he couldn't put his finger on it. "Huh?"

Annoyed, Greasly turned to Penny. "Explain to him what it is you are supposed to explain to them."

She turned to Throom with a sigh. "He wants us to tell them the whole Raul Grimshaw story."

"And make it snappy. We're about to land."

They were on the ground and standing in the airlock about to leave the ship by the time Throom and Penny told everything they knew.

"Okay," said Hardegar, "but none of that explains how he jumped forward in time over a hundred years. I mean I remember his disappearance being a big deal when I was a kid."

Penny and Throom looked at Greasly. He blinked back at them.

"Well?" Throom prodded.

"Didn't I explain that?" Greasly inquired.

"No," answered Throom. "That was when you and Penny started—"

There was a "clunk" and a female cry of pain as Penny elbowed Throom in the side. "Damn you Throom!" she complained, rubbing her elbow.

"How was that my fault?"

"Anyway," Greasly grumbled impatiently, "it was that thing where time gets slower when you go really, really fast: time expanding or stretching. What's that called again?"

"Time bloating?" Penny ventured.

"That's it. Time bloating. He blasted off into real space at close to the speed of light for a while then did the same thing to come back. He did it to try and rid himself of Notable Raul. He thought that by traveling into the future he could outlive even the memory of Raul. Didn't work, though. Raul never really went away. In fact just before Bartholomew Methane returned they introduced fission chips, and Raul went through another renaissance."

Throom and Penny instantly broke into song. "Fission chips, the taste will glow on you!" Then, as they each covered their crotch with their hands, "My nuts!" They laughed as they both remembered and mimicked the ad down to the expression on Raul's face.

Klorf looked to Hardegar for some sort of assurance that the two had not lost their minds. Hardegar only shrugged.

"Yeah, right," Greasly said, sounding somewhat embarrassed for their horrible singing. "So are we all caught up? Good. Let's rock!"

With a gleam in his eye, and before anyone could protest, he reached over and opened the outer door of the airlock. Penny screamed and everyone grabbed their weapons as a dozen or so slavering beasts swarmed in through the opening.

"Yeah! That's what I'm talking about!" the cap'n shouted with glee as he blasted away at the rat-like things with his spazzer. As he hit them, they fell into twitching fits with their barbed tongues hanging out from between jagged teeth.

Penny tried to fire, but the gun only flashed a red light at her. One of the things leaped at her face. She quickly knocked it aside—right into Hardegar.

Hardegar screamed as the thing recovered in mid-air and clamped its jaws into his arm. He dropped the discombobulater he had just used to discombobulate one of the things and tried to shake the furry bear trap from his forearm.

Meanwhile the discombobulated rat-dog-thing looked sheepishly around with its large, baleful eyes as if it suddenly felt very out of place and backed out the door.

Three of the things hung off of Throom as they damaged their teeth on his rocky body. He irritably plucked two of them off of himself and crushed one in each hand. Hot pink goo splatted out onto Klorf as he blasted away with his spazzer. Klorf didn't react. He just kept firing.

Throom crushed the last one clinging to him, then squished the one hanging off Hardegar between his two stony hands. The hot pink goo covered Hardegar from head to foot. He wiped it from his eyes in slow, burning exasperation.

"Don't worry," promised the cap'n, "it comes off with soap and water." He was sweeping the twitching balls of fur and teeth out the door with his feet. No more were coming in.

"Why the fark didn't my farking gun work!?" Penny screamed as she beat her palm against it. Throom hastily snatched it from her grasp.

"That's a heat flinger," he pointed out patiently.

"I know that!"

"See this red light? That shows the ship's safety is on. No weapon strong enough to damage the ship will work within 50 meters of it without a special override." Throom slowly handed the gun back to her. "It prevents blasting a hole in the side of the ship."

"Now you tell me," she growled as she sulkily snatched back the gun.

"The farking thing punctured my arm," Hardegar railed. He held up his arm to show the twin half moons of deep but bloodless lacerations. "Look at that!"

"You're not getting vain are you, Hardegar?" the cap'n teased jovially.

"I think you're forgetting I don't heal any more," Hardegar snapped. "I'm stuck with these now."

"You're right. I wasn't thinking about that," Greasly admitted apologetically as he finished kicking the last of the furry things off the gangway. He turned to face Hardegar. "I didn't mean anything by it."

Hardegar nodded sarcastically but let his anger ebb away anyway.

"I would appreciate more of a warning next time, Cap'n," Klorf requested stiffly.

Greasly stopped and looked at him questioningly. "What do you mean? I told you this place was dangerous."

Klorf's chest puffed in indignation. "You did not give me time to prepare before opening the door."

"And you didn't tell me the heat flinger wouldn't work," Penny sniped.

Greasly looked at her sideways. "Are you sure I didn't mention that? I'm pretty sure I said something."

"Not to me," she accused.

"Really?" He shrugged. "Well, I can't do everything around here." He started checking his weapons and turned to exit the door. "You'll all just have to stay on your toes."

"I'm sorry," Throom offered. "It's my fault. I should have briefed everyone better." He shook his head as if to clear it of the thing that he had been trying to remember.

"Come on guys!" the cap'n had turned around and was pleading to them from the base of the gangway. He stood on the dusty and debris strewn remains of an old-fashioned city street. "You're gonna miss all the fun!"

Just then, an iridescent lizard the size of a cougar leaped from the side and bowled the cap'n over. Greasly's spazzer skidded across the pavement. Every one leaped into action and ran down the gangway to where the cap'n and the lizard rolled about in a tangle of furious violence. Penny and Klorf were the first to arrive.

"Spaz it!" Hardegar yelled from behind them.

"No, you'll hit the cap'n," Throom warned from behind Hardegar.

Penny and Klorf only hesitated an instant. With a quick conspiratorial smirk at each other, they aimed and fired.

Chapter 25

"I had to do it," Penny claimed to the cap'n a little later, after the effects of the spazzing had worn off. "The thing was killing you."

"A leaping lizard?" the cap'n mocked. "They're harmless. They don't have any teeth! No teeth. No claws. No pupils. They're just a nuisance."

"We acted on the only information available to us at the time," Klorf informed him. "It appeared to be a threat."

"I know, I know." Greasly waved his hand as if trying to wave the whole ugly incident away. "You did the right thing." He stood up, and though his legs were still a little wobbly, he had enough control to walk. "Still, I think you may have enjoyed it."

Penny winked at Klorf. "I never said I didn't."

"So where are these records we need?" Hardegar interrupted in an annoyed tone.

"In the hall of records most likely," Throom answered.

"Then let's go get them and get the hell out of here."

"What? You're not having fun?" Greasly asked in surprise.

"No. Are you?"

"I *was*."

"Well, I for one am ready to leave," Hardegar complained. Although he, like the others, had used the cap'n's twitch time to clean himself off, he still had traces of the pink goo in his ears, in his eye sockets, and seemingly in every crevice of his head pattern changing it into a hot pink vampire's peak.

"Me too," added Penny.

"I agree," Klorf concurred.

Throom shrugged, "It's not dangerous for me—whatever you guys want."

"What the fark!?" Greasly looked around at them in amazement. "You think this is suddenly a democracy? You're all free to do as you want, but if you want a ride home on my ship you're going to follow orders."

They were silent for a moment; then Hardegar exclaimed, "Oh, now you act like a cap'n!"

"Yeah." Greasly swaggered toward him. "That's my prerogative as cap'n."

"What about your responsibilities as cap'n?" Penny chided.

Greasly held out his arms in standard "give me a break" attitude. "What is this, an away mission or an intervention?"

"There is an implicit agreement between the governor and the governed," Klorf intoned. "If the governed receive nothing for their service, then the government is a dictatorship and is in its very nature wrong."

Greasly was about to speak but stopped with his mouth still open and turned along with Throom, Penny, and Hardegar to look at Klorf.

"What did you say?" Penny asked.

"That we have a right to expect something in return for our services. Otherwise we are slaves," Klorf summarized.

Greasly and the others stared at Klorf in stunned silence for a moment. Then a smile blossomed on Greasly's face as he walked to Klorf with his hand out. Klorf uncertainly took the hand offered him. Greasly clasped it and shook it as he looked into Klorf's eyes with sincere pride. "Klorf, I'm very proud of you right now."

"You've been reading," Penny asserted.

"Yes, I have," Klorf affirmed.

"This is great," Greasly pronounced, meaning it. "It's like the defeat of Xerxes at Salamis, or the fall of the Berlin wall, or the third Arab Spring."

Penny and Hardegar were looking at him as if he were speaking Flootian.

"Or Xunglunkan the Tharfamite's rebellion against the hump-fitters union."

That they knew. They nodded in agreement.

"This is really great Klorf," Penny said with her hand on his back. "You stood up to authority."

"I meant no disrespect, Cap'n," Klorf assuaged, casting his eyes down. Greasly grasped his hand tighter to get his attention.

"Klorf," Greasly said. Klorf looked up at him. "Saying what you think is right is never disrespectful—though it will almost always be seen as such."

"When authority is wrong, it's your duty to say so," Penny added.

"That's right," Greasly agreed, "though whether authority was wrong in this particular case is still an unsettled point."

Penny rolled her eyes and shook her head, unable to find words.

"Thank you, Cap'n," Klorf said.

"No," —Greasly let go of his hand and tapped him on the arm with his fist—"thank you." He breathed in deeply. "So. Let's go shoot some shit!"

Penny stood in amazement as both Hardegar and Klorf fell right in step behind Greasly as he marched off into the ruined city. She looked at Throom, who only shrugged and followed the group.

She ran to catch up with them as they walked purposefully along the remains of a land road that divided walls of very tall buildings made of stone, metal, and glass—all in poor repair.

"So we are going to get the record?" she asked, jumping over a large pothole.

"Yes," Greasly verified without slowing down.

"I mean right now. Are we on our way to the hall of records?"

"We are traveling on a route that ends at the hall of records." Greasly pointed ahead. "I saw some rat-faced scab melons through there as we landed. If you use your heat flinger on them, they explode. It's great!"

"Are we going by the most direct route?" Penny pressed, more suspicious than ever.

"Sure," Greasly said unconvincingly.

"Stop!" Penny shouted. They stopped. She asked the cap'n directly, "What is the most direct path to the hall of records?"

"We'll get there if we go through the scab melons, then left to this place that had a bunch of purple lung pluckers last time I was—"

She spoke slowly and deliberately. "Is it possible to get to the hall of records from here without going through the rat-faced scab melons or the purple lung pluckers?"

"If we go-"

She interrupted him. "Yes or no? It's a yes or no question."

Greasly took a deep breath and let it out before he answered, "Yes."

"Okay, what is the shortest route that avoids all known monsters?"

Sulkily and without looking, he lifted his arm and pointed at the building they were standing in front of. They looked and saw the words "Hall of Records" engraved above the door.

"You mind if we take this route?" she asked smugly. He flopped his arms in resignation, and they all walked to the door.

Chapter 26

When Throom entered the building, he was surprised to see a large counter with a receptionist behind it. He turned to Greasly. "I thought you said it was deserted?"

The others muttered agreement.

"I never said that," Greasly said matter-of-factly. "I said they changed, not died."

Hardegar was at the desk already leaning over to talk to the receptionist. Her brown hair was elaborately piled atop her head. Her fingernails curved in a four centimeter arc and were decorated with glittery patterns over a base paint of blood red. Her clothes were on the flashy side of professional and heavily accessorized.

"Hello," Hardegar said suavely, "I was wond—"

Her hand shot up faster than the eye could follow and formed a wall between his face and hers. He moved to look around it.

"Take a number. Have a seat," she said.

"We're looking for the records—"

"Take a number. Have a seat," she repeated. Her hand moved again to obstruct his view. The fingers all formed a fist except for the index finger, which wagged back and forth in admonition.

"Hey, Hardegar," Greasly warned, once he noticed what was going on, "I wouldn't do that if I were you."

Hardegar brushed the cap'n's admonition aside and turned back to the receptionist. He reached up and tried to move her hand out of the way.

In a flash she was holding his hand bent back in a direction that caused his receptors to register potential damage to his infrastructure and was forcing him down to the counter by twisting his arm. Her eyes were staring at him in righteous indignation. "Take a number. Have a seat."

"Okay! Okay!" he yelled.

"Take a number. Have a seat." She began hitting him over the head with a hand bag as she spoke. "Take a number. Have a seat. Take a number. Have a seat."

"Help," Hardegar whimpered beneath her blows.

Penny pulled her discombobulater and fired. It seemed to have no effect.

"That won't do any good," said Greasly. "All receptionists are immune to discombobulation." He deftly spazzed her.

She fell to the floor twitching, but the fount of verbiage continued to flow. "Take a number. Have a seat." He spazzed her again. "Do you have an appointment?" she asked, then went right back to "Take a number. Have a seat." He shrugged and gave up.

Throom helped Hardegar, who was stunned and shaking, stand up. They followed the cap'n, along with the others, to a pair of metal panels in the wall. The cap'n pressed a button of ancient design, and an upward pointing arrow lit.

"Nice." Throom smiled as the metal panels slid apart to reveal a small room.

"Everybody in," Greasly invited as he entered the tiny space.

"I haven't been on an elevator since Cran." Throom said.

"The Solians were past elevators, Throom." No sooner had Greasly said this, than Throom noticed that the tiny room had no ceiling. It was actually the bottom of a square tube extending out of site. "This is a heaver."

They all instantly found themselves being heaved upward with face melting force. Their velocity diminished, and just when Throom thought they would all fall back down to their deaths, a floor shot out of the wall, and they landed on it as gracefully as cats.

"They're much faster than elevators." Greasly finished as a new set of metal doors slid apart to reveal a corridor lit by fluorescent rectangles all along the ceiling.

They all exited the heaver. Throom noticed that Penny was pale and shaking a little.

"I don't like that," she muttered weakly. "Let's not do that again."

"No need to," promised Greasly. "We have to take the plummeter down."

"Oh, goody." She shuddered.

"Yeah," Throom agreed, with spirit.

A door opened nearby, and a Human Solian male came out dressed in a white shirt with a blue tie. His pants were beige and fairly baggy. The Human seemed to have most of his body weight, which was in no short supply, around his middle and hips. Throom wondered if maybe this was the natural result of using the heaver too often.

When he noticed that the Human wore thinly rimmed glasses, Throom had to smile. He chuckled at the quaint absurdity of them. "Doctor, I can't see well." He imagined the patient saying. "Well, let's just wire these lenses in front of your face, and you can walk around all day looking through them," would come the response. Then, remarkably, the patient would say, "Hey, doc, great idea!"

The white-collared Solian walked past them and through another door labeled "IT." Greasly shrugged and said, "This must be it." He then went in after the Solian.

The room was huge but divided up into tiny pens by panels that rose just to eye level. Each pen was open to one of several narrow paths that cut through the room like cramped alleyways. The room was alive with a low mumbling of dozens of voices coming from the inhabitants of some of the tiny pens.

A pen near Throom was occupied by a pasty, lumpy Human that had a very similar weight distribution plan to the one they had seen in the hall.

"Reboot," he was saying again and again.

They walked through the room to see if any of it was different, and from every occupied pen that they passed they heard either "Reboot" or "Upgrade."

"I think they're tech support," Throom concluded. "This might be a good place to get into their system and search for the information."

Greasly agreed. "You want to try that while we keep looking for a public interface, just in case?"

"Sure." Throom started looking for a cube with an active interface.

"Are you sure you'll be all right alone?" Penny asked.

Throom looked around at the flabby, white, fading images of Humanity. "I can handle them."

Just then, they all gasped and jumped as a door at the end of the path they were standing in suddenly burst open. Several larger-than-man-sized wolves with glowing red eyes ran into the room and down the narrow corridor toward the crew.

Penny was shocked into inaction as she stared at the massive canines running in her direction, but the cap'n's voice snapped her out of it and she leaped behind Throom.

"Buh-duh-guh, guns! Guns!" Greasly fumbled with both his words and his gun. The others grabbed and fumbled as well, while the wolves nearly flew toward them down the path between rows of cubicles.

Just as the crew had their guns out and aimed, Throom yelled, "Wait!"

The wolves were stopping each time one of them found an occupied pen. They would dart in and drag a technician into the pathway and out the door.

"Let them go unless they get too close."

The last one ducked into a pen just ten or so meters from the crew. It dragged the technician out by the shoulder. They heard the tech saying "Reboot?" all the way down the hall and through the door.

"My god, that's horrible!" Penny exclaimed.

Hardegar was reciting a prayer under his breath.

"To die like that. . ." Klorf muttered and searched for the words, "I'd rather die."

Penny looked at Throom, who looked at the rest of the crew. He seemed to be thinking the same thing she was. Several of them would look very tasty to a creature like that.

"Maybe I should stay with you," he suggested. "We should all stay together."

"No," corrected Greasly, "an away team should always split up."

"What?" Penny turned quickly to face him. "Why?"

"You must have at least one person from your crew split off from the rest, so that when the rest are in a real tight spot, and there is no way for them to get out of it, that person can show up unexpectedly and save them."

Penny blinked, waiting for the punch line. "Are you joking?"

"No," he declared as if offended. "It's basic cap'nology. They teach it to you the first week, right after 'Don't get in the way of the real Galactic Guard.'"

"But it's crazy." She looked around at the rest of the crew but didn't find the rousing support she had hoped for.

"It's probably based on sound research," offered Throom in a noncommittal tone.

"Probably." Hardegar nodded.

"The Galactic Guard Lite has a long and prestigious history," Klorf added.

"It is based on sound research," the cap'n confirmed. "It's based on a thorough study of history."

"R2D2 did save Luke and the others from the trash compactor," argued Hardegar. "It's right there in second Luke."

"I don't care what it says in the Bible—I don't care what they said in Cap'nology 101—it's stupid." Her face was getting red. "Throom should stay with us, because having him with us is much more likely to save our lives than not having him with us."

"Maybe you're right." Greasly nodded thoughtfully then asked Hardegar, "How about you? You want to split off and show up to save us later?"

Hardegar thought it over.

"Lets all just stick together, okay?" Penny pleaded. As a last resort she looked Greasly right in the eyes and gave him her soft look. "Please?"

"Ah fark!" he snapped, turning away. "Don't do that."

"I'd feel a lot safer," she cooed softly.

"Alright, alright!" he gave in, waving her away. He pointed at Hardegar. "But if things start looking bad, I want you to turn and run as fast as you can."

"I can do that," Hardegar avowed with confidence.

"Okay." The cap'n turned to Throom. "You get busy trying to break into the system. We'll be looking around in here if you need us."

That seemed a lot like splitting up to Penny, but she felt that if she brought it up, she might jinx the victory she had just scored. At least they would be in the same room.

"Right," Throom affirmed, then turned to try and find a working interface. He started with the pen that they had seen the last technician dragged out of. It turned out to be a good strategy, because the interface was open and active. He went right to work.

He found that the system only allowed access to some sort of troubleshooting database. It asked questions about the current situation, and based on the answer, took you to either a solution or to another question. Throom began tracing his way through the decision tree in hopes that one of the branches might include some sort of link to the underlying system.

After an hour or so, he hit on a solution that was neither "reboot" nor "upgrade" and found himself with low level access to the system. From there it was an easy matter to get the information he needed and put it on an info chit. He slipped it into a pocket on one of his weapon belts.

Throom stood up and scanned the grid of dividers looking for the tops of his crew-mates heads. He saw no such thing.

"Hey," he yelled, "I've got it. Let's go."

No answer. No sign of the crew—just the panel grid and the soft murmur of "Reboot" and "Upgrade."

Throom thought to himself that if he had skin, it would be crawling right now. How could they all disappear at once? He started walking through the aisles cautiously, careful to look in every cell of the grid. He saw several of the techs and many more empty pens, but no sign of the crew. After he made a complete sweep of the room, he stood on his tip-toes to look for all of the entrances and exits.

He identified the door they came in and decided that was the one they would most likely have gone through if they left of their own accord. He started to wind his way through the maze of cubicles but finally gave up and started just smashing his way directly to the door.

His smashing drove one or two of the techs out of their cubes. They wandered around like lost chickens repeating "Reboot? Upgrade?" uncertainly to themselves.

He reached the door and looked out into the hall. It was empty.

He searched around the door thoroughly for any sort of clue that the rest of the party had come this way. He saw nothing. He started plowing another path to the next door. Halfway there he stopped and shook his head in disgust. He had just remembered that they all were equipped with remote yackers. He tapped his ear to activate it. His eyes grew wide as screams filled his ear.

Chapter 27

"Cap'n, Penny, Klorf!" Throom barked through the remote yacker. "Where are you? What's happening?"

"Throom! Throom is that you?" It was Penny.

"Yes. What's happening? Where are you?"

"Throom, I need you..." What she was saying was sometimes drowned out by screams. "...help me...end of hall."

Throom ran out into the hall and to the door at the end. The door was marked "Lounge". It was locked. He could hear screams through it. He braced himself and threw his shoulder against it, smashing it open. He stumbled into the room.

They were all inside the lounge, lounging. Most of them were sitting in comfortable chairs and watching a holovid of a rock concert. The rock fans screaming in anticipation of the start of the concert were the screams he had heard over the yacker. Penny was at a cabinet. She waved him over. She had to yell even with him standing next to her.

"Help me up!" she yelled, accentuating the last word by pointing in that direction. Then she turned around and held up her arms.

Dumbfounded, Throom grabbed her by the waist and lifted her up. She grabbed a box of vacuum sealed snacks off the top shelf. Notable Raul smiled at him from off the package as he set her down.

"Thanks!" she yelled.

In the holovid, the deep driving bass started up, followed by a wavering electronic chord.

"Ooh!" Penny mouthed. "I love this song!" Then by way of explanation, "Hardegar figured out how to make it work! It still picks up the latest feeds! Great huh?" She danced her way over to one of the chairs, popped the seal on the package and started handing the snacks around.

Throom looked around the room until he spotted the old-fashioned controls of the holovid. He paused the playback. The others complained loudly, except for Klorf, who only sat with his head down.

"Why did you do that, Throom?" Greasly snapped.

"What the hell are you guys doing?"

"We're watching a holovid while you do your thing," Greasly answered. "Didn't Klorf tell you?"

They turned to look at Klorf, who looked away awkwardly.

"I thought we weren't splitting up," Throom accused loudly.

"We're not," the cap'n assured him. "We were just down the hall."

"You don't consider that splitting up?" He turned to Penny. "*You* didn't consider that splitting up?" She felt compelled to look at her shoes.

"Sorry, Throom," she shrugged timidly. "I complained, but then Hardegar found these holovids and..." She looked up at him with a sheepish smile. "I just LOVE the Bouffants!"

He looked at the frozen holovid. On the stage were five men with instruments. They were dressed in leather and each sported hair that looked like the end of a cotton swab dyed black. He shook his head in disbelief.

"I was an easy target in there," Throom asserted. "Come to think of it, you were easy targets in here."

"Not really," Hardegar countered.

"Well, the music is loud enough to attract everything on the planet!"

"I made sure that the room was secure," reported Klorf defensively.

"Right," the cap'n added, "Nothing can surprise us as long as that door remains—Jebus! What the fark happened to the door?!"

"I happened to it, I thought you were all being killed!"

"And you were going to save us?"

"Of course."

"Yes!" Greasly clapped his hands together once and stood up with a smug expression on his face. He pointed back and forth from Penny to Throom saying "Eh? Eh?"

"Oh, shut up," Penny grumbled irritably.

"Chalk one up for Cap'nology 101!" Greasly announced with glee.

Throom looked at all of them. "How can it be that four professional adults would throw caution to the wind on a dangerous planet just to watch five dumb-asses bounce around on stage?"

"The Bouffants," corrected Penny darkly with narrowed eyes, "not Five Dumb-asses."

"They have Five Dumb-asses live at the Hyperdrome, though," offered Hardegar, jumping up and heading for the holovid controls.

"Don't touch that," threatened Throom. Hardegar turned and went back to sit down.

Throom walked over to Klorf. Klorf sank down into his chair. He looked up like a scolded puppy at the stone man towering over him. "Why didn't you tell me?" Throom asked.

"Yeah," wondered Hardegar, "why didn't you?"

At first Klorf could not look at Throom. His shame was almost palpable. Then he took a deep breath and forced himself to stand and look him right in the eyes. "I had hoped that you would be killed, and I would have fulfilled my duty to Kurplupt."

Throom threw his head back and clapped his hand to his forehead with a clicking sound of stone on stone. "That's it. That's what I've been trying to remember!" He looked at Klorf again. "You're trying to kill me."

"But you didn't have the guts to face him," accused Greasly.

"Or he had the brains not to," piped in Penny.

"It was a dishonorable act done for the sake of honor," reasoned Klorf.

"Well, you blew your chance, Klorf," assured Throom. "I'm not going to forget again. Next time you try, you had better make it count."

"Yes," Klorf said, nodding appreciatively.

"No, that wasn't a tip," Throom corrected. "Oh never mind." He took a step back.

"I like and respect you greatly, Throom," said Klorf. "I will be greatly saddened when I kill you. I wanted you to know."

"Can't you hear how crazy that sounds? You don't kill people you like and respect."

"That's true, Klorf," Greasly added. "That's literally the least you can do for them."

"It is not in my nature," Klorf stated matter-of-factly. "I'm sure no dirt-dweller can understand the life and ways of the unbounded. Until you have felt the vast openness of life in a bottomless ocean, you cannot understand how important traditions and mores can be. My race developed clinging to the sides of the croosians. We clung to them through the great pressures and darkness at the very heart of Vadnu, pressed tight against their bodies, depending on them for everything.

"For some of us the flapulates took the place of the croosians. They are just as important, and the dying wish of our master is a sacred thing. To deny that would be to deny everything I am. So even though I understand that I am no longer a slave, I still have a cling-on heart and cling-on blood. I am still a cling-on."

They were all silent.

Throom nodded sadly. "I think I understand—at least a little. Space is even bigger and emptier than Vadnu." He looked Klorf in the eyes. "But I still won't let you kill me."

"Please, don't give me the chance."

Throom reached over and took the matter declumpinizationizer from Klorf. "I'd better carry this."

"Well," threw in Greasly, clapping his hands and rubbing them together. "Are we finally ready to rock?"

Most of the group affirmed that they were indeed ready. So a disgusted Throom stood guard at the door for nearly two hours while they "rocked".

Chapter 28

After the concert, they all readied themselves to go back to the ship.

"So, what do you think?" Penny asked Throom expectantly.

"What do you mean?"

"The Bouffants. Did you like them? Aren't they great?"

He was truly at a loss for how to answer.

"I figured you would be a big rock fan." Greasly looked around awaiting the laughs. "Get it? Because he's a big, rock, fan!"

"We get it," Penny said flatly.

"Maybe it's strange, but I don't really like rock music," Throom said.

"No way!" Penny exclaimed. "You don't even like The Fur? Don't Lick Me There? How about harder stuff—Six Dogs and a Corpse? The Raging Jizz Wicks? Really?"

To Throom's surprise, his not liking rock music seemed to offend her. She was looking at him like he had just said she had a zipper in her forehead.

"I'm sorry," he ventured. They entered the hallway.

"So what *do* you like?" Her voice was picking up a derisive tone now. "Country? Old-Time Joe and the Colon Polyps?" She mimicked the lead singers deep gravelly demon voice building up smoothly into a blistering yell. "Are y'all ready?"

"Not really."

"Good." Penny patted his arm. "That's all they listen to back on Goob. I hate it."

"It would be just horrible if I were to like it," said Throom sarcastically.

"Say what you like about the Polyps," Hardegar chimed in, "but Clyde Funkly plays the meanest monster bass in the known galaxy."

"Oh please." She was rankled now. "Jock Rocket makes him sound like a spastic monkey wearing boxing gloves."

"Look, I like the Bouffants too, but let's be real."

"Yes," Throom threw in quickly, "let's do that. We are on a dangerous planet. Let's be real."

They were at the plummeter. Greasly pushed the button with a down arrow, and the door slid open to reveal a tiny room just like the heaver. They all piled in, and Greasly pressed the button marked "G". Both Penny and Hardegar screamed as the floor promptly fell away.

A floor far below seemed to race up the shaft toward them, but instead of splattering them to pieces when they reached it, the floor gave way and applied just enough resistance to their fall to slow it gradually and comfortably until they were on the ground floor and the doors opened up.

"That was worse than the heaver!" Penny screamed as she stumbled out of the room, grasping her sides. "I'm staying on the ground floor from now on!"

"Yes!" exclaimed Greasly, beaming, but he wasn't agreeing with Penny.

Throom followed his gaze through the windows of the building to see the street outside crawling with hideous, supra-man-sized creatures.

The things were generally Humanoid but their proportions were distorted beyond sanity. Their arms were so long that they moved on all fours without bending over. Their legs were so long that their knees stuck out to the side as they scuttled about like crabs. Instead of skin, they were covered in a reddish brown exoskeleton with spikes and barbs on every dorsal surface and also on their inner forearms. Their heads were elongated with large multi-faceted eyes, and a mouth that reached down to the middle of their chest. Their jaws were permanently open—jammed with dozens of slithering tentacles.

"Heat flingers," the cap'n commanded as he pulled his and readied it. "Aim for the eyes."

"I'm not going out there," assured Hardegar.

"Me neither," concurred Penny.

"Suit yourself." The cap'n shrugged and started to move eagerly toward the exit.

Just then, the creatures stopped and seemed to be looking upward. Greasly also waited to see what was happening. The crab-men in the middle of the street sidled to the side as a large craft landed. The side of the craft bore the insignia of the Solian Public Shuttle System.

A door slid open, and what appeared to be a Xemite stepped out. He looked around. Suddenly the stalks on his head stood out stiffly. He quickly turned to get back on the shuttle, but it was too late. The door was closed. The shuttle ascended. He stood alone in a sea of encroaching monstrous menace.

"Fark!" ejected Throom as he grabbed his heat flinger. "We can't leave him out there."

With four powerful bounds, Throom ran to and through the window, shattering one of the panels of glass and scattering some of the monsters. Before the others could even react, he had downed two of the things with his heat flinger.

"Come on!" he yelled to the crew.

Penny readied her heat flinger in time to see that the cap'n was already leaping through the hole in the window. With a battle yell, he landed and fired. The head of the nearest creature vanished—replaced by a smoldering, blackened slag of charred goo. Its limbs spread out on the pavement as it slumped to the ground.

Greasly fired at the beast behind it but missed. It clicked its way around the body and swung at Greasly with its spiky arm. It was surprisingly fast and knocked him to the ground before he could fire.

Penny reached a position just inside the window and fired. She grazed the thing's arm, blasting away one of the spikes. Another one reached an arm around the panel to strike at her. She ducked and the claw hit only glass, which fell in a shower of dagger-like shards. She half leapt, half fell backwards and rolled deeper into the reception area. Hardegar had to hop over her as she rolled underneath him.

Hardegar blasted at the glass-breaker and hit it in the tentacles. Bits of the rubbery flesh flew everywhere. The thing didn't fall, it only seemed to get angrier. Klorf finished it off with a blast to the eyes.

Three more of the things invaded the lobby in an all out assault. Outside, Greasly was blasting them left and right, but they were closing in. Throom was felling them with one blow each but couldn't keep up with the number of them.

One grabbed the screaming Xemite and pulled him into its mouth tentacles, which wrapped tight around his squirming body. Throom turned and put his fist into the skull of the beast. It slumped with the Xemite still entangled.

Inside, Klorf blasted the thing that was headed for him and took a shot at the one closing in on Hardegar. Hardegar had fired at it but missed. Klorf's shot took some of the spikes off its back but didn't slow it down.

Penny was up on the receptionist desk. The receptionist was standing and saying "Take a number. Have a seat." Penny missed a creature. It swiped at her with its claw, and she narrowly escaped by jumping as it swung under her. The claw opened a huge gash in the receptionist who gasped in indignation rather than terror or surprise. "Do you have an appointment?" she started asking.

Penny blasted at the thing, and missed again. She leaped down behind the counter, and the thing grabbed the babbling receptionist and pulled her into its tentacles.

Hardegar screamed, as he also was being pulled into a crab-thing's tentacles. Another blast from Klorf opened up the thing's side but didn't even distract it. It was holding Hardegar pinned to its tentacles with one arm and slashing at him with the other.

Klorf was fighting another one that had come through the window and had to defend himself rather than help Hardegar.

Penny fired at the one eating the receptionist. The thing's head splattered and the receptionist slid to the floor. "Have a break. Take an appointment," she mumbled as the last drops of her own life's blood drained away.

Penny rushed to a position where she could aim at the thing eating Hardegar. She shuffled around but could not get a clear shot. Hardegar—now desperate, with his heat flinger hand trapped between himself and the beast—fired. The lower left half of his torso was blasted away along with part of the beast.

Penny screamed, "Hardegar, no!"

The thing's claw swung inward and punctured Hardegar's right side. He fired again. More of his left side was blasted away. There was no blood, but hydraulic fluid sprayed out along with chunks of machinery and mummified flesh.

Penny aimed at the thing's head. Hardegar's own head was barely out of her way and with both of them moving about she knew the shot was too dangerous. But Klorf, his forehead a bloody red, was still too busy with his foe to fire from a better angle and Hardegar could be dead by the time she moved to a better position. She had to take the shot.

She fired. As she did, the beast lurched.

The center of Hardegar's back exploded. His head fell to the floor and rolled into a corner.

Penny was frozen with the terror of what she had just done. The thing, enraged, dropped what remained of Hardegar's body and lunged toward her.

She fired but missed. It washed over her and pulled her into its tentacles. She screamed in pain as one of the thing's spikes punctured her ribs. The tentacles pulled her in. Her arms were pinned and useless.

It all seemed to happen so slowly now. She tried to struggle free, but it was only driving the spike deeper. Any deeper and she feared it might puncture her lung.

Plans of possible escape rushed through her mind, but nothing plausible. Was this it? Was it possible that the end was like this? It seemed wrong. It seemed not at all the right time for her to die, but maybe it always seemed like that. Maybe you always had the feeling that you were going to get out of the mess you were in, and you always did, except that last time. Maybe that was the way it happened with a quick death. Maybe they all went wide-eyed and unbelieving. Was that the true terror of death—the shattering of that one last illusion?

She felt her arm burning as it made contact with the digestive juices deep inside the tentacles. She could no longer see. She was being pulled in completely. She would need air soon, but she was being held so tight she could not draw a breath. Suddenly there was a jarring sensation. Jaws? Was she nearing a set of powerful internal jaws?

The world shifted. It began to spin. She thought she must be passing out. But then a firm grip took her by the ankle and pulled her out into the air. She gasped in hungrily. There was light. There was air. She made out a pair of stone legs. She was dangling upside down. Throom stood holding a limp Xemite under one arm and her leg with the other. He was talking, but she couldn't make out the words.

She was sobbing uncontrollably.

Throom noted that Penny was alive, deposited her and the Xemite on the floor, and rushed to help Greasly and Klorf with the remaining few creatures. The pair was inside the windows, side by side, picking the things off as they tried to enter. Soon there was only one left.

"Dibs!" yelled Greasly and took it down. He surveyed the carnage around him, breathing hard, face flushed, grinning broadly.

Klorf was also breathing hard. The ridges on his forehead were standing out like the slats of venetian blinds, and it was obvious now that they were the protective covering on a set of blood-red, gill-like organs. Those crimson gashes, along with his furious expression, took Greasly aback for a moment when he turned to congratulate the cling-on.

"Whoa," he said, holding out his hand to Klorf, "take it easy. It's over."

Klorf forced himself to breathe more slowly. The ridges on his forehead began to pulse. They closed then opened several times, opening a little less each time, until eventually they closed completely. He was then calm enough to brush his palm against that of Greasly.

"Is everyone okay?" Greasly asked.

Penny had rolled into a fetal position and was sobbing deeply.

"Penny's wounded," Throom reported. He paused a moment before saying, "Hardegar didn't make it."

There was a muffled yell from the corner. Throom, Klorf, and Greasly all looked at each other, unsure if they were glad or horrified. Finally Throom went over and picked up Hardegar's head. It was indeed the source of the yelling.

"Oh sweet Father, Son, True Prophet, Holy Ghost, and Force!" Hardegar panted. "I thought you were going to leave me here."

"I can't believe you're alive," Throom gasped. The other two males closed in slowly, gaping in wonder.

"Yeah," Greasly agreed weakly.

"I haven't been alive since Endrosia," Hardegar reminded them. "I am still active, though."

"How can you talk without lungs?" Greasly asked.

"It's all synthesized anyway." Hardegar's eyes turned toward his body. "Hold me so I can see my body."

Throom complied, moving him around so that he could see all the pieces.

"Okay." Hardegar sighed. Throom turned the head so they were face to face again. "It's done for isn't it?"

Throom nodded sympathetically.

"Oh well, I got a lot more use out if than I bargained for. It's been out of warranty for ten years now."

The three with bodies looked uncomfortably at the leather covered talking skull. The eyes were glass and had become more translucent than their original design intended. A light on the mechanism in each one made them glow red in their sockets. It had no tongue. The lips formed syllables but the mouth was empty and you could see through it to Throom's hands when it spoke. The vampire's peak tooled into the hairless leather head only added to the sinister effect.

Greasly wondered if it would really be such a horrible thing for them all to simply drop Hardegar and run for the ship. Wouldn't he want them to do the same if he were in Hardegar's place? He thought what that would be like—to be

trapped and unable to move on this insane planet, probably
to be swept up by one of the quasi-zombie janitors and sent
to a landfill—buried alive and unable to escape or to die until
your power cell ran out some time in the far, far, distant
future. No. Not even Greasly could convince himself he
would prefer that over being a burden on the rest of the crew.

Throom was thinking along similar lines but wasn't sure
how to ask it. How crass would it be to ask someone in
Hardegar's situation if he wanted you to end his life for him?
Throom knew that he could not even hint at that. He would
have to wait for Hardegar to bring it up.

"You want us to finish you off?" Greasly asked.

Then again, maybe he wouldn't have to wait. He held
Hardegar up at eye level to all of them.

Hardegar looked around at them. His expression changed
to one of concern. "No thank you," he uttered nervously.

"We won't unless you tell us to," assured Throom, "but if
you need..." he let the sentence wither and die.

"That would be a sin," Hardegar proclaimed with
indignation.

Penny was still crying but stood up and stumbled toward
the group. "I...I...I..." she gasped, "I killed him. I killed
Hardegar."

"Not quite," Hardegar said.

She perked up at the sound of the voice and scurried to
the huddle. When she caught sight of Hardegar, however, she
leaped back and screamed. She looked around at the others
for confirmation that she was seeing what she thought she
was seeing. Her lips distorted in disgust.

"Now that hurt," whined Hardegar.

"No, no," Penny pleaded, "I'm sorry. I'm sorry Hardegar.
It was just a shock. I wasn't expecting you to be..."

"Hey, this isn't that big of a deal really. I mean I've
had several years to get used to being dead. In a way it has
perfectly prepared me for this. In fact, now I see why God let
me die when I drank that Endrosian water. It was to prepare
me emotionally for this."

"But what's the purpose of this?" It was Greasly asking.

"I don't know yet, but I'm sure something great is going to come from it."

The others nodded politely. "Sure, sure," they said.

There was an uncomfortable silence that eventually Penny broke. "Well, I'm losing a lot of blood so..."

"Yes," agreed Greasly.

They were halfway to the shuttle when Throom remembered something. He ran back to the hall of records. When the others reached the transport, they heard the thunderous footfalls of Throom as he ran up to them with the Xemite draped over his shoulder.

"Forgot the Xemite," he said as he walked up the ramp.

Chapter 29

Back on The Incorrigible, Throom placed the unfortunate
traveler he had saved in an empty cabin and made sure
it would be comfortable when it woke up. Once he had
a chance to actually examine the creature, he found that
instead of eyes on the end of its eye stalks, each was capped
with a Human-like nose. It appeared to be Xemite in every
other respect, however, and from its dress Throom guessed a
fairly important one too.

He moved on to check on Penny, whose wound was not
as bad as it had seemed. Once he was sure she was okay
and had a tissue regeneration bath clamped onto her side, he
went to the bridge to talk to the cap'n about the information
he had found on Sol Deux.

When Throom entered the bridge, he started at the sight
of Flathead. She was there in her usual place behind her
console, but her usually box-like hub was now covered with
lumps.

"Flathead!" Throom cried. "What happened to you?"

"What?" Flathead asked, but her voice was different.
It was as if the word carried the harmonics from a hundred
other voices—as if it were call and echoes all compressed
together. "Nothing's wrong."

"She's pregnant, Throom," the cap'n interjected
nonchalantly.

"Oh." He looked at Flathead and could now see that
the lumps were moving this way and that under her yellow,
paisley skin.

Throom shuddered. How did these organed creatures stand themselves? The idea of being a bag of collected chunks and pieces had always made Throom uncomfortable. As he watched the lumps move under Flathead's surface, he realized part of what made it seem so horrible to him. It was so invade-able!

He turned to the cap'n. "I wondered if you wanted to go over what I found out about the Flummox?"

Greasly leapt to his feet. "Hell, yes! Let's look at it!"

It didn't take them long to have the information up and displayed before them. Greasly shrugged and nodded his head when he saw it. "Not as helpful as I had hoped it would be, but at least we'll know it when we see it now. Thanks Throom." Then he added in a brighter tone, "Next stop, Frag."

"What about that Xemite?"

"Oh yeah. Sol Prime then Frag."

*   *   *

It was a quick stop on their way out of the Sol system to dump the unfortunate Xemite on Sol Prime. It turned out that he was indeed a Xemite, in spite of his mutation. In fact he was a quite respected Xemite named Snerk Rabbledauber, heir to the Rabbledauber banana empire and inventor of the pokeless string banana. He had simply boarded a shuttle and found two entries for the Hall of Records on the shuttle menu.

He had chosen the wrong one.

Before the Incorrigible lifted off from the top of the Rabbledauber Banana Plaza Sol, Snerk had presented Throom with a crate of his finest as a small thank-you for saving his life.

Once they were well underway Throom went to talk to Penny and gave her one to cheer her up.

Throom stood as she lay on her side in her cabin with the portable flesh reconstitution unit strapped to her ribs. She examined the banana like an ancient might examine a fine cigar.

"Looks like a banana," Penny shrugged. Then she grasped the stem end and pulled. A strip of the outer covering pulled back. She pushed the strip back into place and felt along the edges. "Seals back up nicely," she said with a nod. "It must have been hard to engineer such a good ziplock."

"Do you think we should have tried to do something about that shuttle?" Throom asked, getting a little bored with the banana show.

"What?" She started at the idea. "You mean the button that took him to Sol Deux?"

"Yeah. How many other people a year do you think get killed because of that?"

"I don't want to think about it." She turned her attention back to the banana. "Let's see if it's really pokeless." She peeled the banana as he spoke.

"It seems like a danger we should do something about."

"Something should definitely be done," she agreed. She pulled the middle of the fruit from it's skin. Her face lit up with surprise. She held the skin up showing him the inside of the nub where the flaps of skin met. "Look!"

"So?"

"No poke!" She exclaimed. "The little black pokey thing! It doesn't have one!"

"If we know of a danger and leave it, aren't we partly to blame?"

She sighed. "Getting a simple change like that made on Sol, for an outsider would take a lifetime. Literally, Throom, a lifetime. You've never been there. Besides, Snerk lives there. He's better equipped to fix it than we are."

"I hadn't thought of that."

"People have to solve some of their own problems," she fiddled with the middle of the banana idly as she spoke. "I mean it would be great to fix everything—to save everyone. But the galaxy is just too big to...oh my god!"

"What?"

"What? Can't you see?" She was pulling a thick string of flesh free from the meat of the banana. It pulled away cleanly.

"That's not normal?"

"No it's not normal," she said preparing to lower the banana string into her mouth, "it's awesome!"

Throom decided it was time to leave Penny to the delights of her Snerk's Wonder. He had been twice now to see Penny since they left Sol Deux and so far had avoided Hardegar. It was time to stop putting it off.

Chapter 30

"It's okay," Hardegar reassured Throom, "I can endure all things in Jesus H. Christ."

"That's good," Throom replied.

"In fact, I'm already putting all of this behind me and looking to the future. I was thinking of inviting Penny and the cap'n to a Bible study. What would you think of that?"

"The cap'n?" Throom could not keep himself from smirking just picturing it. "I think that sounds like a great idea," but then he added with genuine disappointment, "but it better wait until after we find the treasure. He gets pretty single-minded when he's working on something like this, but after, definitely. And I want to be part of that one."

"Great!" said Hardegar with only slightly dampened spirits. "Sounds like fun."

"Yes, it does."

"So, just Penny for now. I think the Pentity will be a good topic."

"Well, maybe we should all be focusing on the task at hand." He looked at the leather head sitting on the bunk. "No offense," he added.

"No Bible studies until after we find the treasure?" Hardegar was incredulous. "Flathead and I have been having a great time at ours. But now that he—er—she's pregnant, I have an opening."

"Well, I can't forbid it, but it would be best to hold off." Then he added as a convincer, "We are very close."

"Okay, maybe you're right." Hardegar had to admit that he didn't really feel up to the challenge. "Maybe I need some time to adapt to my new body anyway."

"Sure!" Throom blurted, happy that Hardegar had provided an argument he had overlooked. "So how are you doing?"

Hardegar shrugged with his eyebrows, or rather with the tooled strips where his eyebrows had once been. "Not bad. I really think God is preparing me for something. Something big."

Throom thought that he looked more like he was being prepared for something small, like a small box or a bowling bag, but he just said, "I'm sure you're right."

"How is Penny, by the way?"

"Her wound should heal up nicely. A few more days, and she should be as good as new. She'll be in top shape by the time we get to Frag."

"That's good."

They were silent for a few moments.

"She's very sorry for what happened," Throom said. "She says she knew she wasn't a good enough shot, but she had to do something."

"I know, I know," Hardegar reassured, "I don't blame her. If you see her, tell her that for me."

"I will."

They were silent again.

"Oh," Throom remembered, "the cap'n said to say that you are welcome to stay on as part of the crew, and we should discuss how your duties will have to change because of your, uh, handicap."

"I hadn't thought of that," Hardegar admitted. "I guess I might not be able to do everything I was doing before."

"Probably not." Throom stood for a moment searching his memory. "All right, I give up. What were your duties anyway?"

"Oh. I was hoping you would know."

"You don't know?" Throom asked in amazement. "I mean, what were you doing before?"

"Not a damn thing," Hardegar laughed.

"Seriously?" Throom considered making an issue out of it, but realized that Hardegar had actually given nearly everything for the crew so he decided not to berate him for not giving more. "Well, I suppose that you should be able to handle your old duties then."

"I'll do my best," Hardegar said cheerfully.

Chapter 31

The Incorrigible glittered like new-fallen snow as it exited Flitzville and re-entered so-called normal space. The specks of light flashed then vanished until the only glittering was the gleam of the ship's polished curves.

"Set a course for Frag," the cap'n ordered.

"Done," reported Flathead. "We should be in orbit in less than an hour." Her chorus voice was getting worse. Now some of the voices trailed behind the others like an echo.

"Good." Greasly turned to the rest of the crew, who were gathered on the bridge. "Where's Penny?" He spotted her at her console, now free of the portable healing bath. "Penny, the second we are in range, I want you to start scanning for any sign of the Flummox."

"Right." Penny affirmed, then noticed something on her console. "Cap'n, another ship just left Flitzville." She tapped a bit then added, "It's The Other Woman."

"Great. How the hell did he track us here?"

"Maybe they cracked the code too," Flathead suggested.

"Nuh uh." Greasly shook his head. "I checked out that triple-dip lard cone he has working on breaking the encryption. He was fired from every programming job he ever had for incompetence."

"Fired for incompetence?" Throom exclaimed incredulously. "From a programming job?"

"Right," Greasly nodded, "so you know there's no way he cracked it."

"Maybe he got lucky," Penny offered as she started a thorough scan of the Incorrigible.

"I don't think so," Greasly reasoned. "The odds of a lunkhead like him stumbling onto the answer are phenomenal enough, but when you figure in the odds of Groat showing up immediately after we do... He followed us somehow. Raise him."

Flathead started flapping at the controls.

"Aha!" Penny exclaimed as she checked the results of her scan. She disappeared under the console for a minute and came back up with a transmitting device. She plunked it down on the console. "There you go. It was hooked into the navigation circuits."

"Groat must have put it there," Throom proposed, "but when was he ever on the bridge?"

"It couldn't have been him," Penny stated. "I scanned the ship several times very carefully after he left. There was no signal that wasn't accounted for—not even a timer or computer waiting to switch on later. This was not on board at that time."

"Wow, you thought of everything," Throom exclaimed, quite impressed.

"Of course."

"And that was the last time anyone other than us was on board."

"Not quite true," Greasly said, flopping down into the cap'n's chair.

"Rabbledauber!" Throom exclaimed.

"No, not Rabbledauber," Greasly assured with dejected certainty.

Penny and Throom looked at each other and tried to puzzle out what Greasly was talking about. It occurred to both of them at once and an instant later Klorf voiced their conclusion by saying, "The gritch!"

Greasly nodded.

"But how would Groat get a gritch to plant this?" Penny pondered.

"It wasn't a gritch," began Greasly. "There is no such thing."

"No such thing?"

"But there was an intruder," Klorf half stated and half asked.

Greasly sighed. "Oddly enough, yes. But I didn't know it when I told you about the gritch."

"You mean you made it up?" Throom asked.

"It was something they taught me in officer's training—a special command technique."

"Called lying?" Penny sniped.

"In layman's terms, yes."

"Then who did we jettison into Flitzville?" Throom asked softly.

"I don't know. But I think it must have been Willy."

"But once he stole the log, he was supposed to go his own way," Penny countered. "He was on Groat's ship when we left."

"Maybe," ventured Throom, "he was discovered before he could get off The Other Woman."

Greasly knew it was the wrong time for a joke and let the straight line wither and die unfulfilled. It was always sad when that happened.

"Then Groat hired him to spy on us," Throom concluded.

"Makes sense," Penny agreed.

"Somehow he trailed us to Kravits Rock," Greasly pondered.

"Actually," Penny pointed out, "if he found out that it was time for the Kravitsian Big Bang, he would know where we would be and when."

Greasly shook his head. "Of course. Why didn't I see that one coming?"

There was a sloppy popping sound from behind them. They turned idly but only saw Flathead still operating the controls.

"You raise them yet, Flathead?" Greasly asked.

"They are responding now," she answered.

Greasly turned to the front view screen. Ratner Groat appeared there.

"What the hell are you doing here?" they both asked at once.

"What am *I* doing here?" Groat asked. "That's none of your business."

"I could say the same thing."

Groat ignored this last statement because he was smiling fetchingly at Penny. "Ms. Forethought," he said with style, "Our meeting on my last visit to your ship was far too brief."

"Mr. Groat," she returned with something more than neutrality but less than a smile. She narrowed her eyes at the clever devil as she idly fingered the transmitter she had discovered. She could see that he noticed it, but he quickly hid his surprise and went on as if nothing had happened.

Groat turned back to Greasly. "So here we are both randomly showing up in one of the universe's most dangerous systems. How odd."

"True," Greasly admitted, "but we did get here first. So if either of us is following one of us, it's not us."

Groat tried to work his way through Greasly's sentence but just gave up. "I know you stole a copy of the log," he stated flatly.

"And we know you put Willy back on board the Incorrigible."

"You caught him, too, eh?" Groat looked around to see if he could see Willy. "It may be time for him to retire."

"I think he already has."

"So now we both try to be the first to find the wreck of the Flummox?"

"Looks that way."

"Winner take all? Loser takes nothing?"

Greasly shrugged. "You can share if you win."

"Of course, Frag is a dangerous place. A larger party would stand a much better chance of surviving."

"Don't be such a mooch, Groat."

"I'm suggesting a partnership."

"Right." Greasly rolled his eyes. "The way I see it we have everything and you have nothing."

"How do you figure that?"

Greasly held up a finger for each point. "We have a real Fraggart, a top-notch sensor jockey, detailed information about the Flummox, and on top of all that, we actually decoded the log. You didn't."

"What makes you say that?"

Greasly pointed to the transmitter. "Mr. Microphone here."

Groat bowed graciously. "Fair enough."

"So what are you bringing to the table?"

"A Lumarian."

Penny straightened in surprise. Greasly mulled it over. He looked at Throom, who shrugged back a "maybe".

"A real Lumarian?" Greasly queried.

"Genuine."

"Let's see him."

"Her." Groat looked off screen. "Come here Criss, let me introduce you to my arch rival."

A roughly humanoid female entered the view. Her head was like a large watermelon with an anteater snout attached. Two large eyes graced either side of the snout. The watermelon-like striping covered the entire head and continued down into the loose fitting diaphanous gown she wore.

"I send you peace and life," they heard her say, but no part of her head moved when she spoke—as if she were speaking directly into their minds.

"Right back at ya," Greasly retorted curtly. "Are you really a Lumarian?"

"I am a child of the Universe."

"But you were born on Lumaria?"

She nodded.

"And you have Lumarian sensitivities."

She nodded.

"What card am I thinking of?" Throom piped in.

"I am not a mind reader, here for your amusement," she castigated.

Greasly glared exaggeratedly at Throom, who shrugged and walked to his console. Greasly turned back to the screen. "Some people," he commiserated then added, "But you can see the future, right?"

"If the Universe wills it."

"Roughly what percent of the time does the Universe will it?"

"I will aid you in your searching, but I will not be placed under your microscope."

Throom chuckled to himself, "Microscope."

Greasly turned his attention to Groat. "The proverbial pig in a poke, eh?"

She bristled at this.

"She's very good. She told me things about myself that I've never told anyone."

"Like what?"

"You know, there might be reasons I never told anyone," Groat suggested caustically.

"You a bed wetter?"

"No."

"Drug addict?"

"No."

"You sell Amway!"

There was another sloppy popping sound behind him. He looked around but saw no clue as to what it might be. When he turned around, he spoke to the Lumarian.

"No offense, but I need some sort of assurance that you can do what you say you can."

"I do nothing through my own power. I am merely a conduit through which the love and knowledge of the Universe flows."

"That's what I want to know—if you con-do-it. Ha ha!" Greasly looked around to accept the laughter and admiration for his expertly delivered pun. He got only head shakes and glares. He turned back to the Lumarian. She had crossed her arms. "I'm sorry," Greasly continued, "I just couldn't resist."

"Stop being an ass, Lou," Ratner said, seemingly embarrassed for his old friend. He then turned to the Lumarian apologetically. "He means well. Can you give him a little something? For me?"

"For you," she acquiesced. She stood silent for a moment then took a deep breath, closed her eyes, and raised her hands palms-upward. She began to sway gently like seaweed under an ocean. Her hands moved gracefully through the air for a while then moved to cover her heart, which happened to be at her crotch. She continued to sway until she finally stopped and opened her eyes. "Thank you," she whispered softly, apparently to the Universe.

"What'd you get?" Greasly asked.

"You have a dark stain on your past, Mr. Greasly."

"Cap'n Greasly."

"I sense that you have been through a period of rigid discipline. Were you in the military?"

"I was."

"The Galactic Guard. No. The Galactic Guard Lite. You made it all the way to the rank of cap'n."

Greasly was momentarily impressed; then a thought occurred to him. "That's a matter of public record. Anyone could look that up."

"But she doesn't even know how to access a computer," Groat countered.

"I really don't," she assured him.

"Hmm." Greasly stroked his chin.

"This dark thing happened before your years in the Galactic Guard," she continued.

Greasly looked puzzled, trying to guess what she might be talking about.

"Or possibly after. It was after your time in the military."

Now she was in more fruitful territory. He was thinking of several things.

"Recently," she ventured, "have you recently experienced a loss?"

"Yes, actually."

"And you feel you were the cause of this loss?"

"No," he lied, thinking of Willy.

"Although you may not want to admit it."

"Maybe," he allowed cautiously.

"Or someone near you is responsible. Or feels responsible."

Throom looked down at his controls.

"He most likely does," Greasly agreed, happy that she was zeroing in on Throom's transgression instead of his.

"This person, picture the person in your mind. I sense masculinity. Is the person a male?"

"Yes." She had Greasly's attention now. "Pretty much." In fact she had everyone's attention except for Throom, who was busily trying to look busy.

"I sense chaos. Going many directions at once."

The crew was looking at her quizzically, trying to fit her description to Throom.

"He is very solid and stable. A stickler for the rules. Stony."

Throom stopped. He slowly looked up at the screen.

"The one who likes card tricks knows of whom I speak," she concluded, looking at Throom.

"Wow," whispered Penny.

"But this one is very sorry for the loss. I sense that very clearly. He should know that the Universe forgives him." She turned back to Greasly. "As it forgives you."

After a few moments of silence, Greasly admitted, "Impressive."

"So are we a team?" Groat asked.

"I have to talk it over with the crew," Greasly said and was about to tell Flathead to cut communications when the Lumarian interrupted.

"Disaster! Death and Ruin!" she screamed in dramatic tones.

They all turned to look at her. Her body was stiff, her eyes were closed, and her head rolled about as if she were in great pain.

"I see ruin, disaster, and death. Despair! Desolation! Ruin!" Her knees seemed to buckle under her, and she fell to the floor.

Groat looked down at her. "She does that now and then," he apologized, then to Greasly, "We'll check back in a few." He nodded at someone off screen and the view screen went blank.

"So what do you guys think?" Greasly asked the crew.

There was another of the sloppy pops from behind him. He stood and turned around. "Is anyone else hearing those sounds?"

"Yes," Klorf answered. "That is the third time I have heard it."

Greasly walked to Flathead who was standing still except for the lumps swarming under her skin. "Is it you making those sounds, Flathead?"

There was no answer.

"Flathead?"

There was another pop as a small tentacled object burst through Flathead's skin and splatted against the wall.

It flopped to the floor and instantly sprang into motion, scurrying under the console.

"Cap'n," Flathead began, her voice was now back to the female monophonic version, "I'm going to need some time off."

Penny gasped as three more tiny Kravitsians popped out of the ship's pilot. Then she screamed along with Greasly and Klorf as Flathead was torn apart by dozens of explosions. The tiny squid-like things flew everywhere, splattering the walls, the consoles, and the crew then flapping away to dark corners and crevices.

The non-Kravitsian crew members stared in horror as Flathead disintegrated before their eyes. By the time the popping slowed and stopped, the shadows were seething with tentacular motion.

"Flathead?" Greasly squeaked.

There was no reply.

The four of them eased toward the console so they could peek down to where Flathead had fallen. Greasly saw at last and went white. Penny clung to Klorf as she started to cry. Throom grimaced as he saw that what had once been Flathead was now a slimy blob of lacerated blue meat mixed with yellow tatters of flesh.

"Flathead?" Greasly asked again. "Are you all right?"

Throom moved around to kneel by what used to be his crewmate and friend. He gently lifted it up, but when he stood, it fell apart and plopped to the floor all around him. He let what was still in his hands fall and said sadly, "I don't think so."

"That smell," gasped Klorf in a daze. Throom saw that he was breathing heavily—the gill slits on his forehead open and raging red.

"Just like on Kravits Rock," Penny moaned in a husky voice. Throom noted with alarm that her hands were exploring the contours of Klorf's well-muscled chest. Klorf stood with his eyes closed, breathing deeply.

Greasly stood in a state of shock. He was breathing heavily but also weeping.

Then from all around them the schizophrenic voice of Flathead comforted, "It's all right Cap'n." The voices were more disjointed than ever, but the plurality was now made up primarily of Flathead's male voice.

Greasly started and looked around. The voices had definitely come from the undulating shadows.

"Turn off the lights," they pleaded.

"What?" Greasly's voice was quavering.

"Please Cap'n, turn off the lights."

Greasly smiled. "Yes, yes I will."

Throom wasn't sure that Greasly could handle it in his current state, so he reached over and tapped the appropriate panel. The room went dark.

He listened as the Kravitsians swarmed to the remains of Flathead. He did not dare move for fear of stepping on one of them. He heard Penny give a cry that seemed to be a mixture of frustration, pleasure, and anguish. Klorf moaned. Then Throom heard what seemed to be clothes ripping and animal grunts. Soon there were bodies hitting the floor and a symphony of sighs and moans.

Throom felt a number of the tiny Kravitsians climb up him to feed on the juices that had been Flathead.

"Touch me, Klorf!" Penny cried, "Here. No, here."

"Release!" Klorf demanded impatiently.

"Not my elbow!" Penny yelled in frustration. "Here. No. Don't stop," she commanded, then a moment later, "Not there, Klorf!"

"It's so much stronger than on Kravits Rock!" moaned Greasly. From the sound of his voice, he was losing his composure as well.

"Please, Klorf!" Penny begged.

"Let me!" Greasly snapped. Throom heard his hasty footsteps running to her.

"Oh yes! Oh yes!" Penny moaned. Then, "Klorf, stop rubbing my elbow!"

There was a tumbling of bodies and more moans of passion.

"Yes!" Penny sighed with relief, "that's it!"

Throom wanted desperately to leave but was afraid to move for fear of crushing any of the tiny Kravitsians that swarmed over him.

"Klorf, leave my elbow alone!" This time it was Greasly's voice.

Klorf wailed in frustration.

It was just then—when Throom was most thankful that the room was completely dark—that the entire bridge was suddenly illuminated by the light of the view screen. Groat and the Lumarian were checking in to see what had been decided.

Chapter 32

Frag three was the only habitable planet in the Frag system, and for that reason it shared the system's name. Calling Frag habitable, however, was stretching the definition to epic dimensions.

The landmasses of the planet were scarred and barren from the war that had killed off all Human life long ago. The radioactive and biological weapons used during that war had made the atmosphere fit only for the race of stone Humanoids that had, themselves, originally been engineered as weapons. So now those weapons, being the only indigenous form of life on the planet, had inherited all of Frag as well as the name of Fraggart.

Even the oceans were murky and dead, having been covered over by a thin layer of dust that still floated on the surface. That, plus the complete lack of clouds, made the entire surface look from space like a perfectly smooth grey ball, punctuated only here and there by dark splotches.

As Ratner Groat looked at it, he worried about his skin. The radiation at the surface would be deadly. He would have to use extra sun-block even inside his old-fashioned radiation suit if he went outside. If he wasn't careful, he could add years to his face. But then again, he thought, catching a glimpse of the Lumarian reflected in the observation deck glass, he might get lucky and never leave the shuttle.

He ran a finger across one side then the other of his pencil-thin mustache and grinned at his reflection. He turned and spoke to Criss Weller, the Lumarian, "Anything yet?"

"I have a strong feeling that what we seek is on the planet's surface," she said.

"Me, too." There was a hint of impatience in his voice. Since the failed attempt yesterday to get Greasly to join forces, all that the Lumarian had done was reveal to him several digits of his Galactic Security number, tell him that his dead grandmother wanted him to know she was all right, and bend an eating utensil with her mind.

"Look," he began, sitting beside her, "I don't want to pressure you, but you do realize that you are our only chance, right?"

She nodded her watermelon head and blinked the watery orbs on the side of her snout. "Perhaps we are too far away."

"Would you like me to fly closer?" he offered gently.

"Yes," she said like a child.

He patted her hand as he rose. "Tell me the instant you get anything."

"I will," she promised then added, "I'm sorry, Ratner."

"No. Don't be sorry. If you don't get anything, you don't get anything."

"Whenever I try to concentrate, I remember..." She shuddered.

"Don't think about it," he urged, knowing that she was reliving the moment that they had contacted the Incorrigible for the second time. He couldn't blame her. He had to admit that he was a little turned on by it to start with, but when that bloody-foreheaded cling-on rose up out of the sea of squids, back arched in a violent paroxysm, spurting a fine mist from glands all over his chest... And what was it that he had been wailing? Eggs? He couldn't blame her.

"Maybe if I talk to the Xemite, I can reach a deeper communion with the planet," she suggested. "It may help me touch its soul."

"Sure." Groat shrugged. "You can talk to Toby anytime you want. I'm going to the bridge now. He should be there. Let me walk you." She held out her hand, and he helped her up. The door sighed sexily as it opened to let them through.

*   *   *

Cookie looked up when Groat and Criss entered the bridge. He shook his head as he noted that Groat had his hand around the melon-headed female's waist.

"Toby, this lovely lady would like to speak with you." Groat handed her off to Toby.

As he parted company with her, he kissed the back of her hand. She entered conversation with the Xemite, and Groat sank into the rich comfort of his command chair. He noted the look that the Nootian was giving him. "What?" he challenged.

Cookie left his post and came to talk privately with Groat. "What?" he asked as if Groat's "what?" had been a stupid question. "The Incorrigible is here with us."

"I know that."

"And we still have no clue where the Flummox is."

"True."

"And we're getting nothing of value from the brain digger over there."

"Melanie's doing all she can."

"I thought her name was Criss?"

Groat almost blushed. "Melanie is a little pet name I have for her. You know because of." He motioned with his hand as if his own head were shaped like a watermelon.

"By the moons of Noot," the Nootian swore to himself.

"Don't get worked up, Cookie," Groat consoled, "You know I never let women get in the way of business."

"I don't know that," Cookie complained. "You keep saying that, but I don't know that." He nodded to Groat's crotch. "Let me remove it," he pressed.

Groat covered his area with his hands. "No," he replied adamantly.

"You'll feel much better. You really will."

"No. Stop even suggesting that."

Cookie shrugged and gave it up. "Well, let's at least attack the Incorrigible."

"We can't just attack the Incorrigible."

"We are outgunned, true, but with my tactical skill and a surprise attack—"

"No. I mean we just can't do it. It would be wrong."

"How have you Humans survived?" Cookie remarked with distaste.

"By not killing each other, for one thing, and by keeping our testicles, for another."

Cookie did nothing to hide the look of disgust on his blood-red face. "Well, we have to do something. They have the resources that we need, and we have a defective brain digger."

"What do you mean defective?"

"Has she given us anything? Even a hint to where the Flummox is?"

"It's not her fault if the Universe doesn't... what?" Cookie had turned to leave in the middle of his sentence.

He turned back, and with a nod to Groat's privates, restated his answer for the whole mess. "Snip." He went back to his post.

Groat shuddered. He looked back at Criss. She stood listening intently to what the many-eyed Toby was telling her. He was pointing at things on the console, but she was intently looking into some of the Xemite's eyes. She seemed to be studying him. Her hand rose and traced the contours of his body a few centimeters from the surface. She nodded. "Yes, yes," he heard her say.

Curious, Groat got up and went over to them. One of Toby's eyes tracked him as he approached. "I was just telling Ms. Weller about the area of unusual radiation I told you about."

Groat shook his head. "I told you that's not that unusual. I'm not setting foot on Frag until we have something a lot more definite than that."

Toby shrugged. "I'm just telling you what I was telling her—which was what I'd been telling you."

"You see, his aura is intensely purple in this area." Criss spoke as if she was continuing a thought rather than starting one. She motioned around his head. "That indicates that he is tapped into the Universal flow."

"Is that good?" Groat asked.

"His intuition will be unusually strong until the swelling in that chakra goes down."

"Really?" Groat looked at Toby.

"What he tells us will produce positive energy."

"What was that place you were telling me about?" Groat asked him and moved around to look at the console.

Toby debated silently for a moment whether he should point out the unfairness of what was happening, but he finally decided to just play along—at least Groat was listening to him. "This area here. I get occasional traces of Throckmonger's anomaly there."

"And what did you say would cause that?"

"I don't know what would cause it," he said, hiding his impatience at having to go through all of this for at least the third time. "It is just a very unusual thing to pick up on a planet like Frag."

"And you think it's the Flummox."

"I don't know what it is, but since we are looking for a ship that would be of an unusual design on this planet, it might be worth investigating an unusual reading."

"But your gut tells you..."

"My gut?"

"Your stomach."

"None of my stomachs say anything." Toby was puzzled by where this conversation was going.

"I mean do you feel as if the Flummox is at that spot."

"It seems like the most likely lead we have so—"

"But what is your feeling?"

"Feeling?"

"Do you FEEL that the Flummox is there?"

Toby was starting to get an idea of what Groat was looking for. Several of his eyes narrowed in annoyance. Still, he recognized that he could make this situation go his way, and if it turned out not to be successful it would be the Lumarian, not he, who had made the mistake. "I have a hunch," he blurted as if trying to get it past his internal sensors without drawing their attention. He immediately felt dirty.

"Let's get down there and take a look," Ratner Groat commanded.

Chapter 33

As soon as he had felt the tiny Kravitsians move off of his body, Throom had shuffled to the door and then walked quickly to his room. The last place he wanted to be was on the bridge when the lights came on. What he had seen by the light of the view screen had been enough to keep him disturbed for quite some time.

He had had to keep telling himself that in spite of their strange bodies and habits, they were still people and he still liked many of them. He had adjusted to a lot over the years, but at times the utter strangeness of the organed races was overwhelming. What he had needed more than anything else at that time had been solitude. He had closed his cabin door and disabled visitor notification. After pacing the floor for a little while, he had finally settled down and started reading some technical documents.

About fifty hours later, he felt as if he had regained his composure. He locked his console and stood up.

He wondered if the others had recovered yet. He was sure that even after the effects of the aroma had worn off, they would be crippled by shame for at least a week. But then again, they had to eat. Possibly that necessity would drive them back to normalcy. They also had sleep to help them.

The cap'n had once explained to Throom how sleep affected Humans emotionally. Waking up for a Human could be like starting over. It made even the worst problems seem somehow more manageable. It could be like drawing a line in time—turning your back on the past with its failures and focusing on the vast uncharted future.

Well, that was certainly what they needed. Throom hoped they had all slept very well the last couple of nights.

Throom opened his door. Outside sat three tiny replicas of Flathead. They leaped to their tentacles and spoke more or less in unison. "Throom!" they said excitedly. Their voices were all very much like Flathead's male voice.

Throom was taken aback for a minute. He had been working hard to get Flathead's disintegration out of his mind and had apparently succeeded. He hadn't even thought about the dozens and dozens of tiny Kravitsians running all over the ship.

"Hi, uh," Throom wasn't sure how to continue, "Flathead?"

"What have you been doing in there? We've been trying to get you for over six hours," they scolded.

"Oh, uh, I was reading."

"Why didn't you answer your door?"

"I turned off VN," Throom explained. "I needed to be alone."

"There's a lot of that going around," the Flatheads complained. "No one else will come out either."

"I don't doubt it. They are probably wishing they were dead."

"Those are just about the cap'n's exact words," two of the Flatheads said. Throom noted with curiosity that one of the Flatheads had said the same thing, except he had left the phrase "just about" out of the sentence. "When I told the cap'n about Groat's shuttle, he didn't even care. He just mumbled something about deserving it and went back into his cabin. I don't know if he was even fully awake."

"What about Groat's shuttle?" Throom bent over to get closer to them.

"It's on the surface right now."

"Great," Throom sighed.

"Not even Hardegar will let us bring him out of his cabin."

"What's he embarrassed about?"

"Nothing. He's sulking."

"Ah." That made sense. He had missed his second accidental orgy. "Did you remind him that he doesn't have a body?"

"That only made him angrier."

Throom got back to the business at hand. "So no one has done anything about Groat?"

"I pinpointed his most likely location on the surface, but other than that, no."

"You and I should go take a look."

The Flatheads started at this. "I can pilot you down, but if I left the shuttle, the radiation. . ."

"Wear a suit."

"It won't fit any more!"

"Oh. I suppose not."

The environment suits that they had on board the Incorrigible were so old that they relied on enclosing the entire person in an impermeable fabric. The fabric didn't even adjust itself to the body shape of the wearer. You had to find one that was made to fit your body type and size.

The newer environment protection devices were much more forgiving. The dress shield, for instance, was simply tied around the waist, and the field generation fins hung down around you. It was a much more versatile solution than the environment suit but still only really worked well with roughly Humanoid body shapes. Even on humanoids they had some drawbacks: they did not protect from every kind of radiation, they were hot, and they elicited giggles from some when worn by males.

Panty shields were two steps beyond that. They generated a field that protected from every form of radiation, one size fit all, and they were invisible under even the tightest pants. Neither Throom nor Flathead cared about the latter, but the shields were also so small and delicate that you could find some way to fit them onto nearly any body type. Right now, thought Throom, they would be a very handy thing to have. He could wear one as a glove and Flathead could tie one around his hub like a scarf.

Come to think of it, there were lots of things that it would be handy to have, but when you haven't planned ahead you have to work with what life gives you. "What if several of you got into the suit? Do you think you could coordinate your movements?"

The three spoke at the same time. "Are you crazy?" two of them asked, but the third asked, "Are you insane?"

Throom was again intrigued by the discrepancy. "Okay, well I guess having you on the shuttle is better than nothing. Why don't two of you go get the shuttle ready, and one of you come with me to gather equipment?"

"Right," they agreed. "You two go to the shuttle, I'll go with..." They were all saying it at once. "No, you two go..." Same problem. "Okay, one of you two go with Throom." They said, "Oh forget it." They all started walking toward Throom. They stopped and chorused in frustration, "Fine, I'll go get the shuttle ready." They all moved in the opposite direction. They stopped and flopped their tentacles in despair.

"Why don't I get supplies by myself and meet you at the shuttle?" Throom suggested.

"That'll work." With a mock salute from each, they headed off down the corridor.

Throom blinked after them for a few moments before turning and heading for the armory.

He picked up two matter declumpinizationizers, a spazzer, and a belt to hold them. He didn't bother taking a yacker since the only kind they had was of such an ancient design that the radiation would make it useless anyway. He strapped it all on and headed for the shuttle bay.

When he got there, the Flatheads had nothing ready. They were still standing in front of the shuttle telling each other what to do. Throom sighed and shook his head. He left them where they were while he readied the shuttle. They were still at it when he finished. He scooped them all up and tossed them on board.

When they realized what had happened, they all blushed purple. Throom noticed the blushing and admonished, "Now don't you start that too!"

Chapter 34

"I'm just so sorry," the Flatheads said later as the shuttle was drifting toward the surface of the planet. Flathead had always been dependable. In fact, Throom thought this might be the first time he had ever failed to do what he said he would do. The Flatheads seemed shaken by it. "It's just so frustrating. It's like my own private Heck. No offense," they said to themselves then replied, "None taken."

"I don't understand," Throom said, "Are you just having trouble adjusting to having multiple bodies?"

"What do you mean multiple bodies?"

"Well...more than one." Throom tried not to make the remark sound smart-assed.

"I only have one body, Throom." They all held out their tentacles as if to display that one body to him.

"You mean that you are all one body?"

"No, I am me, and I have one body," they all said, each touching a tentacle to themselves. Then they each pointed at the other two. "They each have their own body."

"You're not connected? I mean, you don't all share a mind?"

"That's impossible. Kravitsians don't have thought transceivers."

"So how do you do it? How do you share thoughts?"

"We don't share thoughts. We're just having the same thought at the same time."

"So how do you do that?" Throom was no less amazed.

"All Kravitsian minds start out identical to their mother's. Only eventually do they become individuals.

They diverge as each reacts to different stimuli and as the effects of the different genetics of their donor—you would say father—continue to alter their chemistry."

"Wow." Throom was awed at the concept. "So each of you remembers being Flathead?"

"Of course."

Throom was struck with a troubling thought. "But none of you really are."

"I am," they said.

Throom didn't want a confrontation, but he wasn't satisfied. "So do you remember being inside?" he queried squeamishly.

"Yes."

"But you don't remember having others inside you."

"Actually I do. All during gestation we are experiencing what the mother is experiencing and also what we are experiencing."

"What about at the end? Do you remember..." Throom's voice quavered slightly.

The Flatheads were silent.

"Do you remember the birth?" Throom asked at last.

"Yes," they answered in a subdued tone.

Throom paused a moment, not certain he wanted to hear more about it, but his curiosity won out. "From both sides?"

"No," they admitted. "We lose contact. That's what starts the whole process. Do you know what I mean?"

Throom shook his head.

"Well, when we lose input from the outside world it's just... well it becomes very... It's hard to take." They seemed reluctant to continue.

Throom was getting the picture. He nodded sadly and turned to look at the planet slowly moving towards them. He had a lot to work out. He had watched Flathead die, yet here were three miniature versions of him—three out of how many? Dozens, at least. They each remembered everything that Flathead had experienced in his life. Every moment that he and Flathead had spent together was in the mind of each of these offspring. So why was he feeling this sense of loss? If anything he should be feeling a sense of multiplication.

Throom pondered it for a while. He heard another argument among the Flatheads starting up—if it could really be called an argument. After all, the problem was that they were in complete agreement. Maybe coincidence was a better word. He ignored it. Something would have to be done to help them work as a team, but for now Throom's mind wandered back to the moment of their birth. As he thought about that moment, the reason for his sense of loss gradually became clear to him.

Throom pictured being a Kravitsian inside its mother. Unlike other internally gestated species, a Kravitsian experienced the outside world. Its confinement was not the only thing it knew. If it never knew what it was to be outside, it would make being contained inside another being bearable. But to know what it was to be outside and then to have that contact revoked—to have known the world of sensations and interactions and color and then to lose it— to be trapped inside another being—it would be terrifying. They would be driven to escape out of sheer panic.

The mother, on the other hand, would be left to experience the pain of their escape. The idea struck Throom with terror—to be ripped apart from the inside.

Throom closed his eyes and shook his head slowly. That was the source of his sadness over the event. These things might be copies of Flathead up to the point just before birth, but only the "real" Flathead had disintegrated. That Flathead, his friend and comrade, had faced that moment of horror and pain and—and this next thought hit Throom the hardest— faced it entirely alone.

They were getting close to the surface of Frag. He would have to do something to solve these contentions before he left the ship in case he needed Flathead's assistance somehow. He pushed his pain down and faced the problem.

He turned and interrupted their discussion. "Look, I can't have you doing this while I'm out there. You need to be ready to help me out if you have to."

"I know," they agreed.

"So I'm going to appoint one of you leader."

"What?" They were appalled.

Throom touched the one closest to him. "You are the leader."

"No!" they all protested, to Throom's surprise.

"What? Why not?"

"We are all equal. There's no basis for this one to have authority over the other two," they said, except that the one he had pointed to said "me" instead of "this one."

"You're right, of course, but it is just something you will have to put up with for a while."

"For how long?"

"Until we come up with something better."

"I can't do that," they all decided.

"Well, look," Throom explained, his frustration growing, "When you need to split up to all do different things, one of you has to be the one to pass out the tasks. You know it doesn't work otherwise."

"I know, but you can't just pick one of us and give him authority over the others!" Their tone suggested that Throom should damn well know better than to suggest something like that.

Throom sighed. He hadn't counted on the emotional baggage Flathead had from growing up in a caste system. An idea occurred to him.

"What if it was randomly decided which of you would do each task?"

They thought that over. "So no one of us would have authority?"

"Not a one."

"Okay."

Throom got up and went into a storeroom. After a few minutes of searching for some suitable items, he emerged with three small objects in his palm. He knelt down by the Flatheads, smiling at his own ingenuity. "These are spacers used in the flibbernaster. One side is red, the other is purple."

"Okay." Each took one as Throom handed it to him.

"Now any time that you need to split up to perform different tasks, you chose one of the tasks and all toss your spacer in the air. Each one will land with either red or purple facing up. The one that doesn't match the other two is the one that goes and does that task." Throom smiled.

They made the Kravitsian equivalent of a shrug. "Let's give it a try."

"Okay, suppose someone needs to go check the bamboozler."

"Okay." They flipped the flibbernaster spacers in the air. They all landed purple side up.

"That's okay. Just do it again."

They complied—all red this time.

"Again."

All red again.

There was a click as Throom put his hand to his forehead. They all flipped the farking thing the exact same way! "Let me see those." He took them and handed them back making sure that one was facing the opposite of the other two. "Now try it."

They did—two purples and a red.

"Good," Throom said, then to the one that got red, "You would check the bamboozler."

"Let's try it again." The spacers came down two reds and a purple, but the purple was the same Kravitsian that got the red last time.

"So this time the purple would go do the task. See? Different this time." He hoped he could sneak it past Flathead but had no such luck.

Without saying anything, they flipped the spacers three times in rapid succession. Every time the same Flathead was the odd man out.

Throom was crouching with his hand over his face. "Okay, hold on."

He went into the storeroom again and came out with a small transparent box and a marker.

He crouched down. "I'm going to write on you."

They permitted it.

Throom had thought at first to number them but thought that would be too close to a rank. Instead he drew a circle on one, a square on the next, and a triangle on the last. After each, he told the Flathead what he had just drawn and told him to remember his symbol. Then he took the spacers and drew the same three symbols on them so that each spacer corresponded to one of the Flatheads. He put the spacers in the box and sealed it.

"There," he said, "you all shake this together and look at the spacer that is the odd color. The Flathead with that symbol does the task.

They tried it a few times and it seemed to be quite random this way. They were satisfied.

"Good!" Throom exclaimed as he rose. "If all the colors match, just do it again. to choose between two of you, shake it until one of you is the odd color."

They understood.

"So do you think all the rest of you are having the same problem back on the ship?"

"No. They have more differences than we seem to. I think we all had the same donor. It was our similarity that made all of us try to rouse the same people in the same order."

"True brothers," Throom mused.

"Also, spontaneous cloning isn't unheard of in Kravitsians."

Throom liked that idea. It would be even more as if Flathead had survived.

The auto pilot chimed. They had reached their destination.

Chapter 35

The Incorrigible's shuttle hovered over the Guy's Night Out—as the shuttle of The Other Woman was named. The Guy's Night Out sat in a moderately level valley between some jagged crags. It still had power and seemed to be in good working order.

There wasn't enough level space near the Guy's Night out for the shuttle of the Incorrigible to land, so they landed on the other side of a nearby ridge. Throom prepared to exit the ship.

"I won't be able to communicate with a yacker because of the radiation," he told the Flatheads, "so one of you will have to keep an eye out for me."

"Will do. Be careful out there."

"Will do," Throom responded. He checked his weapons one last time and headed for the airlock.

Once outside and walking through the bleak and erose landscape, he was at once flooded with feelings of nostalgia. He had played in an area similar to this when his mind was young. These broken hills, these fractured valleys, from the look of them they could be the very place where he spent hours playing classic Fraggart games like smash-the-rock, crush-the-stone, and throw-the-boulder. (The young Fraggart mind was so easy to entertain.) He pondered idly that the very shattered stone he now walked past could well be what remained of one of his playthings.

He had been very good at rock throwing and smashing. It seemed strange to him now that it could have been so important to him at one time. It had been only later in his development that he had grown bored with those rock-based games and had moved on to smear-the-queer, war, and the ever popular chum chucking. He had been very good at those games too. You didn't get to be a Fraggart of Throom's age without being good at those games. That was the period in his development that he regretted the most. He pondered idly that the very shattered stone he now walked past could well be what remained of one of his playmates.

How many of those he had known were now nothing more than gravel? He remembered with sadness how, when he finally saw the senselessness of the violence and tried to explain it to his formation-mates, they only stared at him as if he were speaking Flootian, then went back to smashing the Fraggart they had captured from a rival group. Not one of them had had any idea what he was trying to say. Not even—and this was the part that shook him most deeply— the prisoner himself. Throom had decided that day that he did not belong with these people. That was when he set out into the wastelands.

Soon he had come across the villages that others like himself had built out of the rubble and learned that he was not alone in despising mainstream Fraggart culture. He had joined this tiny band of barbarians, and his life changed completely. He stopped being ashamed of curiosity and instead indulged in it. They taught him to read, and he educated himself from the remains of the ancient libraries.

He wondered what would have happened to him if he had never deviated from the Fraggart way of life.

The answer seemed to lay at his feet.

He snapped out of his reverie. Right now, he needed to know if anyone was alive on the Guy's Night Out.

As he approached, he noted with alarm that the door of the shuttle was open.

"That's not a good sign," he murmured to himself. He readied the matter declumpinizationizer and cautiously moved to where he could see into the open airlock. It was empty. The inner door was shut.

Throom moved up into the airlock. There was no sign of a struggle. He started the entry procedure. It wasn't even

locked. He thought that they must have left in a hurry—
unless they left someone to guard the ship, but if they left
a guard he was doing a very poor job of it.

He pondered what to do about his weapons. If a member
of The Other Woman's crew was on board, he would want
to set his weapons down to show he was not hostile, but
if the ship had been taken over by some hostile force, like
Fraggarts for instance, then he would very much need his
weapons.

He checked his matter declumpinizationizer and the red
deactivation light made up his mind for him. It would not
operate on board anyway. The weapons that would operate
on board would be useless against Fraggarts, and he would
be able to handle anything other than a Fraggart barehanded.

He set his weapons down.

The air purification and pressurization cycle finished, and
the inner door opened. There was no one there. Cautiously,
Throom stepped into the shuttle.

"Hello?" he ventured softly. No reply.

He advanced slowly, scanning the ceilings and walls for
nasties that might leap onto him as he walked past.

The shuttle was just as pimped out as The Other Woman
herself. The walls of the cabin were covered in a rich
burgundy velour with a prismatic purple stripe running
parallel to the floor at about waist height. The chairs were
rich and plush and trimmed with chrome. The floors were
covered with deep shag carpeting.

Throom noticed two piles of clothing. He walked over to
them and picked up the garments. There were two complete
sets of clothing, down to the under-things, both in a pile as if
the persons that had worn them had been instantly vaporized,
leaving the clothes to fall into heaps. Throom looked around
nervously. What could have done such a thing without even
singeing the clothes?

He dropped the clothes and began cautiously looking in
all the places in the cabin that were not readily visible. He
ended up near where he had come in. He decided to start
opening doors.

The first door he opened was across from the airlock. In
there he found two more sets of empty clothes. These were

less orderly. They were tossed about as if the people that had worn them were in motion when they were vaporized.

A scenario was forming in his mind. Whoever wore the first piles of clothes that he found were probably the first to go. They were taken completely by surprise. These others knew what was happening. They ran in here trying to save themselves but were taken as they tried to–

It was then that he heard the sounds that first startled him, then blew his entire theory, then terrified him. He heard a door sigh open, followed by the voice of Ratner Groat saying, "Come here, my little melon patch!" Then a female and a male giggling as they apparently ran around the main room in pursuit of each other.

He peeked around the edge of the door. Groat and the melon-headed Lumarian were frolicking through the deep pile shag, stark naked.

He moved out of view and revised his scenario. This was even worse than the first. In this one Groat and the Lumarian waited impatiently for the away team to suit up—he noted that this room did indeed have environment suits and some seemed to be missing—and the instant the inner airlock door had closed, Groat and what's her name started their fling. Throom pictured the pair of them rushing into the other room so fast that their clothes were left behind to fall in heaps, but it was more likely they had simply removed them then and there. They had been romping around ever since. Throom closed his eyes and shook his head. What a nuisance these sexual urges must be; if they were not to the Humans, they certainly were to him.

He was snapped out of his righteous indignation by the Lumarian letting out a short scream—one that sounded genuinely alarmed. Throom pressed his back against the wall. Had they seen his weapons? No, he had left them in the airlock, and that door was closed. Maybe he had left some clue that he had been in the main room? He heard them hurriedly getting dressed. He glanced down and noticed at once the footprints that his mass had pressed into the deep pile of the carpet. Of course!

He tried to decide if he should hide or just announce himself.

Then he heard Groat say to the Lumarian, "There, I've overridden the protections so this will work. But only use it if you have to. If you miss you'll declumpinizationize a hole right through the ship."

"Whoa, whoa, whoa!" Throom cried out loud enough for them to hear. "This is Throom from the Incorrigible."

"Throom?" Groat sounded both surprised and relieved. "What are you doing here?"

"I'm looking for treasure," Throom said in a "well duh" tone as he rounded the corner.

There was a flash of white light and a clap of thunder as Criss Weller fired her matter declumpinizationizer square at Throom's chest.

Chapter 36

Groat and Weller both covered their heads and turned away as the area where Throom had been standing exploded with fury, dust, and debris. The cloud rolled over them, and their skin was pelted with what felt like tiny rocks.

The blast seemed to last an eternity. At last all was quiet except for the fierce ringing in their ears.

Groat was afraid to see the results of the blast, but finally looked toward Throom.

Throom was standing there motionless, with his eyes closed, and covered with shimmering metallic dust. He was in one piece.

Criss had aimed directly for his chest. Luckily for Throom, what Criss aimed at and what Criss hit had never once been the same object.

Throom's eyes opened slowly. He glowered at the hastily dressed couple.

Groat quickly pointed at Criss, who was shaking herself off. She smiled apologetically and shrugged. "Sorry."

Throom looked around to survey the damage. The inner door to the airlock was completely declumpinizationized along with a large chunk of the walls near it, but at least the hull had not been breeched.

Groat snatched the gun from Criss. He quickly ran to a console and turned the safety back on.

"Well, now we have a problem," Throom informed them as he dusted himself off.

Groat came over to examine the damage. "It can be fixed," he concluded. "It'll make it back to the ship."

"Sure, but I'm in here. Your crewmen are out there. And you don't have a working airlock."

"Marklar!" Groat cursed as he realized that if they opened the outer door, the deadly air of Frag would rush in. If even one of the remnant viruses got in and found a host, they would be dead before they knew what had happened.

"We can't open that door," Throom said, in case Groat needed a summary of the situation. Then he realized that was not entirely true. "Well, I could," he amended. Then, when he saw the look on Groat's face, he added, "But I won't."

"Thanks."

"How many people do you have out there?"

"Toby and Cookie."

"How much air do they have?"

"A little less than two hours left now," Groat reported after checking the time.

Throom thought the situation over. "They need to get to the Incorrigible's shuttle. Can you get word to them?"

"The only yackers we have are sort of old and have a very limited range because of the radiation."

Throom nodded. "Same here."

"Is anyone on your shuttle? Can they go out and find them?"

"There are two problems with that. One, they don't have environment suits and two, we can't contact them either."

"Or The Other Woman," Groat added.

"Or the Incorrigible," Throom finished.

"Death! Disaster! Ruin!" They looked up as the voice of the Lumarian interrupted their ruminating. "I see it— the clouds lowering—darkness growing. Death!" She was growing more intense. "Death! Ruin! Destruction!" She fell to the floor in a faint.

Throom and Groat went back to what they were doing.

"I wonder if we could make it to one of the ships and back with help before Cookie and Toby returned," Groat pondered out loud.

"What kind of help? Do you have another shuttle?"

"Not that works."

"Neither do we." Throom thought some more. "I've got it! You two get in environment suits, and everyone stays suited until you get back to your ship."

"That could work." Groat smiled. "Cookie and Toby can recharge their suits on the way."

They walked into the supply room that held the environment suits. There were two suits left. One would fit Groat, but there was no way that Criss would be able to fit her huge head inside either one. Groat's optimism drained from him as he held the two suits limply in his hands.

"Are any of the interior rooms airtight?"

Groat shook his head.

They both stared at the suits.

"I know it would be tough, but it's the best option so far..." Throom didn't have the heart to put his idea into words. "I mean you only lose one crewman."

"There has to be another way." Groat had thought of it too.

"Yeah," Throom agreed and started thinking about it again.

"Deathhhh," Criss moaned, apparently in her sleep.

"If we get Cookie and Toby back here we might be able to communicate with them somehow to get them over to your shuttle," Groat continued.

"Does the shuttle have some sort of public address system?"

Groat shook his head. "No." Then added uselessly with a shrug, "A private undress system but..."

"Let's take it a step at a time. Does it have any exterior lights or something like that?"

"Yes," Groat answered, curious how that helped them.

"Show me."

Groat headed to the control panel.

Chapter 37

Several of Toby's eyes blinked behind the lenses of their environment suit sleeves. The stalks moved about, surveying the monotonous surroundings. "I think maybe that one looks familiar," he suggested in reference to a jagged rock.

"Which one?" Cookie asked. "The one that looks like an oblejag snout?"

"I don't see any that look like an oblejag anything." Toby's frustration was beginning to find its way into his voice.

"That one right there." Cookie pointed.

"Where?"

Cookie grumbled, stomped over to a rock and kicked it. "This one! The one that looks like an oblejag snout!"

"That's the one I was talking about," Toby snapped, "but it doesn't look like an oblejag snout."

"It looks exactly like an oblejag snout, you farking moron. There's the abrader, those are the incisors, that's the impaler."

"You have quite an imagination, Cookie." Toby chose to ignore Cookie's hand gesture. "Anyway, does it look familiar?"

"No."

"The problem is they all look different depending on what direction you look at them."

"No shit," Cookie retorted.

They had been trying to find their way back to the shuttle for nearly an hour now, after failing to find anything of interest in the direction of the anomaly that Toby had noticed. It was starting to get dark. If they had to use their environment suits' power for light, it would be used up that much faster.

Toby sat down on a large rock that looked like an oblejag snout. "We need to be systematic about this. I think we should be trying to move from high point to high point, and we should be marking everywhere we have been."

"That's a good idea." Cookie came over to join him. "If you had thought of that when we left, we wouldn't be in this mess."

"What do you want from me? I'm a sensor jockey, not a navigator."

"You're also the science officer."

"You didn't think of it either," Toby pointed out.

"Well, neither did you."

Sensing the possibility of an infinite loop, Toby dropped the subject and stood up. They both knew that it had not been wise to go out onto a planet on which geo-navigators didn't work. There was no point assigning blame. "Let's climb to that point and see if we can see anything. Then we can build a pile of rocks to mark the spot."

Cookie started immediately for the point. Toby fell in behind.

When they reached the top they scanned the dimming saw-like horizon. Suddenly Toby's eye stalks all faced the same direction. "What's that?"

"I'm going to guess a rock."

"Not this time." Toby pointed. Several beams of light were searching the sky in a tight circle. "It just came on." The two looked at each other in surprised exuberance.

"Yes!" they said in unison. They immediately scampered down the slope toward the light.

Behind them the lights of the Guy's Night Out flicked on and scanned the heavens. As they started to mount the next slope, Toby caught sight of this second set of beams with some of his backward-facing eyes.

"Hold on, Cookie." Toby stopped to compare the lights. "Cookie. Cookie!"

Cookie continued climbing. He was moving at a pretty good pace. Apparently they were already further apart than the meager range that the yackers in their environment suit had in this radiation.

Toby ran after Cookie. They were at the bottom of the next hill when he was close enough to get a message to him. "Cookie! Cookie!" he panted from inside his suit, which seemed unusually hot at the moment. "There's another set of lights!"

Cookie stopped and turned to see what Toby was pointing at. There, above the dark broken hill, another set of searchlights was scanning the sky. "What the..." he muttered. He looked again at the lights they had seen first.

"Maybe another ship?" Toby suggested. "A shuttle from the Incorrigible?"

"Maybe." Through his visor, Cookie's blond eyebrows were knit in concentration. "But which is ours?"

"If either of them are," Toby reminded. "We can't be sure that either one is a shuttle, let alone our shuttle."

Cookie checked his suit. "Well, whatever those are, they're too far away." He turned to the lights they had been following. "And whatever these are, they are not just another pile of rocks. We better head toward these." He started off and called over his shoulder, "Fast!"

A quick check of his own suit's supplies of air and energy convinced Toby of the wisdom of that course of action. "But don't run!" he yelled, "You'll only deplete your suit faster!" Cookie was already out of range. Toby shook his head and started after Cookie at the fastest walk he could manage without increasing his breathing.

Chapter 38

Greasly stepped out of the people cleaner for the third time in as many hours and still felt dirty. He looked in the mirror and futilely straightened his hair. He stared for a moment at the man looking back at him and wondered again how Penny was doing. He hated the thought of her feeling humiliated or used. Maybe she was still sleeping. He had been unconscious for two days and the pheromones seemed to affect her more deeply than they did him. Did that mean that when she woke up, she would feel even worse than he did now? Worse emotionally that is.

He had to admit that physically he felt fantastic. In fact, he hadn't felt this good for a very long time. He was full of energy and his skin was still alive to every sensation. (He had never realized how much fun the squeegees in the people cleaner could be.) It was as if he had overdosed on pseudo-sex. It was only his mind that troubled and oppressed him with an overpowering feeling of regret.

As he dressed he tried to reason his way through this thing.

Why should he feel regret? He hadn't planned any of it. He had tried his best to control himself. Penny certainly had no complaints at the time. Just remembering the fervor and abandon with which she had refrained from complaining made his body reapportion its blood supply. Had he really taken advantage of her? Couldn't it just as easily be said that she had taken advantage of him?

No, it could not. He sat down and pondered why as he pulled on his socks. Why, since time immemorial, had it always been the man's fault? Maybe it was because modern Human females nearly always—to one degree or another— had to be convinced that having sex might be fun. The lead was nearly always left to the male. Maybe it had really been the same in the past as well, in spite of what most of the late twentieth century Hume histories showed.

But whether or not she had taken advantage of him, he most definitely had not taken advantage of her. It had been a mutual mishap. He hadn't planned it; he repeated it to himself. She had to know that. If he had planned it, he certainly wouldn't have included Klorf.

Klorf. He must really be taking this hard. His annoying pride and honor would make any embarrassment harder to take, and not only had he been as humiliated and embarrassed as the rest of them, but he hadn't even had satisfying sex—the poor fish-headed bastard.

He put his newly dressed feet on the floor. He really should contact Penny. He wanted to make sure she knew he had no idea that all of this would happen. He wanted to make sure she understood that this had been his first experience with this stage of Kravitsian reproduction—that Flathead had never turned female before.

Flathead. Greasly fell back onto his bunk. On top of all of this, he had seen one of his oldest friends disintegrate quite messily right in front of him. Greasly rubbed his temples with thumb and forefinger. Or had he? He had seen Flathead fall apart, but he had fallen apart into a hundred smaller versions of himself. How the fark is one supposed to feel about that? Actually, he guessed he knew the answer to that question. Apparently the answer was horny.

How could he have known the pheromone would be involved in the birth process? He hadn't even expected the birth to happen the way it did, and once it had started, what could he have done about it? The pheromones had just been too strong. It wasn't his fault. He was back to Penny. It wasn't anyone's fault. It was just something that happened. There was no way, and no need, to undo it.

But it didn't feel that way.

Greasly shook his head. This had to be some after effect of the pheromone. He could think of no logical reason that he should feel this guilty; he, of all people, afraid to leave his cabin because of the chance of meeting one of the others. It was ridiculous.

He stood and walked to his cabin door. He could not bring himself to open it.

He went to the console to call Penny. He could not bring himself to use it.

He needed something to take his mind away from all of this—something other than more pseudo-sex. He took a crystal puzzle off the shelf where he had tossed it in exasperation a few nights earlier after struggling with it for hours. He looked at it and saw that he was only six moves away from the solution. He quickly manipulated it to the finished state.

That had been easy—as easy as things used to be. He wasn't sure whether to be amazed that he had solved the puzzle so quickly or annoyed that it could no longer take his mind off things. With a shrug he tossed it aside.

He lay on his bunk again. It wasn't really the act of sex, he thought, it was what he knew would happen now. That was it. He felt he was wronging her now because he could not continue the relationship.

He felt the feeling inside himself like when his sinuses suddenly cleared up after taking some destuffinizer, except this clearing was in his emotions. That was it. He hated feeling as if he were teasing her. If he could only be certain that she didn't want him.

A sudden pang overcame him. No, that wasn't it at all. He realized with not a little terror that he would not be satisfied if he knew that. He realized with sudden and brutal clarity that if he knew she didn't want him, he would be crushed. He realized suddenly how much he wanted her.

"No," he said out loud as he sat up on his bunk. "I can't do that." He looked at the console he had considered using to call Penny.

He had long ago come to grips—so to speak—with solo sexuality. He was used to getting by on pseudo-sex— that merciful combination of drugs and holovids that was designed to substitute for the real thing. Why should he need her? What did she offer that he didn't already have?

It was a stupid question; he knew quite well the lesson of Onan One colony.

It had been in the early years of Human exploration into other solar systems. A small exploratory colony had been established on Onan One. The atmosphere on Onan One was acidic and thin, so the colony had to be entirely enclosed and controlled. As a result, the Humans there lived in close proximity to each other.

That would have been fine except that pseudo-sex had just been invented and the head of the colony implemented a no-real-sex policy to cut down on dissent and petty squabbles.

The plan seemed to be paying off until the suicides began—five hundred and forty two in one year—nearly thirty percent of the colony. A committee of Onanites was formed to study the problem. After examination of the suicides, they found that for an overwhelming majority the cause had been, simply put, loneliness.

Pseudo-sex had been proven to be a perfect simulation of having sex. It had all the bodily benefits of an actual roll in the sack. So the committee set out to find out why it had failed. It took them some time to finally come to a conclusion. They reported that sex is more than a bodily function. It is a very intimate thing that people do together, and that somehow that intimacy itself is very important for emotional well-being. All of this information was transmitted across the light-years of space to Hume. The scientific community looked over the report and sent back their reaction to the findings. The reply consisted of three words. "No shit, Sherlock."

Greasly had always thought the Onan One colony had had all the brains of a bag full of other bags, but had he been making the same mistake? He never put himself in the same category with Onan One because he had always felt that he didn't miss the intimacy. He didn't need anyone to share his life. He had never sat around wanting it. He had never really missed it. Surely you would have to feel the lack of something before it could affect you, yet now, without warning, just the possibility of having it was affecting him with a vengeance.

Greasly looked around his spartan cabin. The bland utility of it now seemed sad to him—even pathetic. Was this going to be the rest of his life? No color? No richness? No sensuality? No Penny?

He needed to talk to Throom.

Chapter 39

Greasly found Throom's cabin empty. It didn't take him long to find one of the Flatheads.

"How are you feeling?" he asked the sky-blue little bugger.

"Not too bad," Flathead replied.

"Do you know where Throom is?"

"Yes. He's on Frag."

"He went down alone?"

"No, three of, uh, three Flatheads went with him."

"Even so," Greasly pondered, "why would he do that?"

"Didn't one of us tell you?" Flathead asked. "Groat's down there."

"Oh right, I remember you telling me."

"Not me, but..." Flathead struggled with how to talk about himself, "another me."

"Have you heard anything from Throom yet?"

"No. We can't communicate because of the radiation."

"Oh, Jebus, of course." Greasly didn't notice how the little blue Flathead tensed at his swearing. "Our farking antiquated yackers. Well, ready the shuttle and we can..." Greasly realized that the shuttle was on the surface with Throom. "Fark! Get up to the bridge and put us directly above the shuttle."

"But we can't get a reading..."

"Just make your best guess," Greasly commanded, already on his way down the corridor toward Penny's room. "Penny will take care of the detail work."

Greasly had to override Penny's privacy lock to get into her cabin. She was still asleep. He went over and sat on the bunk beside her. Mini Penny appeared to be unconscious as well—hanging half in and half out of her zipper. Penny's cheeks were still flushed a delicate red and her lips were parted in a relaxed smile. He noticed the small gap between her two front teeth. The imperfection filled him with such delight that he had to smile.

He reached up and brushed the back of his hand across her cheek. She breathed in quickly and closed her mouth. With her eyes still closed, she rubbed against his hand the way a kitten does.

"Penny," he spoke softly.

"Mmmmm," she purred. Mini Penny stirred and withdrew inside her head.

"Penny," he repeated a little louder. Her eyes opened slightly. She saw him and was awake. She sat up and took stock of her surroundings, rubbing her eyes and blinking.

"Oh," she mumbled, "Cap'n."

She blinked some more, then squinted at him, trying to focus. Then her expression changed to surprise and shock as she apparently remembered what had happened. Her hand went to her mouth. "Oh fuck!" she gasped. "We did it again, didn't we?!" She couldn't help laughing.

He smiled at her—having trouble not laughing himself. He had to look away. His cheeks were hot. What the fark was that about? Blushing? He looked over at a mirror. He was blushing.

Still laughing, she shook her head. She too was red as a Nootian. "I'm so sorry Cap'n. I never..."

He held up his hand to stop her. "Never tell a guy you're sorry you had sex with him."

"Well, that's not what I mean," she blurted, "I mean..."

"I know," he assured her. He was trying to be serious but couldn't stop his smile. He looked away to regain composure. He had never guessed she would react like this. He was thrilled at her sense of humor.

"We can sort all of this out later," he suggested, unable to look directly at her. He glanced at her and saw that she was trying to be serious too, with similar results. They both broke out laughing again.

He closed his eyes and concentrated. "I'm a cap'n, for Christ's sake. I can't sit here giggling."

"Right," she concurred.

"Throom's on the surface, and we need to contact him."

"Is he okay?" She was shocked into sobriety.

"We don't know. That's why we need you."

"Of course." She was up and getting dressed. "I'm sorry, Cap'n."

"Don't be," he almost pleaded, "I'll meet you on the bridge." Just before leaving he stopped and looked back at her. "Penny..."

She stopped dressing and looked at him.

He struggled to say something but didn't. Then as if it were not what he intended in the first place he said, "Call me Lou," then went to the bridge.

Chapter 40

Criss Weller grabbed on to Ratner Groat and screamed as a sudden impact shook the Guy's Night Out.

Throom looked up in surprise. "Uh oh."

Ratner freed himself from the Lumarian's clutch and ran to one of the consoles. "Looks like we got hit on the port side."

"By what?" Throom rushed to join him at the console. Ratner brought up an echo image from one of the sensors on that side of the ship. In the distance on one of the hills stood two stone Humanoids. They seemed to be high-fiving.

"Fraggarts," confirmed Throom with exasperation. "I was hoping none of them would find us."

"What are they doing?" asked Criss.

"Throwing rocks at us," Ratner answered.

"Why?" she pleaded. "We didn't do anything to them."

"Doesn't matter," Throom explained. "We're a target that's not a rock. That's a rare thing on Frag."

"Well, let's tell them to stop."

"How? We can't leave the ship, and none of the usual means of communication work because of the radiation," Throom complained.

"I'm not sure I could blast them from here," Ratner offered, "but I could probably hit close enough to scare them off."

"Fraggarts don't scare. It would just make it more fun for them. On Frag it's all good fun until someone gets killed—then it's a blast."

"What do we do, then?" Criss asked.

"Leave," Ratner answered.

Throom was in agreement. They took control positions. The ship rocked again.

"Fark!" Ratner spat. "That was damned close to being a breach."

"Maybe you should suit up."

Ratner glanced at Criss. "No time now." He continued with the controls. The ship lurched again, this time upward.

On the display, the Fraggarts started as the ship rose into the air. Seemingly elated, they scurried to gather smaller rocks and began rising to the new challenge. The rocks flew at and past the ship. When the ship was nearly out of range, one headed straight at the display.

Throom felt the impact through his feet, and the display rocked, but the artificial gravity was on now, so they didn't otherwise experience it.

They had escaped.

Throom and Ratner sat next to each other, watching the display as they skimmed over the craggy surface of Frag. The idea occurred to both of them at about the same time. Throom closed his eyes and shook his head at how stupid he had been.

"You know," Ratner was the first to speak, somewhat sheepishly, "since we are up here, we should probably..."

"Look for Cookie and Toby." Throom finished the thought for him.

"In fact, you know we probably should have, you know..."

"... thought of this sooner?" Throom suggested.

"Yeah, probably so."

They skimmed the abrasive surface of Frag in silence for a while.

"I just don't usually think of a shuttle doing this," offered Ratner. "I mean a shuttle is for shuttling right? Going from point A to point B."

"Yeah, I guess I sort of had that idea stuck in my head too."

They rode in silence for a bit longer then Ratner added, "We should really call it a runabout or something."

Chapter 41

"Anything yet?" Greasly asked Penny. She looked up from her console on the bridge of the Incorrigible and shook her head.

"I'm going to try a pseudo tachyon Mumford conversion." She made some adjustments.

"Cap'n," called one of the five or six Flatheads that were on the bridge with them. "The Other Woman is in range."

"Good," replied Greasly, "try and raise them. Put them on as soon as you do."

"Lou, I think I have something," Penny said.

Greasly quashed the urge to say "You didn't get it from me!" and moved over to her.

"Some movement. I think it must be a shuttle."

"Ours or theirs?"

"Can't be sure yet. Let me do a Fingle refraction on the harmonic retrograde inversion signature." She fiddled some more.

"Penny?" Greasly asked in a low voice.

"What?" She asked as she worked.

"Do all those things you say really mean anything?"

She smirked and without looking up, responded. "That is a trade secret, Cap'n."

"Cap'n," Flathead interrupted, "I have The Other Woman on the display."

Greasly looked up and saw what looked like a blob of clear gelatin with warts doing an impression of a melting scoop of ice cream. It bubbled and hissed from atop a control console.

"Hey, Jones," Greasly responded, "is Groat there, or did he go to the surface too?"

Jones fibrillated and sighed.

"He took Cookie and Toby, too, eh?"

A flop, a trickle, and a shiver.

"Even the Lumarian? Have you heard anything from them?"

A long low flatulence.

"We have three people down there too. We've spotted what seems to be one of the shuttles, and it's moving along the surface."

The display suddenly jumped, and the gelatinous splop was replaced by a gelatinous Humanoid. It was Stuart.

"You must help me," Stuart demanded breathlessly. "I'm being held prisoner on The Other Woman. I've broken into the main communication link, but I won't be able to hold it for long."

"You're Stuart, aren't you?"

"Yes." Stuart was clearly puzzled that Greasly knew him. "You have to help me. They are trying to starve me to death."

Greasly looked at Stuart. If he was not a mountain of fat, he was certainly a foothill. Behind him Greasly could see a half eaten package of rice cakes. "Can you put Jones back on?"

"Aren't you going to help me?"

"Sure," Greasly said in a non-committal way, "you try and hang on, and I'll see what I can do. Put Jones back on."

"If you don't help me, I will be forced to report you to the Galactic Guard."

"Jones! Now!"

Reluctantly Stuart put Jones back on.

"Your prisoner says he's hungry," Greasly told Jones.

Jones communicated his lack of surprise at that bit of news then asked what Greasly was thinking of doing about the shuttles.

"Well, we only have that one shuttle. Do you have a spare?"

Jones said that they had one other shuttle, but it was out of commission, and they had no mechanic to fix it.

"Jebus. They left you alone with a broken shuttle?"

Jones complained at the truth of the statement. On the bridge of the Incorrigible, some of the blue and green Flatheads were complaining among themselves about something the cap'n had just said.

"Great," Greasly grumbled. "Well I suppose that unless I can come up with a mechanic and some way to get him over to you, we'll have to take the Incorrigible herself down there."

Jones bubbled.

"I'd rather not do that because there's a chance the radiation might make a ship this size, and this age, hard to handle, so if you get any ideas let me know."

They broke communications.

"Flathead."

Six Flatheads answered. "Yes Cap'n."

"Think you could fix their shuttle?"

They all answered with some variation of "Maybe."

"You." Greasly pointed at the Flathead closest to him. "If I can get you and some of the others over there, do you think you can fix it?

"It depends on what the problem is, but it is possible."

"How many of you would you need?"

"I don't know—two or three should be fine."

"Okay, go gather up that many then check the system specs of both ships to see if we can dock together. If so, let me know. If not, start brainstorming other possibilities."

"You know who was a much better mechanic than me," the Flathead informed the cap'n.

"Who?"

"Hardegar."

"You want to take him along?"

"I think it would be a good idea."

"Well, that's fine with me if you don't mind toting him. It probably won't happen anyway. I'm just covering all the bases."

The miniature Flathead nodded and was on his way out the door.

Greasly moved to Penny. "Any more information?"

"The way it is moving back and forth, it seems to be looking for something."

"Probably the Flummox."

"Probably."

"Any other news?"

"Well, every now and then I get traces of Throckmonger's Anomaly from the area."

"What could cause that?"

"I have an idea, but I want to run a trilateral Leibniz transform before I say anything."

"Just go ahead and tell me."

"Okay, well, it is possible that the anomaly is caused by Notable Raul Fission Chips."

"Really?" The cap'n was pleased by that news.

"It's possible," she warned, "but it could also be one of a few types of low-grade nuclear waste. I'll know for sure which it is in a few minutes."

"Good, let me know." Greasly did not move away. Instead he stood where he was and pondered. "If it really is fission chips, how many bags would you say there were?"

"Crates. Several."

"So what would they be doing on the Flummox? Grimshaw would have hated them, wouldn't he? I mean they were the reason that his little time fluffing maneuver failed."

"Time bloating," Penny corrected, "and maybe he just stole them to sell them."

"I guess that makes sense."

"Look. See this spike?" She pointed at the display. "Definitely fission chips."

"So is the shuttle moving toward that location?"

"Sort of. It'll get there eventually. But wait—with a spike like that, the fission chips can't be over 10 years old."

"Really?" Greasly tried to digest this new information. "It can't be the Flummox, then."

"You wouldn't think so."

"And Fraggarts don't eat."

"Right."

"Could be a recently crashed ship. Would you be able to detect any survivors?"

She shook her head, making the zipper pull on her forehead jingle. "No way. But I'll see what else I can find."

Greasly turned to the rest of the crew. "Flathead, can you get us down there to a specific spot?"

"And land us?" the five of them asked in unison.

"You." Greasly pointed to a blue Flathead. "I'm going to call you Levelhead."

"All right," Levelhead said without enthusiasm.

"I'm not sure yet about landing—possibly."

"I don't think the radiation will be a problem, Cap'n, but landing will depend entirely on what the area looks like."

"Okay, change of plans," Greasly announced, "I want you to get us down there. Penny will give you the exact position, but if it starts to look too difficult, pull out. I don't want to get stranded."

"Got it."

"You." Greasly pointed to a green Flathead. "You're now Plateauhead."

"Must I be?"

"No good?"

"No."

"How about Planehead? Better?"

"Why not just use my real name, before you started calling me Flathead."

"I changed your name? Why? What was it before?"

"Hoo-Ba-Stank."

"Greenie," he said to the Kravitsian, "I'll call you Greenie. You contact Jones on The Other Woman and your brother I sent off to see about docking the ships; tell them what we're doing."

"Okay," Greenie sighed and went to work.

The Incorrigible began its descent to the surface. As they approached, Greasly pondered the odds of a huge supply of fission chips crash landing on the same planet as the Flummox. The most likely solution that he came up with was that the chips were on another ship that was looking for the Flummox. Why someone would load up on a huge supply of fission chips to go treasure hunting, however, he had no idea.

He started mentally testing hypothetical time bloating scenarios to see if he could think of one that would leave 10-year-old fission chips on the Flummox when that crashed over 50 years ago. Penny interrupted his mental permutations.

"Cap'n, I'm picking up a tiny point of radiation in the Humanly visible spectrum. There are two strange things about it—at least for Frag."

"Really, what?"

"For one thing, it seems to be rotating, and for another it is on the edge of a large rectangular space of very low radiation."

"What?" Greasly quickly moved to her console. She showed him a display of radiation levels. Most of the display was one shade or another of purple but in the center of the display was a rectangle of light blue. Greasly stared at the spot with his brows knitted in concentration. "What the fark would do that?"

"I don't know. All I can think of is some sort of radiation barrier."

"And where's that Throckfinger thing coming from?"

"Throckmonger's anomaly," she corrected, "and it's coming from right in the middle of that."

"Why didn't you see this earlier?" he asked by way of curiosity, not accusation.

"We were too far away. You see, the radiation is only blocked a certain distance upward. That causes diffractionary recombination of the sub ether signatures to—"

"Never mind," he backpedaled, waving her explanation away. "I've got enough to think about right now. The bottom line is that our fission chips are sitting in the middle of a big chunk of non-radiation."

"With a searchlight," she added.

"Curiouser and curiouser," he quoted, looking quite concerned.

Chapter 42

Toby knelt with his palm in the middle of Cookie's back and shook the Nootian's body as it lay prostrate in the gray dust of Frag. "Cookie, Cookie!" he called out then rolled him over to check the environment suit's status. Cookie was still breathing, but barely.

Toby looked in all directions at once. It looked as if the lights they had been moving toward were right over the next hill, but then again, it had seemed that way since they started—not that any of that mattered. There was no alternative available since the lights behind them had switched off.

Toby lifted Cookie onto his shoulders and started up the hill. He wasn't even at the top before his own suit was warning him of imminent power failure. He stopped, and without putting Cookie down, let his breathing calm. He then trudged up the last few meters to the top of the craggy hill—the warning signal of his suit ringing in his ears the whole time.

As he reached the top, he looked down and saw the large spotlight beams they had been following. They were not attached to a ship. In fact they were not attached to anything. They seemed to appear in the middle of the air and shoot upward. They were still moving around as if all of the beams emanated from the same point on the ground, but that point was not there. It was if something had erased the lights from a certain height downward.

Toby shook his head. His vision was getting bleary. He must be hallucinating. Toby descended the hill and walked toward where the source of the lights should be. His vision became more and more fuzzy, his breathing more and more labored. His eye stalks wilted so that he only saw the ground as he walked.

Then he realized that he was no longer walking on the gritty jagged surface of Frag. He was instead on a flat, paved surface. He looked around.

He had apparently walked out onto a huge flat area covered with the rubberized material used on parking lots. A signpost was mounted at the edge of the parking lot and on it were two signs. The top sign had a cartoon picture of an ancient blade weapon called a cutlass and the letter C. The bottom one had words. Toby tried to read them but they blurred and danced before him. He reeled and blinked his many eyes. He brought more of them to the fore to try and focus the sign. It was a warning of some kind. That was clear. Something about shields—protection—something about ending. At the bottom in large letters it said, "STAY BACK".

He was gulping at the stale air of the environment suit. His vision doubled then doubled again, then again. His lungs started to hurt. He needed air. The suit was smothering him. He couldn't take it any more. He lost control and reached to open his suit. He tugged at the fastener to open it but was too weak. He tried again as he felt himself falling to the rubberized surface of the parking lot.

He was hovering at the edge of death—moving down several dark tunnels toward several bright lights at once. It was like being in the center of a dark, perforated, spherical shell that was shrinking. He knew somehow that the in those lights he would find peace. He rushed on toward them but then stopped suddenly. The lights began receding. At first he tried to resist the movement, but it had no effect, so he relaxed and let it happen. Some part of him knew that this was what he really wanted anyway.

A pair of his eyes flicked open, followed by several more of them. His eye stalks snaked as he looked around. Nothing had changed since he passed out. Then he realized that he was breathing something remarkably like fresh Class M air.

One of his eyes peeked down to his right hand. The hand was holding his environment suit open. A wave of terror overcame him, and he quickly closed the suit, but soon he realized the folly of that and stripped off the suit altogether. The air was crisp and sweet and, as far as Toby could tell, non-toxic. Frantically he checked his suit's radiation gauge. It showed that the radiation level was within acceptable limits.

He quickly got Cookie's suit off of him. He slapped the Nootian lightly on the cheeks, trying to revive him. He opened one of Cookie's eyes. The pupil constricted; the eye moved to look directly at Toby. Cookie suddenly gasped in air like someone emerging from underwater just in time. He thrust his chest upward and breathed in greedily. Then he stopped suddenly and sat up. "Where are we?" he demanded in a panicked tone between breaths. "Is this Frag?"

"This is Frag," confirmed Toby. Two of his eyes were reading the warning sign on the post.

"We're dead!" the Nootian yelped.

"No, we're in some sort of protective field."

"Protective field? On Frag?"

"Not only that," Toby continued, rising to his feet, "it seems to be protecting a parking lot."

Cookie looked around and crawled to his feet in amazement. They were on the edge of a parking lot that stretched off as far as they could see. The Fraggart moon was setting in the North. The parking lot around them was illuminated by lights on poles set into the parking lot at regular intervals. The same grid pattern of lights stretched into the distance. The large spotlight that had drawn them there whirred nearby.

"What's that?" Toby pointed behind himself at a light low to the horizon beyond the barrier.

"It's moving," Cookie noticed, "and fast!"

"The shuttle!" Toby yelled. They began running about waving their arms to get the attention of the pilot.

Chapter 43

On board the Guy's Night Out, Groat and Throom watched the instruments and saw nothing out of the ordinary for Frag, just sector after sector of craggy broken rock.

"You see anything?" Groat asked.

"Not a thing." Throom shook his head.

"You picking up anything?" Groat addressed Criss this time. She was standing toward the front of the control room with her arms outstretched, fingers spread, eyes closed. She shook the watermelon at the top of her neck. "Nothing. It's as if the Universe has hidden its face from me."

"Hey," Throom remarked, pointing to the display, "I see some movement."

Groat quickly moved to look at the display. "Where?"

"There. I'll magnify it."

The image zoomed in, and the movement was clearly that of a large group of Fraggarts. They seemed to be in some sort of battle.

"Great," Throom and Groat said together.

"What is it?" Criss asked, her concentration broken.

"Fraggarts," Groat grumbled. "Lots of them." He started to turn the ship to head away from the group.

"Wait a minute," Throom cautioned. "What if Cookie and Toby are over there?"

Groat thought that over then reluctantly headed toward the Fraggarts again. "I guess we had better be sure."

On the parking lot, Toby and Cookie stopped waving their arms and stared in disbelief as the Guy's Night Out—having just turned to head directly toward them—turned again to head directly away from them.

"Is it too dark?" Cookie asked.

"Not for instruments," Toby reckoned. "They probably aren't even paying attention to the Human visible spectrum. If they were, they would have seen the spotlight."

"That stupid son-of-a-bitch!" Cookie screamed.

"They couldn't have been more than two kilometers away. Maybe the instruments are broken? Maybe something is distracting them?"

"That stupid son-of-a-bitch!" Cookie reprised. "He couldn't land us at the spot, sent us out to find it without geo-navigators, and now he's abandoning us!"

"Take it easy, Cookie, I'm sure there's a good reason for this."

"Yeah," Cookie barked, "he's a stupid son-of-a-bitch!"

Kragg the Fraggart was the first to see the Guy's Night Out approaching. He tossed the Fraggart he was holding over his head into a chasm and pointed.

"Look!" Kragg screamed to the group.

He was promptly smashed with a huge boulder. He plummeted into the chasm—screaming in anger as he did—to break into pieces at the bottom.

Although his life was cut short, the message that he had dedicated the final several seconds of his life to had lived on. The Fraggart that had thrown the fatal boulder turned to look. Then, like a candle in the dark spreading its flame to candle after fellow candle, the killer of Krag the See-er passed on the message. "Look!" he said.

Look they did, and those that had looked passed on the message. Soon the entire group was looking at the strange glinting craft skimming effortlessly through the air toward them over the dark and jagged surface of Frag.

This young group had never seen anything like it. It was miraculous how a thing so large and so beautiful could remain in the air for so long. None of them even had a word for what the thing was doing. No wait, yes they did.

From deep inside themselves the word bubbled up from the murky depths of their minds. There was indeed a word for it. Each of them knew it, but none of them had ever had the occasion to use it before. Flying. That's what it was doing. This strange and wondrous thing was flying!

"Dibs!" yelled one of the Fraggarts and scrambled to get a rock of just the right size to knock the strange thing out of the sky. The rest quickly followed suit, each wanting to be the first to bring the thing down.

"I think they've seen us," pronounced Throom on board the shuttle.

"We need to keep looking," Groat insisted—perspiration breaking out above his pencil thin mustache. "Just stay out of range."

"Too late for that." Throom had noticed the barrage of boulders about to envelop them. He grabbed the controls and steered the Guy's Night Out toward the surface. From the display he could tell that one of the boulders had caught the back of the shuttle. They were now flipping over and over as they headed toward the stony surface of Frag. He managed to regain control just in time to turn their imminent crash into a mere rough landing. He quickly took off again, heading away from the Fraggart tribe.

The tribe followed in hot pursuit.

Back at the parking lot, Cookie was pacing like a caged oblejag. "That stupid son-of-a-bitch!" he growled again. He grabbed his suit and took the matter declumpinizationizer.

"Cookie," Toby asked cautiously, "what are you going to do?"

"If they come back, by the moons of Noot, they WILL notice us this time."

"Don't shoot the shuttle," Toby suggested.

Cookie pointed the matter declumpinizationizer at the Xemite. "Look," he growled between gritted teeth, his eyes seemingly glowing from within his blood red face, "where I come from, you never ever leave a man behind."

"That's very noble," soothed Toby, pushing the barrel of the weapon away from him.

"Because if you do, they hunt you down and kill you!" Cookie turned back to watch for the shuttle.

"But Cookie," Toby offered calmly, "if they come back, they haven't left us behind."

Cookie thought that over. He could see the logic of it but held on to enough of his anger to avoid admitting he had been foolish. "I won't shoot the shuttle," he mumbled at last, as if he was only giving in to Toby's cowardly whining.

"Good," said Toby, "because there it is."

Cookie reeled and fired. The lightning-like beam shot out and barely missed The Guys Night Out.

"Where the fark did that come from?" Groat yelped on board the shuttle as he watched the beam come out of nowhere and nearly hit them.

"I have no idea," Throom admitted.

"You said you wouldn't shoot the shuttle!" Toby screamed on the parking lot.

"I didn't," smirked Cookie, lowering the gun and swaggering a little as he stood. "I shot *at* it."

Then the ground shook as a boulder half the height of Toby smashed into the ground next to them and bounced into the searchlight, which crashed to pieces in a spray of sparks.

"Death!" screamed Criss on the shuttle. "Ruin! Destruction! Chaos! Deaaaaaaath!" She fell into another faint.

"She's sure been doing that a lot lately," Groat commented, adjusting the controls to get them above the many dangers of their surroundings.

"Is it, you know..." Throom kept watching for Cookie and Toby as he spoke, "women trouble?"

"I don't know. I don't think Lumarians do that."

"Hey, did you see that?"

"What?"

"There." Throom was pointing at a display. "A rock disappeared. Right there." As they looked, another rock was flying through the air and then disappeared as if swallowed up by the air itself. "See?"

"A camouflage field," they realized together.

"That is very unfraggy," Groat exclaimed, and Throom agreed.

"And whoever is behind it is very unfriendly. Look, they're shooting again." Throom pointed at the display; energy beams shot out of nowhere and blasted away at the countryside.

"Cookie," Groat said in recognition.

On the ground, a Fraggart named Rocky spoke to the others. "Wait! The flying thing is too high, and see, tongues of flame lick at us from the forbidden place." One of the Fraggarts standing atop a crag exploded into bits as if to underscore his comment. "Let's go back and regroup."

A few of them tried one last time with all their might to lob a stone at the shuttle. They all fell short. Another Fraggart exploded as it was hit by the matter declumpinizationizer. Grudgingly they all started trudging away—several of them glaring over their shoulders at the flying thing that was now heading for the forbidden place.

"They're going away," Groat said as he saw the migration begin. From the height of the shuttle, they looked like a slow-motion uphill avalanche. One or two of the stragglers were disintegrated by the energy beam.

"What's that?" Throom was pointing out a strange strip of black on the surface in the distance. The black appeared to be dotted by a grid of lights.

As the shuttle moved on, it became obvious that the camouflage field only went up a certain distance. They moved over it.

"It looks like a parking lot," Groat remarked.

"And that looks like your crewmen," Throom added happily. He gently high-fived the slick commander next to him. When they looked back to the consoles, Groat pointed out a Buick Roadmaster landing on the parking lot.

"Isn't that the Incorrigible?" Groat asked, pointing it out on a display.

"I believe it is," agreed Throom, smiling.

Chapter 44

"Okay, so now what?" Greasly said to Groat as they stood together next to the Incorrigible and the Guy's Night Out. The hatch of the Guy's Night Out was twisted and broken open—the result of Throom leaving the shuttle even though the hatch had been fused shut by the declumpinizationizer blast. Around the leaders, Cookie, Toby, Criss, Throom, Penny, and Klorf stood waiting to see what would happen next.

Greasly had confirmed on the way down that their position was at the edge of a large rectangular parking lot and at the center of it, about two kilometers distant, was a wrecked ship that fit many of the specifications of the Flummox except that it had an annex built onto it and contained large amounts of fresh fission chips. (Ten years was considered fresh for a snack with a shelf life of about 50 years and a half life of over 40.)

"Well, it seems to me that we have no choice but to work together," Groat put forth.

"How do you figure that?"

"Well, I mean, we're all here."

"Yes."

"So how would you stop us from going with you?" Groat held his hands palms upward and hunched his shoulders. "Shoot us?"

Greasly blinked but didn't otherwise change his expression.

"Lou, I know you too well. You won't pull off that bluff."

Greasly shrugged. "All right. Let's talk shares, then."

"Don't you always give even shares?"

"To my crew."

"Won't we effectively be on your crew?" Cookie interjected.

"Will you be taking orders from me?" Greasly asked.

"Hell no," Cookie growled.

"Well then. . ." Greasly rested his case.

"What are you proposing?" Groat crossed his arms to listen.

"You and your crew get one share among you."

"What!?" Cookie barked.

"Too little," Groat reported calmly. "We should get at least half a share each."

"And I suppose you are counting your captive as one of your crew?" Greasly accused.

"Captive?"

"Stuart."

Groat rolled his eyes. "I fired him weeks ago."

"He contacted me and said you're starving him to death."

"Not to death, Lou," Groat shook his head, "just till he fits through the door and we can send him home."

"I figured that was it," Greasly nodded. "So nothing for him, right?"

"Right," Groat confirmed, "but Jones is up there. He should get his cut."

"That's five people," Greasly complained. "Didn't you lose anyone?"

"Not this trip," Groat said proudly. "How about you?"

"One," Greasly admitted then remembered Hardegar, "and six sevenths."

"So does the one seventh get a full share?"

"Yeah," Greasly repined with a shrug and a nod. "It's the noisy one seventh that's left. Oh, and we lost another one, but technically he was working for you when we lost him so. . ."

"Who's that?"

"Willy."

"Really? How?"

"It's a long story," Greasly waved it away, "I'll tell you later."

"All right. So you have how many?"

"Me, Throom, Penny, Klorf, Hardegar, Flathea—" He froze. He looked over at Throom, Penny, and Klorf. Their eyebrows went up as they realized the dilemma. "—d," Greasly finished slowly.

"You forgot you lost Flathead," Groat surmised sympathetically. "I'll miss him too."

"We didn't lose him," Greasly corrected. "Actually, we sort of multiplied him."

"Right. You don't have to count his children," Groat assured.

"But they are not exactly his children," Greasly explained. "They are more like him broken up into 60 or so little pieces."

"Ah. Well then, they all split one share."

"I don't know," Greasly pondered, eyebrows knitted. "Do you think that's fair?"

"Well, how many were there when you offered him a share?" Groat reasoned.

"One."

"Okay then. You offered him one share. You only owe him one share."

"That doesn't quite work," Throom interjected while stepping forward. "You see each one of them remembers Greasly making the deal, so each one of them is going to get one sixtieth of what he was promised."

"But they were all one unit when he made the deal," Groat countered.

"Well, yes and no," Throom cautioned, "technically speaking, the Flathead that he made the deal with died in childbirth."

"Ah, then you don't owe anything," Groat brightened.

Penny spoke up. "But the mind of Flathead, including the memory of the deal, was passed on to each of the offspring."

"That doesn't matter, does it?" Groat was asking a real question, not a hypothetical one. "The person you actually made the deal with is gone."

"Not according to the Grand High Council of Galactic Wisdom," Toby interjected. "In the Universe versus Filbert

Smaz they ruled that the mind is the holder of all contracts, and if the mind changes bodies, the contract follows the mind."

"The Grand High Council of Galactic Wisdom," Groat and Greasly both snorted dismissively.

"Their decisions are non-binding anyway," Greasly waved the notion away.

"These arguments are irrelevant," Klorf's stern voice insisted. "Your deal was not that Flathead was to receive one share. Your deal was that the treasure was to be divided equally among the crew."

Greasly shut his eyes and pinched the bridge of his nose with his thumb and forefinger. "That's right." He nodded. "That's always the deal."

Greasly heard something behind him and looked back briefly to see Hardegar walking down the gangway of the Incorrigible on eight or so tiny green legs.

Legs? He looked again. The legs belonged to one of the Flatheads and Hardegar's head was stuck on its brick shaped body. The entire unit approached the group. It looked like the Flathead he was riding was just barely large enough to carry the skull even though it and all its kin had been growing at an amazing rate. The thing was lucky Hardegar's head was mostly hollow.

"Sorry I'm late," Hardegar greeted.

"We were just starting to discuss shares," Greasly informed him. "I'm wondering if we should get all of the Flatheads out here."

"What's to discuss?" asked the Flathead under Hardegar. "Isn't it always equal shares for all the crew?"

"Yeah," Greasly began, "but we have two problems. One is that we're now working with the crew of The Other Woman, and two is that one of our crew members has split into 60 smaller members."

"Oh yeah, so you don't want to give me a full share, right?"

"Well does it really seem fair," Penny asked, "that we suddenly have to split the treasure 70 ways instead of 6?"

Greasly sighed. "How do they handle things like this back on Kravits Rock?"

"I don't think it ever comes up," the Flathead claimed.

"It has to," Penny insisted. "Don't you have contracts on Kravits Rock?"

"Oh sure, we have contracts."

"So how do you handle it if the person who is part of a contract reproduces?" Greasly probed.

"Well, all contracts have an orgy clause. When the orgy comes, all contracts are suspended. After the orgy the contracts are back in effect if all parties are still male." The Flathead waved some of his green tentacles from underneath the red-eyed leather skull as he spoke.

"So females can't be part of a contract?" Penny asked.

"Well, they can, but the contract is changed in that case. The males have a chance to back out of the contract or to keep the contract in effect."

"Okay," Greasly led on, "so if they keep it in effect what happens after she pops?"

"The contract is inherited by one of the children," Flathead said.

"Aha!" Greasly and Groat exclaimed together.

"Which one?" Penny asked.

"The other people in the contract decide after two months."

"Why after two months?" Hardegar seemingly asked himself in a different voice.

"It gives the personalities of the young time to diverge fully. That way they can pick the one that is closest to the original participant."

"I thought you were all the same," Penny remarked.

"We start out the same but eventually the personality traits of what you would call the father begin to mix with the experience and the personality traits of what you would call the mother. The results can be drastically different."

"So anyway," Greasly summed up, "We really only owe one of you one share."

"That's how it's done on Kravits Rock. But this is not Kravits Rock."

"I don't think I would like your father," Greasly grumbled.

"Wait a minute," Penny blurted, "did you hire Flathead on Kravits Rock?"

Greasly thought it over, "I'm not sure. I think maybe..." He looked at Hardegar/Flathead, who remained silent. "Yes. I did."

"Actually I did," corrected Throom, "and it was on Kravits Rock."

"Well, in that case," Penny continued, "the agreement to accept you as a crew member has the implicit orgy clause and only one of you is actually a member of the crew."

Greasly smiled at her, "Are you sure you're not a lawyer?"

"But we have been acting as members of the crew since our release," Hardegar's legs countered, "thus suggesting a de-facto contract of—"

"Payment for services rendered," Greasly insisted, "those services being transporting and feeding you."

"But we entered your ship in space. It's against Galactic law to charge people you pick up in space for transport."

"We're not in space now." Greasly smiled a checkmate smile. "Do you want to buy a ride back?"

"Alright," Flathead slumped taking Hardegar with him, "you win."

"Cheer up," Greasly consoled, "we'll do something for you. Not a full share, but something." He turned. "Well Ratner, it looks like..." Ratner Groat was not there, nor was his crew, and their shuttle was skimming away into the distance. Greasly turned to his crew. "Did anybody see them leave?"

They all shook their heads. Even Hardegar was shaken.

"They didn't fix their hatch did they?"

"How could they?" Throom shrugged.

Greasly relaxed. "Okay, then there's no hurry. They'll have to land The Other Woman before they can leave, and Jones couldn't do that by himself even if they could get a message to him. Let them do the legwork. If they want to leave Frag, they will have to let us in on the haul." He smiled. He had been waiting anxiously to play that particular ace in the hole on his old rival, but he now realized that if he played it when Groat actually had the treasure in his well-manicured little hands, it would make the coup even sweeter. "We can pick up our shuttle then catch up with them."

Chapter 45

When the Incorrigible arrived at the shuttle, they found it surrounded by Fraggarts and taking a pelting.

"Why haven't they taken off yet?" Greasly worried on the bridge.

"They may be waiting for me," Throom suggested.

"Flathead knows better than that," Greasly countered. "He wouldn't expect you to fight your way through to the shuttle. The engines must be disabled."

"We better do something," Penny said. "From the looks of it, if they don't have a hull breach now they soon will."

"I'm afraid we may have to be inhospitable guests to your planet, Throom," Greasly said as he sat down at the weapons console.

Throom looked on with trepidation. He turned to Penny. "Are there life signs on board?"

"I'm sure there are," she assured him without looking at her readouts.

"Hold on, Flathead," Greasly mumbled as he laid down a line of energy blasts along a ridge atop which there were several Fraggarts. When the debris settled, they were gone.

"Don't let up now." Throom was watching the events carefully on his display. "They won't give up that easily."

The ship wheeled to blast another set of Fraggarts into rubble.

"Incoming, port side," Throom warned.

Greasly raised the ship above the apogee of the boulders' paths.

"They missed us, but two of them hit the shuttle," Klorf reported.

"Flathead!" Greasly barked.

"Yes, Cap'n," the two Flatheads, one pink and one blue, on the bridge responded.

"I want you to do something for me," Greasly began, then described the thing.

"Right," they responded and went to work.

Greasly blasted again, but the Fraggarts dove for cover. "They're catching on," Greasly complained. "You'd think a ship this size would intimidate them."

"We've been hit," Klorf barked, "aft, port side."

Greasly wheeled and blasted the culprits to gravel. "Flathead, you guys ready?"

"Not yet," one of them replied.

"Well, hurry up. We've got a window of opportunity."

"Cap'n," Throom advised, "twenty degrees port."

"Got 'em." Greasly laid down fire. The ridge exploded in a shower of rock fragments.

Throom watched as one of the Fraggarts ran out onto a crag then leaped off onto the shuttle. "You better hurry Cap'n," he relayed, "there's one on the shuttle."

"On board!?"

"On top."

"That could work," Greasly said with a sly grin.

"Ready Cap'n," the blue Flathead announced.

"Booya!" Greasly cried as he deftly flipped the Incorrigible upside down and popped the trunk.

The Incorrigible quickly descended to the surface, close enough that the trunk lid was within a meter of touching the rock.

The Fraggart on top of the shuttle was frozen with terror—arms upraised to shield his head, thinking that the entire space ship was falling on him. But when it did not pulverize him, he looked up with relief and joy.

"Now," Greasly snapped.

The Flatheads hit the controls.

The shuttle was suddenly enveloped in a carefully designed artificial gravity bubble that caused an instantaneous shift in perspective for the Fraggart atop the craft. One second he was standing on top of a shuttle that was resting comfortably on the surface of the planet Frag while an upside-down shuttle bay hovered above him. The next second he was falling headfirst into a right-side-up shuttle bay followed immediately by a shuttle that was falling off the underside of the planet Frag.

The Fraggart fell into the shuttle bay and was crushed by the shuttle that crashed in upside-down upon him. The shuttle bay lid closed. The Incorrigible righted itself in relation to the planet and skimmed off toward the parking lot.

As cheers and congratulations were bandied about the bridge, Throom quickly made his way to the shuttle.

Chapter 46

Throom arrived at the shuttle hole just as the air purification had finished. The shuttle had its legs in the air like something dead in a cartoon. He pounded on the side. "Flathead!" he called out. "Are you all right?" He placed his hand on the ship and felt for any sort of sound.

Nothing.

More nothing.

Then...

Something.

He felt a stirring inside the shuttle as if rubble were being moved aside. He pulled himself up the side of the shuttle and hurried across the bottom of it to a round hatch. He entered the security override code, and the hatch slid open.

He leaped feet first into the hatch, but the artificial gravity on the shuttle was still in operation, so before he was completely through the hatch, he reached a point where most of his body was actually upside-down in the shuttle—poking up through a hole in the floor. In this point of view he fell back into the hole.

In the other perspective, he shot back out of the hole as if he had landed on a trampoline. He caught himself with one foot on either side of the hatch. He then got down and crawled head first into it. This was easier than he anticipated because any of his body that was outside the ship was falling into a hole and only what was already in the shuttle was being pulled up out of one. As a result, he used too much force and ended up falling forward gracelessly onto his face.

Grumbling, he got to his feet and headed for the control room. When he arrived, Throom saw that the plastiglass dome had been crushed down. True to the promises of the Plastiglass Corporation, it had not broken through, but it was opaque and milky blue and it had changed shape from a dome to a flat panel with a Fraggart-shaped lump in the middle.

Apparently the rough dorsal landing had been enough of a jolt to overpower the gravity momentarily because the rest of the control room was a jumble of displaced tools and equipment. Lying in the detritus were two hot pink Flatheads. One was extricating himself from a bunch of tools and the other was limp and unmoving.

Throom quickly moved to the limp one and carefully picked him up in one hand. This one had a circle on it. Throom has very happy to feel it stir. He gently tapped it on the side. "Hey wake up. You okay?" Throom asked hopefully.

"What happened?" The circle Flathead asked.

"Yeah, What happened?" The Flathead still on the floor, the square Flathead, echoed.

"Where's triangle?" Throom asked.

"On the wall of the engine room," they said together.

Throom put circle down and moved quickly to the engine room. He entered the door and looked around. The far wall was bulging inward. A junction box on the wall was hanging, broken loose by a sudden reformation of the wall, and strands of broken light fiber were bristling out of the hole where it had been. Slowly Throom turned to look behind him.

The wall with the door was plastered with hot pink and blue carnage. Throom grimaced.

"The first rock disabled the engine control," Circle related as he arrived in the doorway.

"The second hit as he was working on rerouting control," Square finished, arriving right behind. He poked a tentacle at the bulge in the far wall.

"Well, at least you two are okay."

"Yes," they both said together. "At least that."

"Well, let's get up to the bridge," Throom sighed. "I think we're about to find the Flummox."

Chapter 47

Cap'n Lou Tok Greasly stood before the sign, his mouth hanging open. He read it again for the fifth time but still didn't believe it. The sign said "Closed".

Behind him, Ratner Groat, Cookie, Toby, Criss Weller, Penny, Throom, Klorf, Circle, Square, and a green Flathead with the head of Hardegar perched on top stood engaged in various loud and chaotic discussions. They all stood in front of another sign that had taken quite some time for Greasly to digest the meaning of. That sign marked the location as the Methane Galactic Historical Site, listed a number of restrictions placed on visitors (no recording devices, no pets, no recording pets, no pet devices, etc.) and the hours of operation—the closing time of which Ratner Groat and crew had missed by some ten minutes.

Greasly stepped back to look at the structure again. Whoever built the place had apparently left the Flummox as it had been after the crash but paved out around it in all directions. He looked at the crumpled silver frame of the Flummox. It gleamed brilliantly under the floodlights surrounding it.

Greasly rubbed his chin and walked over to the rest of the group. Groat and Penny were in a heated discussion that seemed to be about the fact that Groat had "made a grab for the loot" on one side and about how fiery Penny's eyes were when she was angry on the other. Cookie and Klorf were commiserating about their positions on their respective crews. The three Flatheads and Hardegar had somehow gotten into another heated discussion comparing the Bible to the Floppy. Toby and Throom were the only ones that seemed to be trying to make some sense of the situation, so Greasly chose their conversation to join.

"The sign says that the place opened ten years ago," Toby was saying. "There was a big increase in government projects at that time. This may have been part of that big kickback scandal."

"So why didn't we find out about it in our research?" Throom pondered.

"I don't know. You know how they write some of those projects. You might have read about it and not even known it."

"True."

"That seems right," Greasly added. "Look at this grossly mis-proportioned parking lot. You know how crazy the farking government is for paving."

"Right." Both Throom and Toby nodded in agreement.

"But where does that put us in regards to the treasure?" Greasly asked. "Where are we legally?"

"Visitors at a Galactic historical site," Toby stated flatly.

"If we break in there, it will be a Galactic offense," Throom added.

Greasly rubbed the bridge of his nose. "Do you suppose the treasure is actually still in there?"

"Could be." Throom shrugged.

"If it is, I suppose we can count on tight security," Greasly surmised.

"You never know." Toby looked at the building.

"They wouldn't set up a place like this in the middle of nowhere and not have it protected."

"Maybe not. But then again, I would've said the same thing about them building a tourist site on Frag in the first place."

"True. I suppose we could find anything in there." Greasly looked at the entrance. "Behind those glass doors."

"Are you giving me an order?" Throom asked.

"No, just thinking," Greasly stated. "Let's not pull a Thomas á Becket."

"A Thomas A-who-ket?" Toby asked.

"Never mind," Greasly waved the allusion away. He glanced over at Groat and Penny. They were no longer arguing, and Ratner was standing closer than he had before. He couldn't tell what Ratner was saying, but he could tell that Penny liked it, even though she didn't seem to want to let Groat know that. Greasly sighed a little. He looked out at the parking lot lights. "Do you suppose they've ever had a single visitor?"

"Possibly not," Throom answered.

"But it does seem to be well cared for," Greasly added, "from what I could see through the doors."

"Robots," Toby stated.

"Why not people?" Greasly asked.

"I don't see any sort of transportation around here," Toby replied. His eye stalks were scanning the area. "They surely wouldn't strand somebody on Frag just to run a museum."

"Might be the only way to get them to do it," Throom threw in.

"True." Greasly nodded. "Or maybe they had transportation, and that's why they're not here now."

"Or maybe they hired Fraggarts," Throom suggested.

That was a new idea to both Greasly and Toby.

"I guess they could, couldn't they?" Toby admitted.

"As long as they hired barbarians," Greasly clarified.

"Maybe we should just knock and see if anyone answers," Throom proposed.

Greasly shrugged and walked over to the door. He cupped his hand over his eyes and put his face close to the glass to cut the reflection of the brightly lit crew and ships behind him. Inside, beyond a second set of glass doors, was what looked like a carpeted waiting room with various plaques on the walls. He could just make out a picture of Notable Raul on one of them. There was what looked like a ticket window of some sort with a set of shutters drawn over the opening. There were several doors in the room.

Greasly pounded on the glass.

Nothing happened.

He pounded again, longer this time.

Nothing, except that the conversations behind him died down as people paid attention to what he was doing.

He tried one more time.

"There's someone there!" Greasly blurted.

A man, who appeared to be in his eighties and opposed to youthinizers for some reason, had walked into the room. He was carrying a bowl in one hand and a spoon in the other. On his feet he wore fuzzy, pink slippers. He was otherwise nude. He looked around, cocking his head to the side as if puzzled as to where that sound had been coming from.

Greasly pounded again. The man looked toward Greasly and moved his head from side to side to try and make out what exactly he was seeing. He quickly set his bowl and spoon down on a nearby table and walked to the door. He opened the inner set of doors and peered out through the glass at Greasly.

"Hi," Greasly yelled to be heard through the glass.

The man rubbed his eyes and looked again.

"Can we talk to you?" Greasly asked loudly.

The old man looked around at the crowd. They had all stopped talking and stood watching silently. Then he looked at his hands for some reason. He felt the flesh of them as if testing that they were real. He looked around at the crowd again. Greasly noticed that tears seemed to be welling up in his eyes. The old man started to talk, but his voice was weak. He cleared his throat and tried again. His voice was still too weak for Greasly to hear, but he could tell by the movement of the lips that the old man was asking if they were real.

"Yes," Greasly nodded. He motioned back at everyone. "We are all real. We want to talk to you about the Flummox."

The group nodded and assured him they were real—several of them stepping up to the door.

The man was visibly shaking. A quivering smile revealed his incomplete set of teeth. He was too moved to speak. He quickly reached to unlock the door but then froze and pulled his hand back, shaking his head. He sheepishly pointed to the "Closed" sign.

"We don't want a tour, just to ask some questions."

"Tomorrow," the old man mouthed. Greasly could just make out his voice now. "Security," he apologized with a shrug.

"We won't tell anyone."

The old man shook his head and held out his hands palms upward and shrugged. "Sorry. Security rules. Very strict." Then he motioned at his body. "I'm not even dressed."

"Right," Greasly concurred.

"Tomorrow," the old man said as he started to dance in a giddy way from foot to foot, an action that made his nakedness that much harder to bear. "Tomorrow." He stopped his jig and put his hands together in prayer and pleaded with his eyes.

"Will you be dressed tomorrow?"

The old man nodded vigorously.

"Okay, tomorrow."

"Thank you, thank you!" He started up his little jig as he quickly reentered the lobby area and picked up his cereal bowl. He waved at them with his spoon, and it looked like he said "Tomorrow." Then he exited through a door.

Greasly turned and looked at the group. "He said come back tomorrow."

"Was he naked?" Penny asked.

"No. He had slippers." He turned to Groat. "Ratner, you and your crew are welcome on board the Incorrigible. It'll be a little crowded, but at least our front door closes."

"Crowded? So we might need to share bunks, eh?" Groat eyed Penny.

"In your dreams, Cassanova," Greasly warned.

"Cassanova?"

"Jebus!" Greasly threw up his arms. "Am I the only guy in the universe that knows his history?"

Chapter 48

The night passed uneventfully. Ratner and Criss spent the night together in a storage room after Greasly made sure that Criss was aware of Ratner's advances on Penny. Ratner would have been warmer in space.

Toby and ten of the Flatheads spent most of the night listening to Cookie complain about how they were letting one old man stand between them and the treasure. News of the "Flathead's share" situation spread throughout the on-board Kravitsian community, and they did some complaining of their own.

Eventually everyone rested, and in the morning three of the Kravitsians and all of the non-Kravitsians were at the door, alert and ready for the historical site to open.

When the old man appeared at the door to remove the "Closed" sign, he was dressed in what appeared to be a brand new uniform of gold and green. What little hair he had was slicked down and in perfect order, the stubble had been removed from his chin, and he was smiling genially. On the left side of his chest was a small placard that read "Benny Gund", and beneath that, "Concierge".

"Welcome," he greeted as he opened the door and let the entire menagerie in. He walked into the lobby and exited through another door, which he closed behind him. The others stood looking at each other.

"Are we supposed to follow him?" Throom asked.

Just then the shutters in front of the ticket booth opened. The old man was there, but now his jumpsuit was gold and purple, and his placard said "Ticket Sales" under his name. "Would you like tickets for the tour?" he asked politely.

"Uh, sure." Greasly stepped up to the ticket booth.

The old man counted those present. "Ten adults. That will be seventy moolas."

"Seventy moolas!?" Greasly spat.

"Adult tickets are seven moolas each," the old man explained.

"That's pretty steep, isn't it?"

"The price has been the same for years."

"Fine," Greasly grumbled as he tossed the old man his moola pod. Then he remembered something. "But wait. Not all of us are adults."

"I'm sorry." The old man smiled. "Where are the children?" He looked around the group with a kindly smile.

Greasly pointed out the Flatheads as he named them. "Circle and Square."

"And me," Hardegar's transportation—Legs, as Greasly had started calling him—put in. Criss stepped aside and the old man saw the leather head with green tentacles coming out of it for the first time. Legs waved. The old man cringed.

"I don't think you counted us the first time," Hardegar added.

"How many of you are in there?" The old man asked, perplexed.

"We're two total," Hardegar summed up.

"One adult and one child," Legs clarified. "He's just the head. I'm acting as his temporary mode of transportation."

"Temporary mode of. . . " Benny turned to Greasly. "Children you say?"

"They're only four."

The old man motioned at Legs. "He has a very impressive vocabulary for a four-year-old."

"Not four years—four days, and yes he does."

"I'm sorry, but I will have to charge adult price for all twelve of you. That makes the total eighty four moolas."

"Four days old doesn't constitute a child to you?" Greasly complained.

"I understand that you find it hard to believe," Circle and Square spoke together, "but we really are only four days old."

"Just pay the man, Lou," Groat moaned.

"I will pay him," Greasly affirmed, "but I won't overpay him."

"I'm afraid they do not really qualify for the children's rate."

"Then you shouldn't call it a children's rate. You should call it an embryo rate."

"The children's rate is intended for children in the Human sense. Other races that are fully developed at birth are not eligible."

"Just pay the man," Penny pleaded.

"That's not right," Greasly reproved and crossed his arms. "You shouldn't base rates on something as subjective as—"

"Pay the man!" the rest of the party yelled in unison.

"Or kill him," Cookie growled in a barely audible tone. Groat elbowed him in the side.

"No," Greasly answered, "He should at least give us some sort of a break."

"Oh for the love of. . . I'll pay it." Groat stepped forward in exasperation.

"No, you won't," Greasly countered.

"Sir, I am not allowed to adjust the rates." Benny Gund stood firm. "It's been seven moolas for adults and six point eight moolas for children since the day we opened."

"Christ, Lou! It's only two tenths of a moola difference!" Groat whined.

"It's not the price I'm complaining about. It's their arbitrary application of the child prices."

"No one else has ever complained about it," the old man offered.

"Well, I'm complaining now." Greasly thumped his finger point on the counter.

"Cap'n," Penny cooed, touching his shoulder softly.

"What?" He turned to look at her.

"Pay the man!" she and the rest of the crew yelled again. He scowled at them and motioned to the old man to continue charging his moola pod. "All right, eighty four."

"Thank you, sir, and would you like to include a tip?"

"What do you think?" Greasly glowered.

The old man handed the moola pod back to Greasly. He reached under the counter and produced a handful of tickets, which he began distributing to the group. The first ticket went to Greasly. Greasly examined the ticket. The number of the ticket was 000000001.

"Is this the first ticket you've ever sold?" Greasly asked.

"Yes, sir, it is."

"Are we the first people to visit this place?" Penny asked in disbelief.

"That's right."

"And how long have you been open?" Groat queried.

"Over ten years now." The old man had finished handing out the tickets. He stood up straight and smiled. "Your tour begins in ten minutes. I hope you find it informative and worth the trip."

"Why not start now?" Greasly asked.

"The first tour is at 8:30," the man answered.

"But why wait?"

"Because it's only 8:20. Other guests may arrive."

"We're the first guests in ten years," Greasly reasoned, "what are the odds of someone else showing up?"

"It never rains but it pours," Benny Gund said with a smile and a flourish of his bony hands. He smiled and sat back waiting for other guests to arrive.

Greasly closed his eyes and bowed his head.

"It's okay, Lou," Penny soothed, placing her hand on his shoulder. "It's only ten minutes."

Cookie stepped up and spoke to them both in a quiet tone. "In under ten minutes we could take the entire site."

"Groat, leash your dog," Greasly warned.

"Cookie." Groat motioned him away from the cap'n.

"So where are you all from?" The old man asked nonchalantly.

"Oh, here and there," Greasly said, tapping his finger on the counter.

"Those ships of yours," the old man peered out the glass doors, "they carry much food?"

"Huh?"

"Food, you got food on board right?"

"Of course."

"What kind?"

"Various and sundry."

Benny closed his eyes and breathed in deeply. "Various," he said dreamily. "That's my favorite kind, and sundry's a close second."

Greasly looked at Penny. She had no clue either.

"Describe it," the old man demanded.

"My ship? I can give you a tour."

"No. The food."

"The food?" Greasly wasn't sure how to do that. "Well it's... which kind?"

"Cheese," the old man breathed intently.

"Cheese."

"Yes. Do you have," the old man seemed afraid to even ask, "Cheezy-Whiz?"

"I don't know." Greasly looked around at his crew. None of them were sure either. "Maybe."

"Oh," the old man sighed, smiling, "I love how it comes out all squiggly like a caterpillar—a tasty orange caterpillar." He was lost in reverie.

"Yeah, that's good," Greasly played along.

"You know with all the new-fangled foods, it's still the simple foods that are the best," Gund said. Greasly thought he saw a tear forming at the corner of the old man's eye.

"Sure," Greasly said.

"How did you hear about the museum?"

"Funny story, that." Greasly leaned into the conversation. "We just happened to find it, but last night we did some research and couldn't find any information about it whatsoever."

"I remember squirting it right into my mouth," the old man informed him dreamily.

"What?"

"Cheezy-Whiz. I'd coat my tongue with it and just let it melt."

"Quaint. Now as I was saying, we couldn't find any information about this historical site."

"I'm not surprised really." The old man shook his head sadly. "They passed funding to build the place but then wouldn't spend anything at all to promote it." The old man leaned forward and lowered his voice. "Frankly, I think someone got a huge kickback from the whole deal." He winked at Greasly and nodded knowingly as he sat back.

"That makes sense." Greasly nodded. "It certainly wouldn't be the first time a ridiculous project got pushed through just to pad out someone's account."

"Ridiculous project?!" the old man ruffled.

"Well, not the whole project," Greasly back-pedaled, "but the parking lot is pretty ridiculous."

The old man shrugged and nodded his consent to that.

"And putting it on Frag." Greasly's eyes narrowed. "Why did they do that?"

"Well, this is where the Flummox crashed, but they could just as easily have moved it somewhere else." For a moment he was lost in his own little world of bitterness. Then he snapped out of it. "Well, just two minutes to tour time," he said checking the time. "Say, I don't suppose you would consider possibly sort of trading some foodstuffs at all, would you?"

"Sure!" Greasly assured him, happy to have something to bargain with. "Let's do it now."

"I can't do it now. I have to give a tour soon."

"You do the tour too?"

Benny nodded.

"Is there anyone here other than you?" Penny asked sympathetically.

"Nope," the old man said simply, "I run the whole place."

"A thousand spots in the parking lot and one employee." Greasly shook his head. "I guess it's a lot cheaper to pave than it is to hire, train, and maintain a crew."

Benny nodded. "Might be if I'd ever been paid," he groused and crossed his arms, "even once."

"That's very ironic." Greasly grinned. "I mean you sitting here with the treasure of Bartholomew Methane and being owed so much back pay... The treasure is here right?"

Benny Gund smiled and wagged his finger at Greasly. "Oh no, that would be telling. You'll just have to wait for the... oh!" The old man's features fell into a panic. "The tour! We should have started 2 minutes ago!"

"Oh good. Let's go."

"No no no no no!" Gund was pounding the counter with his fist. Tears were flowing from his eyes.

"What now!?" Greasly was losing his patience.

"I'm late!" the old man wailed. "For the very first tour!" He looked intently at Greasly for a moment. "That's not a good way to start things off," he wailed then broke into tears again. The shutters moved back into place concealing the ticket booth. The crew could hear him behind one of the doors trying to get control of himself; the door was not opening.

Greasly turned to Cookie. "So what's your plan?"

"Lou!" Penny chastised. "The poor man's distraught."

"He's a farking nutter," Greasly corrected.

"A distraught nutter," she compromised.

Chapter 49

At last the door opened, and Benny stepped through. His uniform had changed colors to red with black trim. The title under his name was now "Docent." He sniffled and stood up straight, trying to be brave. "Are you the first tour?"

"No, we're the plumbers, here to fix the sink," Greasly grumbled.

"Yes," Throom answered for him.

"Do you have your tickets?"

"The guy at the ticket booth took them."

"I did not," Benny demanded.

"Just checking your memory," Greasly handed him his tickets. The others followed suit. Benny detached a portion of each ticket and handed back the stub. Then he walked over to the exterior doors and hung up a sign that said "Tour in Progress. Please Wait," locked the doors, and came back to the group.

"I'm very sorry about being late," Benny began, "I got involved talking to one of the customers and—"

"We were there," Greasly interrupted.

"Yes, of course." Benny straightened up and opened his mouth to begin the tour. He seemed surprised when nothing came out. His eyes flitted about as he tried to remember what he was supposed to say. He closed his mouth and rubbed his chin. "Oh dear," he mumbled, "I'm not sure I remember how this goes."

"Don't worry about the spiel," Greasly suggested. "In fact, why not just let us look around on our own."

"Oh no, I can't do that."

"We won't mind," Groat threw in.

"No, it's not allowed on account of the treasure."

"The treasure?" most of the crew asked as one.

Benny's face was anxious. "Oh! I ruined the tour!" His face melted into a mask of sorrow, and he began crying again. "I'm useless. I never should have taken this job!"

Penny stepped up and put her arm around his shoulders. "Hey, hey, don't let it bother you."

Greasly headed for the door behind them and motioned the rest of the crew to follow, but when he had nearly reached it, Benny snapped to attention. "Sir," he warned in an official tone, "you can't go in there alone."

"I'll take them with me." Greasly motioned at the rest of the crew.

"I mean without a tour guide," Benny elucidated.

Penny shook her head slightly to tell Greasly not to go through.

Greasly rolled his eyes. "Okay then, let's get this tour on the road."

"I'm sorry." Benny was back to sobbing again. "It's just that I've waited so long for this day, and now I've buggered it all up."

"No, no you haven't," Penny soothed.

"Well, yes he has," Greasly corrected.

"Shhh!"

"He's right," Benny sniffed.

"No, he's not."

"Yes, I am," Greasly grumbled under his breath.

"Look," Throom suggested, "do you have the tour written down somewhere?"

"Throom," Greasly whined.

"I do," Benny realized. "Wait right here." He hurried into another room.

Greasly moved to open the door Benny had been going to take them through.

"Cap'n," Throom discouraged.

When Greasly turned to look at them, most of his crew was looking at him disapprovingly, but Cookie and Groat pushed their way through to join him.

"Let's go, Lou," Groat said with a jerk of his head.

Greasly looked at his crew again and sighed. With a shrug he conceded. "Let's give him a minute. We don't know what kind of security they have in there anyway."

In spite of himself, Groat had to agree that made sense. They ignored Cookie's exasperated growl.

Benny returned, carrying what looked like a small green plastic rectangle in one hand. He took his place in front of the door and straightened out his jumpsuit. He cleared his throat and held up the rectangle to view it. Paragraphs of text appeared in the air above the rectangle and scrolled smoothly as he read aloud in a stilted and nervous manner.

"Bartholomew Methane is one of the most notorious pirates the space ways have ever known. With a career of crime that began over two centuries ago and lasted until this very ship"—Benny stopped and gestured woodenly at the walls around him—"crashed on this very spot." He motioned around him at the floor. Greasly sighed and shook his head.

"But few people realize that the feared and hated Bartholomew Methane is more widely known under a different name." The old man paused to build suspense. He paused half a second too long.

"Notable Raul," his guests supplied in one voice.

Benny was shocked, but continued anyway. "He was also known as Notable Raul. Can you believe that?"

"Yes, we can," Greasly confirmed.

"Nonetheless, it is true," Gund said, his voice beginning to shake. He mastered his disappointment and continued. "Believe it or not, the lovable 'My nuts!' man is also the notorious pirate, Bartholomew Methane."

"Look," Ratner Groat interrupted, "we know all about this part of the story, so would you mind just skipping ahead?"

Benny looked at his script. "I'm not sure I can do that. It all builds on itself and—"

Greasly snatched the script out of Benny Gund's hand. "Here, let me help." He advanced quickly through the script and then handed it back to the old man. "Here, start here."

Benny looked at the script and read aloud, "And that final most valuable cargo is preserved here behind this very door."

He looked up, tears beginning to well up in his eyes. "But you skipped nearly everything. Aren't you interested?"

"Yes, of course," Penny soothed.

"But we are also in a huge hurry," Groat explained.

"Yeah, we expected to do this tour yesterday after all," Greasly jibed.

Benny was suddenly belligerent. "Well, you can't blame that on me. The hours are the hours!"

"We understand that." Penny put her arm around his shoulder again. "No one's blaming you. Are we, Cap'n?"

"I suppose not."

"There, see?"

"You just don't know what it's been like," Benny blubbered. "I've been alone here since the paving crew left. I thought when I took the job that I would have co-workers or would at least be able to get to know the Fraggarts, but they made some contract with the Fraggarts to keep them outside the protection field."

"A contract with Fraggarts?" Throom was surprised.

"I don't know exactly. They paid some of them to spread stories about the place to scare the rest off or something."

"Ah," recognized Greasly, "That's called a Chopper Sic Balls. They use it with primitive races sometimes."

"Whatever it is, it worked." Benny's bottom lip was quivering. "And even worse than that, I've had nothing to eat but Notable Raul products—Radee-Yums, Sniff-n-Pops, Bran Bombs, Fission Chips. God, I am so sick of Fission Chips!" His whole body was shaking now. "What I wouldn't give for some good old fashioned Cheezy-Whiz!"

"Really?" Greasly thought the time had come to make his offer. "I'll tell you what, Benny. Here's the deal. You come with us, and we buy you all the Cheezy-Whiz you can squirt. We drop you off anywhere you want—within reason—and we give you a decent amount of spending money to boot."

Benny looked at Greasly with rapturous attention. "Away?"

"Yes, and all you have to do is turn off the security around the treasure."

"But why would you want me to do that?" Benny asked in confusion.

"We're going to take it."

"The security system?"

"The treasure."

Benny was stunned. Slowly the light of reason crept across his face. He was obviously having an epiphany. "Of course! The treasure!" His hand slapped his forehead. "Why didn't I think of that? It's the perfect revenge. And... and..." His eyes rolled back in his head as he contemplated it. "Cheezy-Whiz," he said passionately. Greasly and Groat caught him as his knees buckled under him.

"So can we take that as a yes?" Greasly asked.

Benny's head was spinning. "Yes, yes, yes! Oh god, yes!"

"This isn't exactly the situation I was hoping to hear those words in." Ratner quipped with a wink to Criss. She tried to ignore him.

"Benny"—Greasly looked him in the eyes—"the sooner you turn off the security, the sooner you can get away from here."

"Right." Benny stood up and straightened out his jumpsuit. "Right," he reiterated. He scratched his head and stared at the floor. "Now, how to do it." He paced as he mulled the problem over. "Where would those controls be?"

The crew exchanged worried glances.

Benny gently pounded his wrinkled forehead with the side of his bony fist. "Think, Benny, think," he mumbled. Finally he shrugged and said, "I just keep coming back to Cheezy-Whiz. You wouldn't have any on you, would you? Just one can? I'm sure I could think better after that. Do you have any?"

"I don't know!" Greasly exclaimed in exasperation.

"We don't have any on the shuttle," Ratner apologized, "but we do have a hot tub's worth of whipped cream."

"Not quite the same," Benny whined.

"Throom. Go back to the ship and see if you can find some Cheezy-Whiz," Greasly yammered.

"Right," Throom responded and headed out the door.

"While he's doing that why don't you show us around?" Greasly suggested. "Maybe we can help you find those controls."

Chapter 50

Throom exited the Methane Galactic Historical Site annex
and moved across the pavement to the Incorrigible, his
footsteps sounding eerie in the silence. He walked up the
gangway and entered the ship. The exterior door of the
airlock closed, but while he was waiting for the interior door
to open, he felt several strange sounds through the soles of
his feet. There was some sort of commotion occurring on
board.

When the door of the airlock opened, a green Flathead in
the process of fleeing from something was hit by the beam
of a spazzer. He fell, rolled, and came to a stop inside the
airlock to lie there twitching.

Throom quickly stepped into the corridor. A green and a
blue Flathead, both holding spazzers, started at the sight of
him.

"Flathead," Throom snapped, "what's going on here?"

The Flatheads flapped something to each other in
Kravitsian and quickly disappeared around a corner. Throom
pursued as quickly as he could safely pursue, not wanting to
grease any of the Flatheads by accident. As he rounded the
corner he saw that the pair of them were now firing at three
other Flatheads, two green and one hot pink. The targets
were in a panic because there were two more blue Flatheads
at the other end of the corridor trapping them in the middle.

One of the trapped greens fell to the floor twitching,
followed quickly by the other green and the hot pink.

"Hey!" Throom yelled. "Cut that out!"

The spazzers gathered the spazees and dragged them away as quickly as they could. One of the armed Flatheads called out, "Just stay out of it, Throom."

"Not everything is about you," a blue Flathead added.

"At least tell me what's going on."

They were gone. A door opened next to him and a hot pink Flathead poked his hub into the corridor to see if it was safe. Then he motioned Throom into the room with a twitch of his hub. "Come on!" he snapped. Throom quickly obeyed.

When the door closed, Throom squatted down to talk to the pink. "What the hell's going on here, Flathead?"

"I'm not sure what to call it. What's the opposite of a revolution?"

"I don't know." Throom shrugged.

"The Shemps and Jeffies are trying to institute the caste system on board by force. They've even turned some of the Porkies."

"The who and the what?"

"I told you all about the castes before."

"Oh yeah," Throom remembered, "I always just thought of them as colors. I forgot the names."

"The Shemps are blue."

"Those are the top caste, right?"

"Top..." Flathead had to remember how Throom and the Human's thought of top. "Yes, they are the top. Then the Jeffies are next—they are yellow."

"Jeffies are yellow," repeated Throom, trying to memorize it.

"The Porkies are green, then the Caners." He motioned to his own hot pink body. "We're pink."

"Porkies green, Caners pink"

"Then the Mooks are those with mixed color. They are what you would call the bottom."

"Okay, so the Shemps and Jeffies aren't as sold on equality as you are."

"Right."

"But how can you have such different opinions?" Throom puzzled. "Aren't they all you?"

"Yes and no," the pink said as he held up a tentacle and twisted it back and forth.

"I know, I know," Throom dismissed, "Circle and Square explained it, but a few hormones and a few days different experience can't erase all of your old memories."

"Who said my memories were erased?"

"Well, how could they want to go back to a caste system if they remember how much you—I mean they—hated it?"

"We never see the past, Throom, except through the lens of the present," Flathead explained, "and our vision of the present is very much affected by our moods, needs, and wants—things with strong genetic components. Those things can be overcome if you pay attention to them and know them for what they are, but it takes work." Flathead bowed his hub sadly. "I should have seen this coming. This is all my fault."

"You've never been through this before," Throom offered supportively.

"Well, I must have, actually, but it was so long ago I don't remember. But that's not important. It's all part of Kravitsian reproduction, and it hasn't been that long since my last refresher course."

"Oh."

"Naturally they call what they are doing reintegration; each new person adjusting to his proper place." Flathead shook his hub sadly. "Maybe they're right. Maybe I am a freak."

"If you are, then you're my kind of freak." Throom patted him gently. "Let's just worry about this mutiny."

"You're right."

"How serious are they? Would they kill anyone?"

"I don't know. Maybe."

Throom thought the situation over. "Okay, I need you to slip out and go tell the cap'n what's happening. I'll cover you."

"Then what are you going to do?"

"I'm going to get a spazzer and start collecting Shemps and Jeffies."

"Some of the Porkies too—the green ones. Look for the ones spazzing Caners and Mooks."

"Okay," Throom confirmed. "You go tell the cap'n."

They checked to see that the corridor was empty then headed for the airlock.

Throom made sure that the Caner got out of the airlock safely then returned to convert the storage room into a makeshift brig. He started by looking around the room to make sure that there were no weapons or tools that could help prisoners escape. The room appeared empty except for a few crates of vacuum-sealed pork bellies that the cap'n had picked up due to rounding errors when playing the futures market.

Next, Throom went to another supply room and returned with a piece of metal tubing about a meter long and about 20 centimeters wide. From the hallway he punched his fist through the wall of the storeroom just above eye level and stuck the pipe through the hole. He started welding with a pocket welder. When he was done, he had created a tubular chute slanting down from the hallway into the room. He disabled the control console inside the room then exited into the hall and gave the door a quick spot weld to keep it shut.

At last he headed off to start collecting mutineers. Whenever he found some, he spazzed them, gathered them up, and stuffed them ingloriously down the chute. To keep them in, he pinched the end of the tube when he left.

Everything was going quite well until he returned with an armload of spastic Flatheads and found that the pinched end of the tube had been cut off with a pocket welder. Apparently some of the mutineers had happened by, or maybe he had missed a welder when he searched the room. However it happened, several of his captives were working their way out of the chute and scurrying away.

Throom grumbled and deftly stuffed his cargo down the chute onto those attempting an unauthorized egress. He picked up the section that had been cut away and stuffed it into the tube to block the exit. He would have to be much quicker on his raiding trips—especially now that word was out about him being on board. He rushed off to make another collection.

When he rounded the corner into one of the Incorrigible's few wide corridors, he suddenly felt his traction vanish. In fact his weight vanished as well. He was lifted into mid air and was levitating just out of reach of every surface he tried to grab.

Further down the corridor, a yellow Flathead (a Jeffy) was operating a control panel. He waved at Throom with one of his tentacles. "Sorry Throom," the Flathead called, "you should have stayed out of this."

"I'm the first mate, Flathead, how can I ignore a mutiny?"

"It's not a mutiny," Flathead assured him, "it's just house cleaning. For so many years I've been running from some very fundamental truths. I'm finally ready to face facts."

"You haven't been running from anything, Flathead."

"Oh yes I have. I've been denying the entire order of the universe and my place in it."

"Whatever," Throom dismissed. He motioned the thought away with his arm, but it sent him rotating. He twisted until he was steady again and facing his little Jeffy friend. "It still doesn't give you the right to steal the Incorrigible."

"I really am disappointed in you, Throom." Flathead positioned two tentacles in an approximation of arms akimbo. "I'm sharing something very deep and personal with you, and you act as if it's nothing."

"You're right. I'm sorry," Throom apologized as if he meant it. "I was just trying to focus on the point I was trying to make."

"Which was?"

"It doesn't give you the right to steal the Incorrigible!" Throom snapped a little more loudly than he intended. He was spinning in the air again.

As he regained equilibrium, Flathead spoke. "I'm not stealing the Incorrigible. Who said I was stealing the Incorrigible?"

"You did, or rather, another one of you."

"What color?"

"Pink."

"Throom," the yellow Flathead chastised, "are you going to take the word of a Caner over mine?"

Chapter 51

The Caner that Throom had sent to warn the cap'n flapped
his way down the gangway, across the pavement, and
through the glass doors. When he entered the lobby he found
it empty.

"Hello?" he called out.

Klorf quickly appeared from the door that led to the
wreck of the Flummox. He had a spazzer in hand. He aimed
at the Flathead and barked, "Who goes there?"

"It's me. Where's the cap'n?"

Klorf relaxed and motioned through the door. "They are
examining the security system."

"Well, I have to go find him. The Shemps and Jeffies are
taking over the ship."

"Shemps and Jeffies?"

Flathead explained as Klorf led him down into the hulk
of the Flummox, past the three-dimensional displays of
famous skirmishes the Flummox had taken part in, past
Grimshaw's richly decorated cabin, to where the rest of the
group stood gathered around Toby, Groat, and Benny, who
were busy working at a console in the wall.

"Cap'n," Klorf reported in an official tone, "there has
been a disturbance on the ship."

"Hmm?" Greasly grunted, somewhat distracted.

"Did he bring my Cheezy-Whiz?" Benny queried
brightly.

"No," Klorf reported.

Benny grumbled.

"He'll be back soon enough," Ratner Groat placated Benny, drawing him back to the task at hand. "What about this circuit?"

"Several of my brothers are taking over the ship," the pink messenger informed, "the blue ones, the yellow ones, and a few of the green ones."

"Okay," said the cap'n mildly.

After waiting for a moment or two, Klorf reiterated, "Cap'n there has been an armed uprising on your vessel."

Greasly snorted. "Good one, Klorf," he chuckled without looking away from what was going on at the console.

"Excuse me, sir?" From the looks on the faces of the others, he was not the only one confused.

"Armed uprising." Greasly flapped his arms like tentacles. "Good one."

"I did not intend it to be humorous," Klorf stated flatly.

"It's not a joke," the pink Flathead chimed in.

"That's it," Ratner exclaimed, pointing at the console. "Cut the power there."

"I know that's it," Circle and square replied together, "but if I cut that, it brings down the barrier too."

"That would be very bad," Penny reminded them.

"Cap'n. The ship," Klorf interjected.

Cap'n Greasly turned away from the console to face Klorf.

"As security officer it is my duty to defend the ship," Klorf offered.

"Okay," Greasly accepted eagerly, "and bring back environment suits for everyone."

Suddenly there was a loud thump and a rumble resonating from the walls. They all felt the ship move under their feet.

"What was that?" Criss whimpered.

"Did you guys do something?" Greasly asked the trio at the console.

"I don't think we did that," Toby responded.

"Check that out on the way, Klorf." Greasly turned back to the console.

Klorf frowned at the cap'n's manner. He turned on his heel and left the Flummox, followed by the pink messenger.

"Why are they doing this?" Klorf asked Flathead as they walked.

"The cap'n can be very single-minded."

"Not them. Why are you taking over the ship?"

"It's not me. Well, it is sort of, but they're not me any more. We share the same hub, but we're diverging quite rapidly."

"You are saying that none of you can be trusted," Klorf more stated than asked.

Flathead thought that over as they passed through the lobby. "No more than anyone else, I guess," he concluded.

Klorf exited the building in front of him then quickly turned and shut the door.

"Hey!" Flathead complained after smacking into the glass door.

Klorf's only reply was to pluck loose one of the fangs used as buttons on his outfit and shove it in the slit between the door and the jamb to jam it shut.

"What are you doing?"

"I don't want to hurt you, but I cannot trust you."

"But I can help you. Don't leave me here."

"I do not require assistance. You will be safe here."

As Klorf turned toward the Incorrigible, he felt behind him a powerful concussion along with a blast of air and tiny debris that threw him to the ground. When he tried to rise, he felt the stinging of a hundred small lacerations, each still home to a sliver of glass. He gritted his teeth and pushed himself to his feet. He stood in a scattering of broken glass. He turned and saw that the entire glass enclosure had been replaced by a boulder nearly as tall as himself.

Shocked, Klorf tried to look under the boulder, but it had been embedded into the parking lot, how far he could not tell. Then he saw what he had hoped he would not—a smear of blue blood and the tip of a pink tentacle.

Klorf stood and looked quickly around. He soon saw another boulder that he assumed, based on the huge new dent in the tail of the Flummox, had bounced off the hull. That must have been what they all had heard initially. He scrambled on top of the boulder in the entryway to try to get into the building, but the metal roof had been bent downward and he could not get into the lobby.

He saw in the distance a group of grey Humanoids running away. Then he saw another group that seemed to be moving, though not as quickly, toward him. That group seemed to be carrying something boulder-sized and boulder-shaped—possibly a boulder.

Klorf mentally reviewed his weapons. He had only a spazzer—useless against Fraggarts. He looked at the Incorrigible. Her weapons were his only option.

He tried to think of some other way into the ship as he ran toward it, but he knew there were no others he could open from the outside. Running up the gangway would leave him exposed to anyone standing guard in the airlock, so instead he leaped toward the nearest spherical lift pod. There was a squishy sort of thwump as he hit the pod with his arms and palms outstretched. He stuck to the smooth black metal.

Once he was sure that he had a good grip with one hand, he let go with the other and reached down to rip his pants over each of his knees. This freed up his knee suckers. With four points of adhesion he moved fairly quickly up the side of the ship until he was hanging upside down just above the entry to the airlock. A few drops of his reddish brown blood dripped onto the gangway. He took his spazzer in one hand and quickly lowered himself down to where he could see into the airlock. It was empty.

Klorf swung down. Just as he landed, the far door opened and a blue Flathead poked his hub in. The Shemp scrambled to aim and fire his spazzer, but the sight of Klorf glaring at him with his blood-red forehead shocked the Shemp such that he took a fraction of a second too long. Klorf spazzed the Shemp, who fell to the floor a twitching pile of blue tentacles.

Klorf pressed against the wall and aimed at the doorway for several seconds. No one else came through. He carefully checked the corridor. It was clear. He cautiously entered the ship.

Chapter 52

"I've finally decided to listen to my center," the yellow Flathead explained to Throom. "What I was doing here all those years seemed right, but deep inside I knew it was wrong. All I'm doing now is correcting it."

"Flathead, you followed your own path," Throom reasoned. "Do you honestly think that was wrong?"

Flathead bowed his hub a little and said with regret, "It was the path I wished was mine, not the path that was right for me."

"How can you possibly know that?"

"Because I was a Caner," Flathead answered with a touch of condescension.

"Flathead..." Throom tried to think how best to express his thoughts.

"Please don't call me that anymore, Throom," Flathead insisted with distaste.

"I've always called you that."

"It was my Caner name. I have taken the name Darjeelee."

Throom continued, "You told me that you always wanted to be a navigator."

"As long as I can remember."

"And you are the best that I've ever known."

"Thank you."

"And do you remember the burning need you felt to see other worlds—to travel across the stars?"

"Yes," Darjeelee admitted with sadness, "I was filled with lust and passion. Jebus warns us of the danger of that."

"Danger? Of passion?" Throom could not believe that he was hearing his old friend talking this way. "That passion of yours drove you to do what no other Caner had ever done."

"Exactly!" Darjeelee retorted with sudden vehemence. He moved closer to Throom and motioned violently with his tentacles as he spoke. "Untold centuries of peace and harmony, and I flapped it in the hub. That sweet center of my being, of my culture, of all creation—I scorned it."

Throom had no clue how to reason with him on this. How can you disprove something that is purely supposition anyway? When you are dealing with the meaning or the intention of something, how do you verify your guesswork? He ended up just shaking his head as he hovered above the floor. "I don't believe it," he disavowed, "I just can't believe that."

Darjeelee laughed, "Well, why would you?"

Throom thought there was something very insulting about his tone. "What do you mean by that?"

"Well, you know," Darjeelee led, taken a little off guard, "you are... well, you're not Kravitsian."

"That's not all you're thinking."

"Well, it's just..."

"Say it," Throom insisted, anger creeping into his tone.

"It's just that the further you are from the hub the harder it is to accept the truth."

"I don't have any problem accepting the truth," Throom declared, trying to contain his anger, "but this is just nonsense!"

Darjeelee motioned with his tentacles as if to say "See?"

Throom closed his eyes and clenched his jaw. He swung out angrily with all of his limbs but could reach no solid place to push against. He spun uselessly in the air.

"Don't get upset, Throom. It's not a problem with you. You are what you are. And I am what I am."

Throom was spinning as he spoke. "And I suppose it's just a coincidence that you buy into all of this only now that your skin color allows you to be a navigator?"

Darjeelee shrugged. "Some are driven to the hub; others drawn."

"But all your skill and all your knowledge comes from Flathead. It comes from a Caner who you say should have never been a navigator."

"Throom, I know that what I did was wrong. I know you won't believe or even understand this, but Jebus cleansed me of that rebellion."

"You didn't even believe in Jebus!"

"Don't say that name!" Darjeelee snapped with anger that took Throom by surprise. "Lips defile it, let alone stone lips!" Darjeelee started at his own words. He shrunk back abashed.

"Ah," Throom realized, "the rebellious limb and his hard parts—the fall. I get it. You just can't get any worse than me right?" Darjeelee was unable to respond. "Fraggarts have got to be the most evil creatures you could imagine."

"You've been a great friend, Throom. Don't."

"But I'm made of stone, so I'll be going to—what's your trash-heap called? Heck, right?"

"Yes, Heck."

"That's real nice, Flathead."

Darjeelee didn't correct the name. After a moment he spoke. "I didn't make the universe, Throom," he tendered sadly and walked away down the corridor.

Throom spun in confusion and impotence, or, from another point of view, the universe spun in confusion and impotence around him. He covered his face with his hands and tried to deal with his frustration and anger.

It made sense in a way. What if his stone body really was what prevented him from seeing the truth? What if he really was blinded so thoroughly that the lie of there being no hub seemed like the truth? Could it be possible? Of course it could be. But then again, it could also be that the Jordanians were right. In fact, it could be the case that X is the truth. You could put anything you want in place of X, as long as it wasn't testable.

Okay, so if it might be true, why not go ahead and believe it? What was the harm in it? Throom rolled his eyes and shook his head. What was the harm in it? His thoughts were really drifting from reality. He was living the harm in it, as were all the Caners and Mooks.

If it were indeed true, he would have to be forced to believe it by facts colder and harder than himself because it conflicted with something that he knew he believed in. Something that was deep inside even his stony frame. Something that he might not ever be able to prove, but that he would also never be able to deny.

"Throom." A deep voice interrupted his thoughts.

Throom craned his head. Standing on one wall of the spinning corridor, in the same spot that Darjeelee had stood, was Klorf—matter declumpinizationizer in hand.

Chapter 53

"What the fark is going on up there?" Greasly asked after the latest thunderous concussion. There had been two more since Klorf left, and it was getting to be enough to draw everyone's attention from their efforts to disable the security.

"Maybe someone should go find out," Penny suggested mildly.

"I sent Klorf," Greasly replied defensively.

"Maybe he's hurt." Hardegar spoke from his position atop Legs, who was hanging off of a conduit that ran along the wall.

Greasly and Penny looked at each other with sudden concern. "That's true," Greasly looked toward where the lobby was then back to where Toby, Circle, Square, and Groat were wrangling about how best to disable the security. He looked up at Hardegar. "Go find out," he commanded then went back to work on the security problem.

"Me?" Hardegar and Legs yelped in unison.

Greasly stopped and looked back. "Yeah, you. Why not?"

"Well, I'm not exactly the most, uh, efficient person any more. You know?"

"I guess that's true," Greasly conceded. "How about you, Cookie? It could be dangerous. There may be a fight."

Cookie hovered for a moment, weighing being here when the security went down versus a bloody, violent battle with forces unknown. Finally the more attractive option won out. "Right," he declared and headed off.

"So," Greasly continued with the rest of the group. "So far our best option is still to cut all power?"

"So far it is our only option," Circle and Square confirmed.

"Well, maybe we should just get serious about that one. We should all get on board the Incorrigible. Then Throom can shut down the power and cart the goodies up to us."

"Hey," Groat complained, "I want at least one of my people here."

"You don't trust me? Stupid question, I know. I should have asked: 'You don't trust Throom?'"

"I supposed I do," Ratner confessed, "but I still want to be here."

"I thought Throom was bringing environment suits back," Penny recalled, "so we could all stay."

"He is. But why risk being here when we don't have to?"

"Why?" They repeated his question with an "are you serious?" flavor.

"It's the treasure of Bartholomew Methane!" Legs and Hardegar intoned together.

"Well, I'm sorry, but you two definitely have to go back to the ship. There's no environment suit that will fit you. Or you either." This last was directed at Circle and Square.

Just then Cookie came scurrying down to Groat. "We are under attack from the Fraggarts," he reported. "They're throwing huge boulders."

"I thought Fraggarts never came here." Greasly turned to Benny, somewhat accusingly.

Benny shrugged. "They never did before."

"The door we came in is blocked by a rock," Cookie apprised—then to Benny, "Is there another way out?"

"No," Benny whimpered, his concern rising.

"Do we have a matter declumpinizationizer?" Toby asked.

"No," Greasly answered.

"Is there any equipment in here that could move something that large?" Groat asked Benny.

"Nothing." He was beginning to shake.

"So we're trapped in here," Groat summarized, "And out there…"

"My Cheezy-Whiz," Benny mewled, choking back a tear.

The room around them shook with another concussion. The lights flickered and dimmed then regained full brightness.

"Where's the power plant?" Penny asked Benny breathlessly.

"Behind the lobby. Next to my quarters."

"If it gets hit, will the power go out?" she asked. It dawned on all of them, even Benny.

"The barrier!" they barked in unison.

Chapter 54

Throom tried to ignore the fact that Klorf was aiming a matter declumpinizationizer straight at his head. He especially tried to ignore the fact that the red deactivation light was not lit. "Klorf," he called out as if nothing were wrong, "get one of the pink Flatheads over here to turn off this gravity field."

"I'm sorry, Throom," Klorf said instead.

"No, don't be sorry. Do it."

"I saw you here and knew I had no choice. I am honor bound to do this thing."

"No, you're not. I wouldn't think any less of you if you just got me free and forgot about the whole thing."

"You are not even a Vadnu. You cannot know of cling-on honor."

"Cling-on honor?" Throom's annoyance at the way his day was going began to bubble to the surface. "Shooting a helpless person because of an accident?"

"You killed my master," Klorf reasserted.

"Do you honestly think I killed Kurplupt on purpose?"

"No, I do not, but his dying wish was that I avenge him."

"So? Maybe this time he doesn't get what he wants."

"But I am honor bound to—"

"Who's honor, Klorf!?" Throom snapped. "I don't believe for a second that this is *your* honor. You do not want to do this, or you would have already done it."

"It is a heavy burden, but I cannot set it down." He seemed genuinely torn.

"So your only problem here is the sense of honor that the flapulates gave you."

Klorf seemed to know he should fire but could not yet bring himself to do it.

"They made it up to fit their needs, Klorf. Not yours."

"Honor is not about what you need," Klorf declared. "It is about what's expected of you."

"Yes. What they expect from you. The flapulates."

"Not only them—all Vadnus. It is not something you can understand."

"Why not? How is it different from the Fraggart code of honor? I understand that."

"And could you go against the Fraggart Code?"

"I have more times than I can count."

"You admit that you are without honor?"

"I'm not without honor," Throom insisted, "but it is my honor—not theirs. It is based on my values—not theirs. It serves me—not them."

"You are self-centered and arrogant," Klorf growled with disgust.

"Does that describe me, Klorf?"

"You dare to re-define honor to fit your own selfish—"

"Does that describe me? Am I self centered and arrogant?"

"I would not have thought so until you said—"

"Do you honestly think the flapulates have any more insight into what is good and right than I do?"

"That has no bearing on this."

"Of course it does, Klorf. Because you are saying that I am arrogant and selfish because I define honor for myself, and yet you accept the definition that the flapulates came up with without question."

"No." Klorf's fist tightened on the declumpinizationizer. "The flapulates did not define honor. It was told to Sliptuplitut by Shlunt himself."

Throom sighed in exasperation. He recognized Shlunt as a Vadnu word for God. Once again it came down to an unarguable; once again he was left with no foothold. "Whatever," Throom breathed sadly as he twisted uselessly in midair. "Shlunt may be real, he may not be. He may know everything, he may not. But this just comes down to you and me, Klorf. Either you kill me, or you don't. You know I've never intentionally harmed you or Kurplupt. You know I've risked my life to save you. You know I've always tried to be a friend to you. You can tell yourself any sort of nonsense that you want, but when you pull that trigger, you, Klorf, will kill me, Throom. And that will be the long and the short of it."

Klorf stood in silence for a moment, his jaw quivering noticeably.

Then he fired.

The back right portion of Throom's head exploded as the declumpinizationizer beam hit it. He was very lucky that Klorf had lowered the power of the weapon to minimize damage to the ship. It only blasted away a fist-sized portion of his head instead of most of his body. Even so, the force of the explosion sent Throom spinning in the air with enough force that his flailing arm slammed into the floor as he spun.

Throom assessed the flood of sensory information surging into his consciousness. He knew that a good chunk of his head had been declumpinizationized, but he also knew something else: his right hand had hit the floor. His hand had hit the floor and because of how he was spinning, it would hit again.

Klorf steadied his shaking hand to take another shot. He was finding this one to be harder than the first. Not because Throom was spinning, but because the entire situation had changed.

The honor and duty of it had gone with that first shot. It had all evaporated as the mind-numbing inexorability of his action flooded his being with a sensation akin to terror.

Now it was just like Throom had said. Now he was acting in cold, harsh brutality. But he had been taught that this was where the soul of a cling-on was truly tested. Here in this twilight of thought. He had had two paths. Only the strength of his spirit would keep him to the right one now— that and the knowledge that the other path had vanished with the pull of his trigger.

Throom's hand hit the floor again. This time he grabbed at the floor with all of his strength. His fingers punctured the flooring material enough for him to hold on. The rest of his body flailed in a complicated motion—his grip acting as a fulcrum. Throom was now essentially hanging upside down from the floor. He quickly thrust with his free hand and pulled himself down with the other. His thrusting hand crashed through the floor.

Klorf fired again at Throom's midsection, but Throom's punch had disabled the field generator and, without the artificial gravity, his stone body was acted upon by the gravity of Frag. He fell to the floor instantly. The floor shook so much that Klorf lost his footing and stumbled. His shot missed Throom and took out part of the wall.

Throom rolled over and pulled the field generator out from the floor. He held it ready to throw at Klorf, who had just readjusted his grip on the matter declumpinizationizer.

"Stop, Klorf!" Throom pleaded. There was no chance of simply disarming him.

Shaking, Klorf took aim at Throom.

There was a simultaneous declumpinizationizer blast and crash. A splattering of brownish red blood sprayed across the wall of the corridor. Throom's body fell to the floor. The blast had taken a chunk out of his right arm near the shoulder. Throom had no blood, but he felt something draining from him none the less as he lay there motionless. He knew that he would still be able to use the arm, but just then he didn't feel like using it or any other part of his body. At that moment he wanted deeply to be like the rocks of the hills—laying silently for ages on end, slowly eroding into dust.

Chapter 55

"Go!" Greasly shouted. He, Groat, and Cookie strained against the rock that blocked the exit. Their feet slid across the floor as they grunted and pushed. Penny leaned in to try to help, but there was only room for three to push effectively—the rest of the rock being blocked by the crushed-in roof. The rock did not budge. They stopped shoving and slumped to the floor panting.

"This isn't working," Groat wheezed.

Greasly agreed.

Benny entered the lobby followed by Criss, Toby, Circle, and Square. They all carried at least one tool or container of some sort. They tossed it all on the floor. Benny got down on his knees and opened the box that he had just set down. Legs entered the room with tools in some of his tentacles and with Hardegar on top of his hub. Hardegar carried a spanner in his mouth.

Greasly and the others made their way over to the pile and, along with the others, started pawing through the tools to try and find something that could help them. "Is this a pivot-pot lancer?" Greasly asked in surprise.

"Yes, left-handed," Benny confirmed off-handedly.

Greasly tossed it away.

"Look at this furtwangler." Penny turned the object over in her hands. "They don't make them like this anymore."

"A spladium. A corvonite thracher, A fleen-woosh mascanon," Toby enumerated. "Where did you get all this junk?"

"What's this thing?" Circle asked, holding the object up for inspection.

"Sonic screwdriver," Benny answered.

"Silly name," Circle mumbled and discarded it.

"Aha!" Benny chortled as he pulled an object out from deep in a tool box. "I knew I'd seen you in here, you little devil." He clicked a button on the pocket welder and a white-hot flame about 8 centimeters long appeared, shooting out of the device. He let up on the button and the flame disappeared.

"Gimmee," Greasly demanded.

There was another concussion. The room shook, and they all had to grab onto something to keep from falling down. The lights dimmed. They all held their breath. Then the lights went back up.

"You keep looking," Greasly headed to where the metal roof was bent down, barring their way. "In case this doesn't work."

Toby met him at the large stone. "I think you should cut here where the metal is creased." He traced the crease with a finger.

"Why there? There's less to cut if I go across here."

"True, but there are three layers of metal, and if you cut where the crease is, you should be able to get through all of them with one cut. The flame is only so long you know."

"Makes sense to me." Greasly shrugged, impressed by Toby's forethought, and started cutting.

"A tropsnart! I haven't seen one of these since I was a kid," exclaimed Circle. "Last time I was a kid," he corrected.

"That looks like a kloop," Hardegar reported to Legs. Legs dropped the kloop and held up another object for inspection.

"By the Travelling Mines of Oon!" Benny suddenly cried out. "I can't believe our luck!"

They all stopped what they were doing and watched—not sure how much to let themselves hope—as Benny dumped the contents of the box he had been pawing through onto the floor. He bent his aged frame and shoved aside items until he got to the metal cylinder. He held it triumphantly aloft then lovingly to his breast.

"What is it?" Penny inquired.

Benny didn't seem to hear her. Instead, he shook the cylinder then tilted his head back and stuck out his tongue. He squirted the bright orange cheeze into his mouth and closed his eyes. As he savored it, a tear ran down his cheek.

The others grumbled and went back to work.

The ceiling bent violently inward as another boulder hit just above them. Sparks and debris flew as the lighting was destroyed. They all dove momentarily for cover. When they stood again, the room was dark, but they could still see due to light filtering through from outside and from the other rooms.

"Jebus!" Greasly cried as if in pain. "I lost the welder!"

Penny and Groat scrambled over to help Greasly look for the missing welder.

"We have to find it!" Penny screamed.

"I know that!" Greasly snapped. "Just look."

"Where were you when the last one hit?" Groat asked.

"Right about here, and I jumped down like this. I'm not sure how I lost it."

"Criss!" Groat called out, "Come here, Criss!"

The Lumarian scrambled quickly over. "What is it?"

"He lost the hand torch," Groat apprised. "I need you to find it."

"But what do I know about hand torches?" she balked.

"It doesn't matter. It's lost—like my keys were. Help us find them."

Reluctantly she closed her large eyes and breathed in deeply. She held her hands out as if examining the area with her fingertips.

"We don't have time for—" Greasly began, but was shushed by both Groat and Criss.

"I sense it," she announced. "It is in this area. But not where you have been looking."

"So, it's not over here." Groat motioned where they had been searching. "It must be here." He turned and started looking in another area.

"This is ridiculous!" Greasly snapped. "How could it get over there?"

"It's the only other choice." Groat insisted.

"It is there," Criss stated with uncharacteristic certainty, her eyes still closed.

"Forget them," Greasly advised Penny. "Keep looking here."

"It is not there," Criss said flatly. "It is over there."

"It is not!" Greasly barked, then to Penny, "Keep looking here."

"I found it!" Groat stood and held the pocket welder out to Greasly.

For a second he stood there, the target of Groat and Criss's "I told you so" looks. Then, scowling, he grabbed the welder and went back to work.

Groat put his hand on Criss's shoulder and looked into her large watery eyes. "Criss, baby," he cooed softly, "you've earned some very good lovin'."

"No, no, no!" Greasly wailed. He pounded the pocket welder against his palm, but the flame still sputtered and died. He tossed it limply aside and looked weakly at the unfinished cut. He turned to the group. "Have you found anything else to cut with?"

"Nothing," Circle reported.

"And we've looked through everything," Square added, tossing a spon detector into an atomic dustbin.

"Help me try and bend this," Greasly snapped. Several of them rushed over and they strained to bend the metal open far enough to let them get out, but failed even to make a gap large enough for a Kravitsian.

Another boulder strike sent them scurrying for cover. The lights in the other room went out. Groat scrambled to examine the situation. "There's still power," he called back. "Just the lights were destroyed."

"So, what now?" Penny cried.

"Well, Klorf and Throom are still out there," Greasly reminded her. "One of them will rescue us at the last minute."

"So, we just sit here and wait for the last minute?" Toby queried.

"But there's two of them out there," Groat pointed out. "Does it still work if there are two?"

"Of course, if they are acting as one unit."

"Are you forgetting all of the Kravitsians?" Circle asked, somewhat annoyed.

"But they're in mutiny."

"Not all of us!" Square protested.

"Oh yeah," Greasly conceded with concern, "so we have 30 or so people out there."

"That doesn't seem nearly unexpected enough," Groat worried.

"Nope," Greasly admitted, stroking his chin. "I don't think we can count on that."

"This is insane," Penny complained. "The more people are out there, the more likely we are to be rescued."

"You'd think so, wouldn't you?" Ratner Groat nodded. Then he shook his head, "But it doesn't work that way."

"I explained this to you once," Greasly lectured Penny.

"I know you did, but it's ridiculous," Penny growled.

"True, though," Groat said with a shrug and put his arm around her shoulder as if about to explain it all in terms that even she could understand. She slapped his arm away.

"Don't touch me," she snapped. "You two and your stupid superstitions are no help at all. What we need is a lever of some sort."

"Right," Toby jumped in on her side. He was standing near the blocked exit and quickly did some estimating. "Looks like the longest we could get in place would be about two meters." He and Penny started sorting through the rubble.

"What about Jones?" Groat posited to Greasly.

Greasly brightened. "Yeah! We are all in trouble, and Jones rescues us. That sounds good."

"Here!" Penny shouted, pointing to a long piece of metal. Toby rushed over, and they pulled it free.

"You really think so?" Groat pondered.

Greasly's expression changed. He shook his head. "Not really."

"Pull," Penny commanded. She and Toby pulled together. They had jammed it into the slit that Greasly had created with the torch and as they pulled the metal roof bent slightly with an echoing creak. "Somebody else help. Benny? Criss?"

Benny and Criss hurried over and grabbed hold, but there was barely room enough along the bar for all of them to pull. "Criss, your head is in the way," Penny informed.

"We're not getting enough torque, anyway," Toby appraised. "I'll hold on to the end and all of you pull on me." They quickly rearranged themselves. Penny wrapped her arms across the Xemite's chest from behind. Criss grabbed Penny's waist. A pair of male hands reached around Criss and grabbed her breasts.

"Benny!" Criss gasped. She turned to confront the old man but was face to face with Ratner Groat instead.

"Hey baby." He winked. She slapped him.

"Hurry up!" Penny yelled.

They quickly formed a chain that included everyone, even Groat and Greasly, and gave a pull. The metal bent back easily.

Penny looked at Greasly and dusted off her hands with a self-satisfied look.

"Good work, Penny," Greasly commended. "Circle! Square! Get through there and head straight to the ship to let Throom know what's going on. Don't stop for anything." They quickly obeyed.

Another boulder hit. It felt like it hit the Flummox itself this time instead of the annex.

Hardegar and Legs exited the annex, followed by Benny, then Penny.

"Criss, will you be able to fit through there?" Groat asked with genuine concern.

"The future is cloudy," she said—eyes closed, hands feeling the Universe.

"Just try it!"

"Oh," she said and bent down to try and crawl through the gap. Her head was too large to fit, so she sucked it in. The melon-like head shriveled like a deflating balloon until it was about the size of a normal Humanoid head.

Groat's jaw dropped.

Greasly's eyebrows rose. "Did you know she could do that?"

Groat shook his head, remembering the trouble they had gone through over an environment suit for her.

She had her head through now, but her breasts were too large to make it through. "Uh oh," Groat mumbled. Then he yelped as Criss' breasts shriveled up as the head had done. She made it through the hole without further incident.

"Come on Ratner," Greasly said to his shaken archenemy and climbed through the hole.

Chapter 56

When Groat exited he seemed very relieved to see Criss back to normal in all of her appendages. Hardegar and Legs were already at the base of the gangway and heading up into the ship. The others were waiting until everyone was out.

"Okay, we're all here," Greasly confirmed. "Let's go."

They started to make a run for the ship, but when they were nearly to the gangway a Fraggart came out from under it. The group stopped in their tracks. The Fraggart called out "Hey! Guys! Over here!" and several other Fraggarts came out from behind the gangway. One of them dropped a large chunk of metal that Greasly assumed had once been part of the Incorrigible.

"Lou?" Penny asked tremulously.

"Uh," was all he could think to say as he watched four Fraggarts come between themselves and the gangway of the ship.

"Back inside!" Benny screamed as he rushed past them.

"Yeah," Greasly agreed.

But before they could get back to the historical site, another boulder smashed into the entrance—blocking it off again.

"We have to scatter," Ratner Groat assessed breathlessly. "They can't get all of us."

"Yes, they can," Penny cried. "All they have to do is stand on the gangway!"

"These are Fraggarts," Greasly assured her. "They won't think of that. Groat and I can try to distract them all, but even if we can't draw them all off, you will have to make a run for it."

"Why us?" Groat yelped. "Are you forgetting the first rule of longevity? I'm not even a cap'n, and I know it."

"I remember it. 'When risk is great, delegate.' " He looked at Penny. "I'm not doing this as the cap'n," he admitted.

Penny's eyes glittered as she absorbed what he was telling her. Greasly turned and ran toward the Fraggarts that were running gleefully with thunderous strides toward them.

"Wait!" Penny cried, but he was already less than two meters from the stone Humanoids. He ducked suddenly to the side and out of reach. All four of the Fraggarts went after him as he lead them toward the tail of the ship and away from the gangway.

"Come on!" Groat called back to them as he ran not toward Greasly but toward the bottom of the gangway.

They followed quickly, silently, and breathlessly except for Benny. He toddled with the speed of a strolling cheetah, his unfirm fist raised to the sky, shouting at the top of his aged lungs: "Cheeeeeezy Whiiiiiiiz!"

Penny lagged even behind Benny because she was watching Greasly dart and dodge to avoid four angry Fraggarts. She noticed with alarm that three more were running at him from behind.

"Lou!" she screamed. "Behind you!"

One of the Fraggarts chasing him turned to look at her. He broke off and sprinted toward the gangway that everyone but she and Greasly was running up.

Penny also sprinted as hard as she could and tried to focus on getting every bit of speed instead of watching the mountain of stone closing in obliquely on her path. It was looking like they would collide at the base of the gangway, but she knew that the Fraggart's huge mass meant he would have to start slowing down before he got to the base; otherwise he would never be able to change direction to go up the gangway. This he did, and she hit the gangway several seconds before he set foot on it. She saw that the doors of the airlock were starting to close. As she ran, she unzipped her forehead and took out Mini-Penny. Criss and Benny were there yelling at her to hurry.

The gangway shook violently. The Fraggart was running on it. The vibration caused Penny to fall meters from the closing airlock. She threw the spider toward the door. It hit the interior wall and flopped onto the floor of the airlock, out of her sight. Penny rolled onto her back and saw the Fraggart thundering down on her. She continued her roll entirely off of the gangway and landed back-down on the shock-absorbing paving material of the parking lot. The jolt was enough to knock the wind out of her. She felt the impact as the Fraggart jumped off the gangway too.

For several seconds that seemed to last several minutes, Penny tried to fill her lungs as she stumbled forward, but her lungs would not respond. Darkness seemed to be closing in around her vision. Her head was feeling light. She realized with terror that her elbow was resting on the ground, which meant she was not running. She lurched forward and only fell onto her face on the pavement. Then she felt hands gripping her sides and hefting her off the ground. At last her lungs responded and gulped sweet air.

She reached down and grabbed the arms that were carrying her to pry them off, but when she touched them she realized that they were not stone but flesh. She looked up and saw Greasly's face, red and panting, as he tried to run while carrying her. He was looking all around and changing direction. She could tell from his movements that he was running out of places to run. She looked around and saw that they were surrounded by over a dozen Fraggarts, and the circle was closing in on them.

"Put me down," she panted, "I can run." When she hit the ground she saw that the Incorrigible was lifting off. The last bit of gangway retracted as the ship rose.

"Where are they going?" Penny yelled after the Incorrigible.

"I don't know," Greasly panted. "Depends on who's piloting."

She started jumping and waving her hands at the ship as best she could in her exhaustion.

"Don't," Greasly said, grabbing her arm. "Rest. Get as much strength back as you can while they close in. You'll need it to try and get through them."

She looked at the circle of Fraggarts and saw that they were closing in cautiously, arms spread out, legs bent, so they could quickly move to block any attempt to escape.

"Concentrate. Breathe deeply," Greasly advised softly. "Close your eyes. I'll tell you when to open them."

She did as he said.

He held her to him, partly to comfort her and partly because if he had to die, he wanted to be in her arms before it happened. She hugged him back tightly.

"Breathe," he reminded himself as much as Penny. She tried to, but her breath caught in her throat and became a sob instead. "Don't cry Penny," he insisted, his own voice cracking, "focus."

Holding her had been a bad idea; he couldn't bring himself to let her go. He wanted her now, and he could not desert her. He held her out at arms length.

"Focus," she said with a nod.

"You're getting out of this."

"Yes," she tried to convince herself.

"When I run, you follow me."

"Right."

"And you jump over them," he said.

"Over them?" she was confused now. "I can't jump that high."

"I'm going low," he said with significance, "ahead of you."

The image flashed in her mind: Greasly leaping toward the ground between two of the Fraggarts and then, as they bent over to grab him, her vaulting over the top.

"You won't make it."

"I will. Just don't stop for anything. Anything."

She nodded. The Fraggarts were very close now.

"Ready?" he asked, but before she could answer he was running toward a pair of Fraggarts. They quickly moved toward each other to close the gap. The others moved to close the new gaps they had left.

Greasly had just ducked down, preparing to dive between the Fraggarts and Penny was close behind when they were stopped short by an explosion. They hit the ground. When Penny looked up, the two Fraggarts were gone, replaced with rubble.

The other Fraggarts had stopped and were shouting and pointing at the Incorrigible, which blasted several more of them. A single survivor yelled with delight and grabbed up a chunk of one of his colleagues but was blasted to bits before he could throw it at the ship. Penny and Greasly breathed a sigh of relief and smiled at each other, each breaking into cathartic laughter.

* * *

After Throom cleared the parking lot of Fraggarts with the ship's guns, he and the loyal crew and guests rounded up the mutineers. They locked all of the Shemps in one cabin, all of the Jeffies in another, and—just for the sake of safety—they locked all of the Porkies up too. Several Caners and Mooks were given spazzers and posted as guards.

Then Throom explained to them all why he was missing portions of his body and what had happened to Klorf. Perhaps there is a limit to how many emotions people can feel in a day, but the response seemed more muted than Throom had expected. Throom didn't know it, but later, when they had some peace and time for reflection, this tragedy would bubble up like the eruption of an undersea volcano. At that time the tragedy and horror of it would be overwhelming for those that had known Klorf, but for now it was simply noted and logged with a weary respect. They had too much left to do.

Greasly used the Incorrigible to blast a hole in the historical site annex and destroy the power supply. The pinpoints of light spreading into the distance across the parking lot fell dark.

The historical site shared the same poisonous atmosphere as the rest of Frag when Throom walked into what was left of the Flummox.

Chapter 57

As Throom pawed his way through the rubble of the pirate ship, he thought about its former owner—how at one time he had been riding high on top of the system that eventually took everything he had away from him—how they had laid claim to his face, his ideas, everything he had. Throom passed the displays representing the battles the Flummox had survived. What had those battles been like? Was it he or one of his crew that was such a brilliant tactician? At least they had never come close to owning that.

Throom found his path blocked with more debris than he cared to move. He instead took a detour through Grimshaw's cabin. When he stepped through the door, he was taken by surprise. The cabin was decorated with objects of art from all over the galaxy. Beside the bed was an ancient oil lamp, and on a shelf were things that Throom thought, from the look of them, could only be books.

Throom tore down the protective plastic that most of the room had been coated with. He moved his stone fingers over the bindings of the books. He pulled one off the shelf and opened it, smiling at the low-tech ingenuity of the design. His fingers were not formed for this sort of fine manipulation, and the first book that he looked at ended up tattered and torn. He dropped the damaged copy of Emerson to the floor and pulled another book from the shelf. He read the title: *Leaves of Grass*. He chuckled at such a large mechanism being used to hold so few words. He set the book on the bed. Then he realized that it was not a bed. The top was covered with a decorative cloth, but there was no cushion under the cloth. Instead there was a plastiglass case.

Throom picked up the book and pulled the cloth away. Inside the clear box were the remains of a Human. The flesh was little more than dust, and the skeleton looked as if it had been broken apart and reassembled, but the eye patch was still in place. Was this really him? Whether it was or not, they thought it was. They had reassembled him here as part of the exhibit. Throom stared at the remains for several moments. He had been wrong to think that they had not owned Bartholomew Methane, the pirate. They had indeed. They encased him in plastic and made even his death a commodity. Throom felt a new sadness for this tortured man.

Throom brought himself back to his task. He moved to another wall, tore down the protecting plastic, and carefully moved the art that hung there to the other side of the cabin. Then he smashed his way through the wall. When he reached the cargo hold, he began smashing through the plastiglass that covered the opening. This turned out to be no easy task. So instead he ripped through the wall next to it.

Inside were a handful of shipping crates—all closed. The museum designers had not displayed the contents. That didn't bode well. It may have been some purist instinct on the part of the preservationists, or (more likely) they knew they could sell a mystery easier than whatever really lay inside those crates.

It took Throom several trips to bring the storage crates and a few other valuable-looking items out of the Flummox to stack them in the airlock of the Incorrigible.

His last trip in was to load up the artifacts from the cabin of Bartholomew Methane, but he found himself unable to do it. He stood there frozen, holding a sculpture over the open crate he had brought in. He could not bring himself to pack it.

Throom could not escape the fact that these had been the things Grimshaw had collected for himself. These were the things that he had found beauty in. This cabin was the world he had built for himself out of the ashes they had left him. Throom knew that the things in the cargo hold represented nothing more than wealth to Raul Grimshaw—that was why he was squirreling them away on a hellhole like Frag—but these things... these things he kept with him. These were the things of true value to him.

Throom pondered the situation. The odds of the rest of the treasure being of any value in the current market were slim, while these things were obviously priceless. The others had sent him in to collect anything of value. They were trusting him.

Throom looked at the eye patch for a long time then picked up the book he had torn, put it together as best he could, and set it carefully back onto the shelf. He replaced *Leaves of Grass* and, with a sigh, returned to the surface empty-handed.

Throom knew that eventually Benny would mention the artifacts, and the rest of the crew would accuse him of underhandedness. At that time he would explain as best he could, and they would have to accept that explanation or come get the goods themselves. Maybe they would do that; maybe they would not. He knew he would not.

Chapter 58

The Incorrigible was floating silently in orbit of Frag when everyone but Jones, Stuart, and those in the brig gathered in the mess to open the treasure. Before they opened the boxes, they went over the distribution scheme again. After about an hour and a half of debate, they finally got it all settled and opened the ancient storage containers.

To everyone's dismay the first storage container was filled with bars of gold-pressed latinum—total value about 10 moolas, 20 moolas if you could find a backwater world where it was still a controlled commodity. The second container was filled with quatloos—useless since the games on Triskelion had closed down. The third, however, contained sporks—the street value of which would be enough to pay for nearly all of the damages their ships had sustained, as long as they were careful how they spent it.

Feeling a little better because they would at least not go in the hole on this expedition but not wanting that to be all they got for their efforts, they prepared to open the last storage container. Groat stood ready to throw the container open, and everyone held their breath. Hardegar seemed to be uttering a silent prayer, while Legs crossed his tentacles. Penny was bouncing up and down, opening and closing her hands. Throom looked on with particular anxiousness. Benny—who was in ecstasy with a can of Cheezy-Whiz— paid little attention.

"Do it," Greasly said.

Groat opened the container and revealed that it was full to bursting with ancient packages of Bran Bombs. General moans, complaints, and curses filled the room. Unable to believe it, Groat started digging through the packages tossing them out left and right—making sounds half way between a cry and a growl as he did.

"Maybe we can still make something off all of this," Greasly was plotting. "How much do you suppose the Galactic Historical Society would pay for these?"

They started a lively discussion on the possibility, but it was cut short when Groat exclaimed, "Hold on! What's this?" They turned to see Groat manipulating what appeared to be a rivet. "This moves. I think it—" There was a click as a secret panel in the side of the trunk popped open.

Groat was afraid to move at first, fearing he would jinx the moment. Then he gingerly reached in and grabbed the thing in the secret compartment and raised it to his eye level.

They all rushed over to where he held a fine titanium case about the size of a deck of cards. No one breathed as he opened the case.

It contained an iridescent marble resting in red velvet.

"Fark me Jebus," Greasly muttered in complete awe—his knees weakening.

"It's beautiful," Penny sighed. "What is it?"

The others looked at her with disbelief. "Are you kidding?" Groat asked.

She hugged herself and figited. "No."

"It's a rebob," Greasly revealed with reverence.

"Are they worth much?" she asked cautiously.

They laughed. They wanted to answer her, but they all laughed instead.

"A lot?" she asked.

Greasly nodded heartily. The others were dancing about in ecstasy.

"A lot lot?"

Greasly finally brought himself to speak. "A lot lot!" He grabbed her and spun her around.

They all danced around the room hugging each other, laughing, and crying.

Throom breathed a sigh of relief.

Chapter 59

Perhaps it was because the haul had been beyond all expectations that they decided not to press charges against the mutineers, or maybe it was because it threatened to be very complicated if they did—what with the ambiguous status of the Flatheads and the fact that they were all engaged in robbing a Galactic historical site when the incident occurred. Whatever the reason, they decided to drop the Kravitsians off at Kravits Rock on their way to square the rebob away on Sol.

Since neither Greasly nor Groat trusted the other, they attached The Other Woman to the back of the Incorrigible and agreed to travel together until the rebob was safely in a vault.

Once at Kravits Rock, the sporks were liquidated and the money used to pay off the children of Flathead. It took some arguing to get the mutineering Kravitsians to be happy with the payoff, but the fact that the alternative was being shot for their crime tipped the scale.

Greasly put Circle and Square in charge of sorting out which of the Porkies had remained loyal. The loyal ones got the same amount that the Caners and Mooks did, which was three times the amount given to the mutineers, and it turned out to be nearly the same amount they had hoped to get in the first place. So all of the Kravitsians except for three went off to Kravits Rock with a very tidy sum to their credit.

While on Kravits Rock, Legs led a memorial ceremony for the Flatheads that had died on Frag. They then returned the remains that they had scraped off the wall of the shuttle and those they had scraped off the boulder to the nearest bio-recycling unit.

Circle and Square stayed on as full crew members—each with a full share, and Legs stayed on as Hardegar's lower members—content to split a share with him. In fact the latter pair were starting to work so well together that by the time the ship arrived at Vadnu the rest of the crew were all starting to think of Hardegar and Legs as one entity. Legs had even started simulating Hardegar's voice when he spoke, so you could seldom tell which of the pair was actually speaking.

The others would often hear what sounded like Hardegar flapping through the corridors arguing to himself about The Bible and The Floppy. Throom noticed that more and more they seemed to be mixing the two together indiscriminately. They would most likely end up creating yet another religion. He had no doubt that he would be considered an abomination in that one too.

After Kravits Rock, Greasly convinced Groat to make one more stop. He said that before they "cashed in" their rebob and all started living a life of luxury, it seemed appropriate to get one last sorrowful task out of the way. So they all headed to Vadnu to take care of one last funeral.

Chapter 60

The Incorrigible hovered over the waters of Vadnu while the cargo bay door opened. Inside the hold, Greasly, Circle, Square, Hardegar, Legs, Throom, and Penny stood gathered to return the remains of Klorf to the place from which they had come.

"Bow 'em if you got 'em," Greasly intoned. They all looked at the body bag that was shaped like Klorf with the notable exception that it lacked a head. "We are here today to say goodbye to a loyal and efficient security officer: Klorf. He was a cling-on driven by duty even to the very end, and he died trying to fulfill the last wish of his master." Greasly paused a moment in silence. "Anyone have anything else to say?"

Penny was wiping away the tears flowing down her face. She looked at Throom as if she expected him to speak. He only stood with his head down. The fist-sized chunks that were missing from the back of his head and his upper right arm were very conspicuous just then. She knew that he could spend a portion of his finite energy to "heal" those wounds. She was sure that in time he would.

Finally she cleared her throat, sniffled, and spoke. "Klorf was a good friend, and we will all miss him," she began, "but I cannot praise his honor and duty," she struggled to keep her voice from cracking, "because they blinded him to the things..." She had to pause. She tried again, "the great things that ..." She wasn't going to get it out. "He didn't know what he had," she blurted then started sobbing.

Greasly put his hand on her back to comfort her. After a few moments he turned to Throom.

"Throom?"

Throom considered what he might say. He was unhappy with himself that he was still bitter about what Klorf had done to him and, worst of all, what Klorf had forced him to do. Maybe it was just too soon to expect himself to forget something like this.

He looked over the smooth surface of water that stretched far into the distance to a gently curving horizon. He was struck with how beautiful Vadnu was on the surface. Off in one direction, the water seemed to be lit from within by the sun that was below the horizon. The other sun was nearly behind them, and their ship cast a long shadow over the surface. The rich gradations of color and texture caused by all of this was breathtaking.

He pondered what it must be like down there. He imagined himself stepping out of the cargo hold and plunging into the warm water. He saw himself sinking through layer after layer to that darkest place where only croosians and cling-ons go. He pictured being completely still in the very center of Vadnu, no reason to struggle, no possibility of movement. He pictured waiting there, caressed by the pressure and soothed by the darkness, until that inevitable day, the day the fire in his breast burned out. Part of him longed for it. Part of him embraced the finality of it—the complete abandonment of options. But some part of him also rebelled. He knew that that part would always long to see the sun, and he knew that longing would turn the simplicity into torture, the comfort into pain. He sighed and shook his head.

"No," he said to Greasly, but then he added, "Wait, just that... I'm sorry."

Penny started crying anew and Greasly nodded; he seemed to know what his old friend must be feeling. He too sighed. They stood in silence for a few moments and then opened the body bag and returned Klorf's body to the watery womb of Vadnu.

Thank you for reading *Tales of the Incorrigible: Flummox or Bust.* I hope you enjoyed it! If you liked this book, please consider reviewing it at Amazon or Goodreads. Your reviews help other readers find new favorites. Thanks for your support!

About the Author Kevin Bowersox lives in Colorado Springs with wife and fellow author Jodi Bowersox. Besides writing novels and writing comedy for QuipTracks.com he also works as a software tech.

Made in the USA
Middletown, DE
31 December 2021

57376680R00159